Bodies in the Boundary

A JOURNAL THROUGH TIME MYSTERY

SARAH M STEPHEN

WZE PRESS

WZE Press
Vancouver, B.C.
https://wzepress.ca

Edited by Janet Fretter
Cover by ebooklaunch.com

Library and Archives Canada Cataloguing in Publication
Bodies in the Boundary / by Sarah M Stephen
ISBN: 978-1-7778330-8-4 (paperback)
ISBN: 978-1-7778330-7-7 (e-book)

This is a work of fiction. Names, characters, places, and incidents are of the author's imagination and used fictitiously.

To Carol and David Freeman,
with love and thanks for your support.

A Note about Language

This book is set in Canada and written in Canadian English (which is very similar to British English). If you're unfamiliar with the differences, we use *our* instead of or in "colour," "favour," and "neighbour" and double the l in "travelled."

CHAPTER 1

Jack (1898)

THE TRILL OF a whistle signalled that Detective Jack Winston had been spotted. He rounded the corner to find a discarded brush dripping with wheat paste lying on the cobbles. On the wall above, a row of posters glistened with paste. He reached to tear down the flyers, and his fingers came away a gluey mess. As he wiped them with a handkerchief, a single fresh page skittered at his feet. He stepped on its corner. In large, ornate lettering, the text announced "The Crasherton Collision! Only $3, including round-trip transportation departing daily. Selling fast!" In smaller text, the address of the railway ticket office was printed at the bottom.

He picked up and folded the clean page. For weeks the city had been abuzz with expectation of the planned spectacle. Even Winston felt a flutter of excitement when he thought about seeing two locomotives crash at high speed. It was surely to be the event of the year, as foolhardy as it sounded. The Coastal Railway Company was selling tickets as a promotional effort.

Winston's mind raced with the potential disasters that could result from this event, especially if the organizers were correct in their predictions—nearly eight thousand people were expected to attend. He'd thought of little else since learning he would be seconded to Crasherton, the temporary town that would host the spectacle. He sighed and tucked the folded poster into his satchel.

Winston squared his shoulders and called out, "Find another wall, boys. The police station is not to be used to advertise." Another whistle trilled, and Winston interpreted it to mean the boys understood.

He pointed to the clump of posters he'd removed from the wall. "Clean those up before you move on." He waited until he heard another trill. "Good lads," he said and continued into the station.

As he pulled the door behind him, he was already running through his mental list of items to discuss with Chief Constable Philpott. Winston greeted the desk sergeant and confirmed that there was nothing requiring his immediate attention.

"The chief isn't in yet," the sergeant said.

Winston gave him a nod and continued to his desk. He had hoped that the chief might come in a little earlier today as Winston was anxious to review the details of his secondment to Crasherton before his departure. He was due to leave that evening.

Winston set his satchel by his desk and fished out a single page. He had deliberately kept the list of items he wanted to review with Philpott short.

1. *Would he release another constable?*

He ran his finger down the list of constables he'd identified to accompany him, with Thomas Miller's name at the top.

2. *Was Philpott satisfied with Winston's proposed plan for a temporary station?*

The tents Winston had arranged were supposed to be erected today so they would be in place for his arrival.

3. *Did Philpott have any concerns about the proposed safety measures?*

Winston breathed deeply to gain focus. He had spent much of the last several weeks preparing for the event. If Philpott was dissatisfied with anything, they were too close to the day of the event to apply any remedy, and—

"My office, Jack." Philpott's frame filled the doorway, and he turned on his heels before Winston could respond. Winston rose to follow him, grabbing his list and satchel.

∗

CHIEF CONSTABLE LAWRENCE Philpott slid a newspaper across his desk toward Winston. He tapped the main article. COUNTDOWN TO THE CRASH, the headline nearly shouted in bold type. OVER 8,000 TICKETS SOLD! "The city is humming, Jack."

Winston pushed the paper back toward Philpott. Though they had discussed the event several times, they never seemed to get past Philpott's own excitement at the prospect. "I leave this evening, sir."

"Do you feel prepared?"

Winston considered his list. "I could do with another man." The other items were beyond his control.

Philpott leaned back in his chair. "How many are confirmed?"

"Five. A sixth would still leave you with eight men here. Though with the number of tickets sold, nearly half the city's population will be there."

"Tourists are expected from all over. There are daily trains running in all directions. I hear there is much interest from Spokane." Philpott tapped at the article. "And others, like your father, who will sense the opportunities for their own businesses."

"It's not his event," Winston said, noting the defensiveness that had crept into his tone.

"Still, he is running trains in the area," Philpott said, leaning across the desk.

People attending the event from Vancouver would be travelling at least part of the journey on his father's trains and steamboats. His father had spoken of building a southern line that would be more direct, but work on that had not yet been completed. Instead, travelers would journey east overnight, then board a steamboat to travel south. The final leg of the journey would take them across the southern part of the province of British Columbia through what was referred to as the Boundary District. Winston looked forward to the journey and to seeing a different part of the province.

"He'll want to see you," Philpott said. "Speaking to you as your uncle, I think it will be a chance for your father to see you in action, so to speak. He can report back to your mother how splendidly you perform."

Winston's toes clenched inside his boots. He hadn't seen his father since George had married. That last family gathering at his brother's wedding had been tense, despite the happy occasion. "Your statement suggests my mother will not be joining him." He forced his feet to relax. If true, his mother's absence would make seeing his father more palatable.

"She hasn't sent any word recently to Clarissa. But my wife has hinted that your mother was considering the journey. I don't need to tell you how your mother isn't particularly adventurous. I think the furthest west she has been is to Hamilton, and she didn't go willingly, if I recall." Philpott chuckled to himself.

Winston stood to avoid hearing his uncle recount a story from his past. The stories, though coloured with detail, were largely fabrications. Where he had once trusted every word his uncle said, Winston now accepted that despite his uncle's role as the highest-ranking police officer in the Vancouver Constabulary, he was prepared to bend the truth if it suited him.

"May I bring another constable?" Winston's question nudged Philpott back to the present.

Philpott waved his hand. "Take whomever you think you'll need. This is to be funded by public money, mind, so none of those grand expenses you like to sneak in." Philpott winked at his nephew and leaned forward. "I have to say that, but I have no issue with you spending what's required."

Winston bristled at the suggestion that he would cheat the constabulary but chose not to rise to his uncle's needling. "I have secured tents to serve as a temporary station. With so many in attendance, I want to be prepared should any of the revelry get out of hand." Winston traced his finger down his list.

Philpott, catching sight of the document, chuckled. "Really, Jack. You needn't be so worried. I would be surprised if you encounter anything more serious than a man who has enjoyed a little too much drink."

Winston's shoulders tensed at Philpott's dismissiveness. "Still, I'd like to be prepared. It would not reflect well on us to be surprised." He slapped the flyer on the desk. "These are being plastered all over the city. Goodness knows who will come out of the woodwork to witness the spectacle."

Philpott gave an exaggerated nod. "Yes, yes—your extra man is justified. You have thought of everything, Jack. You can just focus on enjoying the event now."

Winston placed a tick beside a list item. "And the train company has assured me that additional safety measures have been taken, after what happened in Texas." Two people had died and several were injured from debris in the resulting explosion during a staged locomotive collision there two short years ago. "They have agreed to let me make any adjustments I feel necessary."

"It sounds like you're all set, then."

Winston looked at his list, then at his uncle. Philpott had been no help in ensuring that adequate preparations had been made for fire protection and food and accommodations. While these arrangements were outside his remit, Winston had taken it upon himself to pursue these details with the organizers. With such a large crowd anticipated, failure to consider what was needed on the ground could result in unrest—or worse—that six officers would be useless to respond to. "I'll review the final plans with Constable Miller."

Philpott returned to the paper in front of him, dismissing Winston with an absent wave. "Very well. It will be like a holiday for you, I should think. A few quiet days in the country. Except for the crash, of course. That is bound to be a racket." Philpott smiled at his own joke. "Clarissa is looking forward to it. And it's not something I want to miss."

Duly excused, Winston left Philpott seated at his enormous desk, still smiling.

CHAPTER 2

Jack

CONSTABLE THOMAS MILLER hadn't yet arrived at the station, having been tasked with an early morning bicycle patrol. He seemed to enjoy the two-wheeled contraption, though Winston had yet to master the necessary balance. He preferred both feet on the ground.

While he waited for Miller to return so they could review the final arrangements for the Crasherton event, Winston took advantage of the quiet in the station and opened his journal to read Riley Finch's latest words.

> *I too am going to be in the Crasherton area. I would like to include some of your reflections of the event in an exhibit, if you don't mind sharing them.*

If everything runs as smoothly as Philpott asserts it will, Winston anticipated that he would find time to share his thoughts with Riley. Their correspondence was one of the things he most looked forward to, though he could never reveal that he exchanged messages with a woman—much less a woman who lived in the future! Winston thought, again, of that day when the truth of this unbelievable reality had sunk in. He smiled at the memory—Riley, the archivist, introducing herself more than a year ago now in the pages of what he thought was his private journal. Though the phenomenon still made his head spin if he contemplated the how of it for too long, he'd built a relationship of great value with this woman living 120 years in the future. He picked up his pencil.

Dear Riley,

This evening I depart for Crasherton and while there, will record my thoughts. I have just met with Philpott, who believes the event will be a spectacle to be remembered. I agree with him on this point. The anticipation, even here in Vancouver, as people have prepared to journey to the site, has been building. Philpott also believes that there is little need for a police presence and has all but discouraged me from planning how to ensure the safety of the nearly eight thousand visitors that are expected.

On this point, we disagree. With that many people, even if they are on holiday and about to witness a remarkable event, there will be those in attendance who will take advantage of their fellow travelers. I hope drunks, pickpockets, and gamblers to be the most serious offenders we encounter, but we will do our best to be prepared to respond to more serious situations.

Warmly,

Jack

Articulating his thoughts in writing had eased his mind. Philpott may not be prepared to offer a full police force—and in truth, they were unlikely to need a detective's services—but should they be needed, he would be there.

He set his pen down and was reviewing his list again when Miller entered, his forehead glistening from his ride.

"Hello, sir," Miller called brightly.

"You're back, Thomas. Good. I'd like to review our plans for Crasherton a final time."

Miller pulled a chair alongside Winston's. Although Winston would have preferred his own office where he could close the door against the bustle of the station, he'd settled for a corner of the room shared by the force's fourteen constables and two detectives. Philpott, as the chief, had his own office. Winston had recently occupied it for a short time while his uncle was away for an extended period. The experience was something he could get used to.

In his corner, Winston had positioned two desks against each other for himself and Miller to sit at. He'd had a blackboard hung on which they could write the important details of their cases. Today the blackboard was bare, as if the city's criminals were also taking some time away to prepare for Crasherton. Another reason for Winston to be ready.

Winston turned to his constable. He hadn't missed the sag in Miller's shoulders at the mention of another look at the plans. "This is the final review, Thomas. Indulge me."

Miller sat back in his chair and pulled out his notepad. "Yes, sir."

Winston repeated some of what he'd shared with Philpott about the tents and crowds. "I sincerely hope that crowd management is our biggest challenge. However, I've taken the liberty to speak with Doctor Evans. He and his wife will be travelling to enjoy the show. He is prepared to offer his services if needed."

"You are expecting violence, sir?" Miller asked.

"Not at all. The excitement may prove to be too much for some, and we may appreciate having a physician we know and trust on-site."

Each item on his list now had multiple ticks beside it. "We leave this evening, Thomas. I'll meet you as planned at the train station. Just to review, we will remain in Crasherton for a couple of days after the event to ensure that the visitors have departed safely." Winston locked eyes with the constable. "And, Thomas, we're going there to work. Several of the other lads will join us, but our focus will be on keeping the visitors safe. The thing we're likely to see most often is drunken revellers, though we will also have to keep an eye out for pickpockets. You know how those with a mind to exploit others can pop up when there's a crowd."

Miller nodded. "I understand." He pushed himself away from the desk. "My mother will be ever so jealous, sir. She'd been hoping to save enough for a ticket to the show, but she had to seek out that Spectre woman again. You know how fond she is of taking advantage of others."

Winston stiffened. Melodia Spectre, in his experience, had not taken advantage of anyone. Miller would be disappointed to know how fond Winston had become of her. As with anyone claiming to have second sight or a connection to the other world, she could be fantastical and flighty. But unlike most with "the gift" to connect people to their lost loves and departed children, Melodia cared deeply for those who trusted her. Winston had yet to see her knowingly engage in deception. "Mrs. Spectre has pointed us in the right direction more than once, Constable. That she earns a living listening to people shouldn't be something we begrudge her, even if you don't agree."

"It's not the listening so much as the pretending to be able to hear the other side." As he spoke, Miller waved his fingers near his head as if tickling the unseen spirits Melodia claimed shared space with the living. "Worse, it's charging others for the privilege. There is no way to prove her claims."

On this, Winston conceded Miller's point. Still, he believed the woman genuinely meant well. Would she be making the journey? Would he see her? For a moment he hoped his mother would be joining his father. Imagining Melodia meeting his mother brought a smile to Winston's face. Until he saw Miller's eyes narrow.

"Look, Thomas. Don't be surprised if we see her in Crasherton. A sudden influx of eight thousand souls will no doubt bring the best and the worst in the crowd." *And the opportunity to make a fair few pennies.*

∗

IN HIS RENTED rooms, with his small suitcase and satchel packed and resting next to the door, Winston paced. When he reached the window, he planted himself on the sill and retrieved his list from the inner pocket of his suit jacket. Had he overlooked anything?

He considered different scenarios and how he would handle them. An unruly crowd? He, Miller, and the other constables had reviewed a procedure for quickly dispersing large numbers of people. What if the crash were to result in an explosion as it had in Texas? The organizers had dug two deep wells and confirmed them as a good source of water right in the town. Winston had written ahead to secure barrels of water to have at the ready at the crash site. He would view the planned crash site when he arrived and decide whether to also move the crowd seating area.

What if more people attended than expected? This was perhaps not an issue he directly needed to address, but it would result in a strain on resources. Should the crowd be larger than anticipated, it would be a matter of the train company transporting additional goods from Vancouver or Spokane to meet the visitors' needs.

Enough. There was nothing more he could do until he arrived. He folded the page and slid it back inside his jacket.

After another few minutes of pacing, Winston pulled a letter from his waistcoat pocket and unfolded it on the writing table. He had spread these pages in front of him so many times before. Although he could recall its contents he read the words again, hearing his mother's crisp voice as he did.

My dear Jack,

I cannot undo your pain. But I can tell you about your brother Ellis.

Why, in the years since Ellis had died, had she never spoken these words to him? Why did she write them only when she knew Winston had finally learned the truth about his brother's death? He felt for the familiar shape of the stone in his pocket…Ellis's stone.

Your brother was a caring and thoughtful young man. He loved you and George and would never have wanted to cause you pain. It is because of this love that I decided we must keep the truth from you. From everyone.

Winston clutched the stone in his hand, his nails nearly piercing the flesh of his palm. Ellis had not gone missing as his parents had let everyone believe for so long.

Your brother had been unable to secure the heart of a woman. That is the only reason he made the decision he did.

This explanation rang hollow. A failed love caused his brother to take his own life? He couldn't accept this. There must have been more to it. Winston had not yet responded to his mother's letter, even though several weeks had passed. Again, he folded the letter and replaced it in his pocket. It was time to leave for the station.

CHAPTER 3

Riley (2018)

RILEY FINCH SURVEYED the items stacked in front of the couch and compared them against the list she held in her hand. Did she need another T-shirt? She added another to the pile. What about shorts? She selected a pair and folded them. Satisfied she had enough clothing, she tucked everything into packing cubes and eased the cubes into her backpack.

Next, she turned her attention to the camping supplies. Lucy was sure to roll her eyes when she saw that Riley was bringing two sleeping bags, but the weather forecast suggested the nights would be cool. And who knew what calamity could render one sleeping bag unusable? Two was non-negotiable. Lucy had assured Riley that there would be food available, but she still packed granola bars into a side pocket. What if something happened on the journey to the festival and she needed to eat? With this thought, she prepared a bag of trail mix to add to her snack stash.

What about Johnny? Should she bring snacks for him? Her stomach fluttered as she thought of him. She had been trying to figure out how he fit into her life when her sister persuaded Riley to invite him to the festival. When he'd agreed to come, she took it as a good sign for their future. She stuffed another granola bar into the side pocket. The forecast also called for sunny days, which explained the two tubes of 30 SPF sunscreen Riley slid into her toiletries bag. She strapped her sun hat to the top of the pack and double-checked that her sunglasses were in the front pocket. Four days away required more than she expected, but it looked like she had everything she needed.

A message alert sounded from Riley's phone. A quick glance at the message earned an eye roll from Riley.

> Safe travels, honey. Don't let Johnny drive too fast. And remember to support Lucy. This is a big deal for her.

It was a classic text from her mother. She was off on her own adventure, visiting a former colleague who had retired to the Gulf Islands.

> Thanks, Mom. I'll see you in a few days.

Riley scanned the room. The last item to pack was her journal—her connection to Johnny's great-grandfather. She picked it up and thumbed back to the entry from Detective Jack Winston that had set her on this trip.

Dear Riley,

I write to you as I prepare to spend time at the site of what is sure to be a spectacle: a staged train crash. The event is being organized by an engine maker, whom I believe also has interest in at least one railway. There is, I understand, much interest in laying permanent track in the area to service the resource mines that are flourishing nearby. The event seems an extraordinary waste of equipment, but I've read that the organizers secured two locomotives that were due to be replaced and revamped them for this singular purpose.

I am set to arrive two days before the crash and will remain in the town for another two days following. I had asked for more time to set up ahead of the spectacle and to organize the men for the task. We'll be hard pressed to dismantle our encampment after the event while overseeing what's left of the crowd at the same time, but my chief constable dismissed my protests. He seems set on this, so I'll need to make the allotted time work. A makeshift settlement has been established, with spectators expected from across Canada and the United States.

She had helped Jack on a few cases now, their strange friendship developing through the pages of a book she'd found in the archives of the museum she worked in—Jack's own journal, from the year 1897. In his latest entries, it was now the summer of 1898. He would soon travel to the town that hosted the train crash spectacle, the same location of the music festival named in its memory—Riley's destination.

When she'd first read this note, Riley had immediately looked up the crash Jack referred to. She had found surprisingly little, despite what surely would have been a noteworthy event given the number of witnesses, all of whom would have travelled to view it. His message had sparked an idea for an exhibit that she had pitched to her temporary boss, Nick Blume.

It will be nice to be out of the city for a short time, and Chief Constable Philpott has assured me that the trip will be more of a vacation than work. Still, with the number of attendees predicted to be near eight thousand, there is potential for trouble, and I would like to be prepared.

That the crash site happened to be the same location as the festival her sister was helping to organize felt almost fated. Since she was already travelling to the area at Lucy's invitation, Nick had agreed to let Riley research the crash and the subsequent rise and fall of the community that was initially created for attendees. She hoped that by visiting the original townsite—now a ghost town—she would learn some additional details to develop her proposal further. Jack's first-hand account as one of the attendees would give Riley some colour to add to the mix.

Vancouver newspapers had sent reporters to the crash, and she had read the articles that referred to the excitement leading up to the show. "Electric," one had said. "Highly anticipated," gushed another. "Invigorating," claimed a third. As for the crash itself, the newspapers reported that it had happened with a spectacular and deafening grinding of metal against metal. But the spectacle had avoided the deaths and injuries of a similar event in Texas two years earlier, the result of flying debris from a boiler explosion.

One article mentioned two deaths at the Canadian crash, though neither was directly related to the crash itself. With a community—even temporary—of eight thousand people, it wasn't unreasonable that some might die naturally. Still, she didn't want to mention the deaths to Jack to avoid sharing anything substantial about the future. And if the deaths were natural, perhaps Jack would have a quiet week as he predicted.

Riley ran her hand along the journal page before closing it and tucking it into her pack. She set the bag on the floor and sat against the couch. She was ready for this adventure.

*

RILEY'S PHONE PINGED with a message alert. Her stomach sank as she read it.

> A case needs my attention. I won't be
> able to get away until Friday afternoon.
> So sorry. I'll call later.

Riley felt a pang of disappointment. Johnny couldn't meet her until Friday night. *If he came at all.* She pushed that last thought aside as she started a reply, deleted it, and repeated the sequence twice before settling on "Okay". She took three calming breaths, then dialled her friend Jules.

"Hey," she said when he answered. "Any chance you're interested in going to the Crasher Music Festival this weekend? I know it's super short notice."

"I thought you were going with Johnny," Jules said. "Aren't you trying to figure things out with him?"

"I am. Or at least I thought so. He just sent a message saying he needs to work. But he says he'll join me there later. I thought you might like to come anyway."

"And play third wheel when he arrives?" Jules's tone was playful, but she understood his reluctance.

"You won't be a third wheel. There's lots of room. I'll ask Lucy to reserve another camping spot. It shouldn't be a big deal."

"When are you heading there?"

"Tomorrow morning, first thing. I was going to take a bus up and Johnny was going to follow after work. I guess he still is, just not on the same day. The bus is the closest thing to a train journey—the way people originally got to the crash site."

Jules laughed. "As it happens, I don't have any plans this weekend. My mom is visiting a friend on the Sunshine Coast. I'd love to join you."

"Do you want to come by bus?" Riley had a good idea of what the answer was going to be.

"Nope! I'll rent a car. Do you want me to pick you up?"

The journey by car would be faster. And really, a bus journey was nothing like the experience of travelling by train. Maybe Jack would share his observations about the journey. "That would be great. And if Johnny doesn't end up coming at all, can I get a lift back to the city after the festival?"

"Deal."

The friends confirmed the final details and ended the conversation. Riley listed potential conversation topics for the journey. Even though she and Jules had been friends for ages, she liked to be prepared. As she made her list, she realized that she didn't do the same thing with Johnny. Conversations with him typically flowed smoothly, though they had grown more awkward as they navigated the questions about their relationship. She tucked that thought away, not quite ready to think about what that might mean.

CHAPTER 4

Riley

WHEN THEY ARRIVED at the festival site, Lucy was waiting near the entrance gates. She hopped into the back seat of Jules's rental. "There's VIP parking, but I want you to get the whole picture," she said.

"Hello, Lucy. Yes, the journey was fine. Thanks for asking," Riley said. She swivelled in the passenger seat to take in her sister. "What are you wearing?"

Lucy was a clash of neon colours. She had paired a pink tank top that barely skimmed her belly button with the brightest green shorts Riley had ever seen. "I don't want to be missed."

"You won't be in that," Jules said. "I wish I'd known to bring something so bright."

"Or sunglasses," Riley quipped.

"There are vendors on-site if you need something different," Lucy said. She pointed out the window. "Can you pull over here? Riley and I will get out and walk through the grounds to where we're staying. You can head back out and park in the VIP lot. It will save you having to carry your things very far." She showed Jules where she was referring to on a map on her phone. "Ready?" she asked Riley.

Within a minute, Riley regretted getting out of the car. Blasts of competing music grew louder as she followed her sister through the campground, feet squishing in the mud. The summer had been unusually wet, and the dampness underfoot combined with the thumping bass in the distance to drown out most of Riley's thoughts. People walking around her seemed to bounce as if they were enjoying the sound, but the vibrations were already giving her a headache. "I'm not sure why we're making this trek, Luce. I only agreed to come here at all because you said it was near a site I want to research," she said to her sister's back. Despite the opening of the festival still a day away, the nearby parking lot was already full of campers' vehicles. "Now you're making me walk while Jules gets to drive to our final destination." Riley hated the whine that her voice had taken on.

Lucy glanced behind her, smiling at her sister. "Isn't this great?"

Either she'd heard Riley and was ignoring her, or the music had already deafened her sister. Or some combination of the two. Never the more adventurous of the sisters, Riley was well outside her comfort zone. Despite her sister's assurances that she could leave her bag in the car and retrieve it after their walk, Riley had slung her heavy pack on her shoulders and held a bag of food in her arms. "I need a shower already. I'm not sure I can do this."

"It will be fine," Lucy said. "We're halfway there. If you turn around now and get Jules to pick you up, you'll just be covering the same distance. Keep going." Lucy's voice bubbled with excitement.

"When will Alex get here?" Riley asked. She hoped Lucy's husband would be on hand for the festival weekend. He had a calming effect on Lucy.

"He's staying home to wrap up some projects. The two of us have a getaway planned for next weekend since I've been putting in so much time leading up to this one," Lucy said.

Other festival goers waved as they passed, a few calling out welcomes. None, with their baggy clothing and colourful hair, looked like the crowd Lucy typically spent time with. Until today, Riley would have described her sister's preferred vacation as one involving poolside beverages and sun loungers. This was looking to be a mucky, sweaty weekend without a pool in sight.

"As you can see, most of the guests are camping. But we've got VIP accommodations," Lucy called over her shoulder. "We're nearer the stages, and we've got our own bathrooms. I mean, we'll share another set of toilets closer to the stage, but we won't have to queue like these guys." She jerked her head in the direction of a group of people standing outside a row of blue portable toilets. Relief washed through Riley as she stepped gingerly around a large puddle. Here was the sister she knew and loved—and who Riley was certain had never used one of those toilets.

After five more sweaty minutes, they arrived at a fenced-off area with a muscular bouncer in a shirt two sizes too small checking the passes of people seeking entrance. He smiled at Lucy when she walked up, and they air-kissed.

"Mike, I want to introduce you to my sister, Riley. Riley, this is Mike. He usually works at a club in Vancouver, but I persuaded him to come up to the Crasher."

Riley started to offer a hand before remembering it held a bag of supplies. Instead, she lowered her head in an almost bow. "Mike, nice to meet you. This looks…interesting. I wasn't expecting we'd need a security guard to let us into our campground."

Mike smiled. "You didn't tell her, Lucy?" he asked as he snapped a coloured band around Riley's wrist.

Lucy put a finger to her lips.

Mike winked back. "This will get you in here and all the VIP areas," he said, pointing at the wristband. "Have fun," he called after them as they walked through the gates.

The fences had been lined with a black tarp, limiting visibility into the area. Riley gasped when she saw rows of recreational vehicles parked within. To their right, a circle of food trucks offered various cuisines. She turned to her sister. "You didn't say anything about this, Lucy. I thought we had to camp?" She dropped her backpack at her feet. "Why do I have sleeping bags and a pillow, and why have I carried a bag of food from the car? I thought you weren't carrying anything because you'd arrived yesterday."

Lucy slid her arm around her sister. "Aren't you impressed, Riley? I mean, I organized all this. And didn't I tell you about not needing to worry about anything?"

"When I asked for a packing list, your response was 'Fun Riley.'" Frustration had crept into her voice.

Lucy gave her a smirk. "You've always been overly cautious. I can't help that you decided to bring two sleeping bags, just in case one got wet." With her toe, Lucy nudged the sleeping bag strapped to Riley's backpack. The sleeping bag teetered and knocked the pack into Riley's leg, buckling her at the knee as she lost her footing. Riley stifled a curse. She plastered a smile on her face as she rose. This was, after all, supposed to be a fun weekend. "I didn't bring Fun Riley because I'm always Fun Riley." The words didn't come out quite as lightly as Riley had hoped. "It never hurts to be prepared," she said under her breath.

She took in the scene again. The ground here was drier. Broad umbrellas created welcome shade from the valley's scorching sun, and small groups of VIPs stood under them, sipping from their festival cocktails. All of them were glamorous, with sleek hair and stylish clothes. Riley looked down at her dusty shorts and tank top. She would need to shower and change before making her way to the VIP lounge area. "I am impressed. This is really incredible."

Lucy beamed. "This is the first year the festival has had a VIP area, and my friend Shelley—remember her? Shelley is part of the company that organizes the event. Because of my work for the boutique"—she placed her hand on her chest as she said *my*, drawing the word out—"Shelley asked me to come up with a theme for the space." Lucy tapped Riley's arm. "And actually, you inspired the name."

Riley tried to think of what she might have said that would have influenced her influencer sister. Lucy spent her days managing a Vancouver clothing boutique frequented by celebrities in town for filming television and movies. Her social media efforts to promote the boutique had led to a few other businesses asking her to manage their promotions, and within what seemed to Riley an incredibly short amount of time, her sister had quickly become a social media influencer. "I did?"

Lucy nodded. "Remember you were telling me that there used to be a town here? Crasher. I always thought it was just a cool name for the festival. But it turns out that town is how the Crasher Music Festival got its name. I looked it up. Did you know that the town was the site for a railway show where two locomotives crashed into each other?" Lucy swept her arm in a half-circle. "I figured, let's call this area First Class, like for the first-class passengers who came here to see the train."

Lucy had so rarely demonstrated an interest in history, or in Riley's work at all, but she couldn't help correcting her. "The actual town was called Crasherton, and it's located about ten minutes' drive from where we parked."

Lucy pushed Riley's sunglasses up her nose after Riley's correction. "I don't think we need to be precise, Riley. It's not like anyone really cares, nerd."

"I care." Riley said as her frustration boiled over. "I care."

Lucy bowed her head. "Fine. The point is you helped inspire the name of the first-class area. Until two months ago, it was just 'the VIP area,' and it lacked a cohesive theme. As soon as you told me about your exhibit idea, I knew we had the perfect theme." She thrust a reusable mug into Riley's hand. "Here is a drink to celebrate." The phrase *To a Crashing Time in First Class at the Crasher Music Fest* was emblazoned in gold letters across the mug. The beverage itself was a beer, which Riley didn't usually drink. But after her walk she was thankful for anything, and she swallowed two satisfying mouthfuls. Afterwards she pressed the mug against her forehead, drawing from it what little relief she could. "Where are we sleeping?"

Lucy led her to a row of camping trailers and stopped in front of one. "I wasn't joking about the toilets. Each of these has its own. But there is also a set of washrooms just for First Class closer to the VIP entrance. You can freshen up if you need to between music acts."

"Thanks, Lucy. This will be great." She clasped the key Lucy gave her in her fist. "Are you in this one too?"

"No, I'm next door. When does Johnny get here?"

Heat rushed to Riley's cheeks, made worse by the beer and the sun. "Actually, something came up. He's not coming. At least I don't think so. He said he'd be able to get away after he finished work on Friday." Riley looked at her toes as they clenched in her sandals. "That's why Jules came. He's in town for a month, and I asked him to join me."

"The VIP lot is just behind there," Lucy said as she pointed toward a group of trees. "I'm surprised Jules hasn't shown up yet."

Riley's frustration bubbled over when she saw how close the VIP lot was. "Why did you let me carry any of this stuff?" She picked up her bag and left before her sister could answer.

CHAPTER 5

Riley

THE CATCH ON the trailer door clicked as Riley shut it behind her. Her sister was really too much. Stomping off in anger had accomplished nothing, but it sure felt good.

She dropped her pack inside the door and tossed the extra sleeping bag in the direction of what she assumed was the bedroom. Afternoon light streamed through the trailer's small windows. Another layer of sweat cloaked Riley after only a few moments inside the trailer. She slid the windows open and tugged the curtains closed.

On top of a small table she found two gift bags. She opened one and pulled out a pouch filled with a selection of cosmetics and toiletries. Her sister was definitely behind this. Deeper in the bag she found locally made goods—candles, honey, and a baseball cap with the festival's logo on it. Riley popped on the hat and continued exploring the trailer.

Across from the small seating area and table there was a two-burner cooktop and, deeper into the unit, a queen-sized bed adorned with expensive-looking bedding. A tiny door near the bedroom revealed a shower, sink, and toilet. The beer fridge in the kitchen area was stocked with fruits and veggies, water, and a bottle of white wine from a nearby vineyard. Being the sister of the organizer had some advantages, even if Lucy had neglected to let Riley know she needn't bring any camping equipment. She grabbed a bottle of water from the fridge and twisted the cap, downing several gulps.

She looked at herself in the bathroom mirror and groaned. The trek from where Jules had dropped her had left her covered in dust. *Thanks, Luce.*

The water in the small shower was warm, and when she emerged, Riley's anger had cooled more than the trailer's interior. She typed a message to Lucy.

What time is dinner?

7 onwards. You have a couple of hours. If you need anything, text. I'll be around.

The dots continued bouncing as Lucy typed another message.

Will Johnny need a trailer?

I don't know. Can we sort it out if we need to?

Lucy responded with a thumbs-up emoji.

Riley pulled on a fresh pair of shorts and a T-shirt. Where was Jules? She checked her phone again. Still no message.

It would be great to spend a few days with Jules. She had missed him after his move to London last year. But no matter how long they were apart, they always picked right up where they'd left off. It had been like that since they were just kids. Jules had to be in Canada while paperwork for his UK visa was reviewed, part of his application for an extended stay. Steve, Jules's boyfriend, would visit Vancouver toward the end of Jules's planned month-long stay. But for these few days, she could have some great one-on-one time with him ... at least until Johnny arrived.

Riley pulled a brush through her hair and twisted it up into a loop, fastening it with a clip. What would they do about accommodations when Johnny got here? Oh, they'd figure it out. For now, Jules could sleep...where?

Riley moved to the table and pushed down on it. Sure enough, it lowered, and the seating pulled out to reveal extra cushions to make another sleeping area. Perhaps not the level of luxury Jules was used to as he jetted about Europe, but definitely a step up from sleeping on the ground.

She pulled her phone from her pocket to send Jules a text.

> It turns out I didn't need to bring any camping supplies, so you can leave them in the car. Unless you want to use them. Lucy arranged an amazing trailer for me. You can borrow the tent and sleeping bag I brought up. Or stay in the trailer.

She snapped a photo of the table-to-sleeping space and included it with the message.

The little dots signalled he was responding.

> The trailer sounds great. I'll bring the rest of our stuff there shortly.

*

AFTER JULES HAD stashed his things in a small storage cupboard, he grabbed a water bottle and downed half of it. "I'm going to explore. Wanna come?"

"Not yet. I'll find you later." Riley swept her arm in an arc. "I need to get this space organized first. You know me. I need to nest for a bit as soon as I land anywhere."

Jules chuckled. "Yep, I know you."

They agreed to meet up for dinner. With a couple of hours to kill, Riley settled on her bed and dug into her backpack. She pulled out the journal to send Jack a note. She'd cranked open opposite windows in the small bedroom, and there was a faint cross-breeze that made the space bearable, almost comfortable.

A rhythmic clanking in the distance sounded like a construction site—stages or vendors' booths going up, maybe? Closer to the trailer, there was chatter and laughter. The anticipation was palpable.

Riley thought of how charged the atmosphere must have been for Jack 120 years ago in the temporary community of Crasherton, bustling with visitors to the area anticipating a spectacle. It must have moved with the same energy as the makeshift community she found herself in now.

Dear Jack,

I'm writing to you from very close to the town of Crasherton. Lucy has been organizing a festival nearby, and I'm trying to imagine how the area felt for you. The setting, I'm sure you will agree, is beautiful, with the deep green of the surrounding forests and the mountainous back-

*drop. I can see the appeal of spending a few days away
from your regular routine—especially in such a lovely place.*

Here she hesitated. The crash was set in a town that, although temporary, had held promise as a rail hub, with lines expected to converge from the north, south, east, and west. The promise was never fulfilled, and the town declined for decades, eventually housing only a handful of residents. She couldn't tell Jack this without compromising her cardinal rule when communicating with him—do not reveal anything about the future that might alter the course of history.

*I'm sure you are busy, but I am curious about the history
of Crasherton and very much hope that you will be able
to provide me with a first-hand account of the crash. I
will do my best to enjoy the event that I am attending.
To be frank, while I'm proud of my sister for all the work
she's put in to organize it, I'm more interested in visiting
the Crasherton townsite.*

Riley

She tucked the journal away and slipped on her shoes and the festival ball cap. She'd do a little exploring of her own before she met up with Jules.

CHAPTER 6

Jack

WINSTON WATCHED PASSENGERS on the platform as they said their
final goodbyes to those who would remain behind. Miller had loaded
their luggage and secured the seats they would occupy until they retired to their sleeper accommodation for the night. After what, if past
experience held, would be a pleasant sleep, they were expected to
arrive at the steamboat launch in Okanagan Landing shortly after
noon.

Winston especially looked forward to the steamboat portion of
the trip. They would pass remote lakeside communities that were serviced only by water, territory he had never laid eyes on. Once landed
in Penticton, they would spend the night at a hotel, then board another train for the final leg of the journey to Crasherton. Their arrival
time was expected to be early afternoon.

Miller sat across from him in the first-class compartment with his
leg bouncing in anticipation of their journey. Doors to other
compartments opened and closed as passengers filtered in. Nobody
had yet joined them, and for a fleeting moment Winston thought
they might have the space to themselves. He held on to his hope until
a short whistle sounded and the train eased forward. Just as he
stretched out his legs, a woman of about thirty years appeared in the
compartment doorway. She held her travelling bag in the crook of
one arm while she tried to steady herself against the train's ac-
celeration. Both men stood, though she motioned for them to sit.
Miller extended his arm to take her bag from her, but she moved her

hand from where she had been holding her hat on her head to clutch the bag to her chest.

The woman removed a shawl from her bag and placed it on the seat across from Miller to claim it. Without a word, she slipped her arm through the handle of her bag and left the compartment. Winston and Miller exchanged glances. From his seat nearest the compartment door, Winston watched as she made her way down the narrow corridor toward the gangway connecting their car to the next one.

"Is it safe, sir?" Miller asked.

"Is what safe, Thomas?" Winston wanted to be patient with the man on his first rail journey.

"Going between the cars like that. It's what she did, isn't it?"

"It's perfectly safe." Winston explained the mechanism. "This way, we can move to the dining car should we need something to eat. Or if we just want to stretch our legs."

Miller sat back against the upholstered seat. This was, Winston realized, the first time he had seen Miller dressed in something other than his uniform. Unsure how comfortable his uniform would be for the journey, he had elected to wear a suit for the first stretch. "I'll put it on before we arrive in Crasherton, though," he'd said. "Will you do the same, sir?"

Winston had been instructed to bring a constable's uniform as the purpose of him being in the town was to be identified as a police officer. "I'll don my uniform after we settle in, Miller. But yes, it's wise that you wear yours when we arrive in Crasherton." Winston turned his attention to the book he had brought—*The Leavenworth Case*. While he seldom found time for reading, he enjoyed a good detective novel. This one, as he'd observed so far, was remarkable more so for its attention to detail than for the fact that it was written by a woman.

"Where do you think she's gone?" Miller asked.

Winston looked up from his book. Miller seemed inordinately interested in the woman's welfare. "The dining car may not be offering service yet, but the seats would be comfortable, I imagine." He lowered his gaze to the page.

Miller stood, approached the compartment door, then resumed his seat. "Are you peckish now, sir?"

"Do you wish to follow the lady, Thomas? Or explore the train?" Winston tried to keep the exasperation from his voice, remembering that not everyone had had his opportunities to travel.

"I don't want to bother you, sir."

Winston moved to sit opposite Miller so they could both look out the window. "As I say, the dining car won't be serving anything yet. This scenery is enough to keep us entertained, though if you need more, we may be able to find a deck of cards to help you pass the time."

Miller's cheeks flushed. "I'll be fine here. Until you want to eat."

"Very well," Winston said as he picked up his novel. After a few pages, he checked on Miller, who was still staring out the window. They were out of the city now, travelling through a heavily forested area. Would the city ever touch these trees? Perhaps Riley would share how far the city's borders extended in her time.

When he next looked up from his book, the landscape had shifted into river delta. Miller had dozed off, and the woman had not yet returned to claim her seat or her shawl. Winston's stomach rumbled. The dining car was sure to be operational now. He nudged Miller's leg with his own and looked away as the man attended to a patch of spittle in the corner of his mouth. He tucked his book into his bag and led the way to the dining car. At the gangway linking the cars, he showed Miller where to place his feet. The dining car was the third they entered and by then, Miller moved almost comfortably in the narrow crossing.

Most of the tables in the dining car were occupied. One sat empty, and Winston positioned himself so he could survey the others. The woman they had seen earlier sat alone, though she gave a slight wave of her fingers when she saw Winston. He nodded in her direction, and she returned her attention to the cup of tea in front of her.

Miller leaned toward Winston. "I see the woman from earlier. If she remains in here, what was the point of her leaving her shawl?" His brow furrowed. "Do you think she will sit in here for the duration of the journey? Is she travelling alone?"

Winston checked his pocket watch. "There are still a few hours until we retire to the sleeper, Miller. She's been here long enough to enjoy her meal, and now she's having tea. We will find her in the compartment when we return, I expect." Winston watched the wait staff bustle among the tables. His stomach gave another grumble. "As to whether she has a travelling companion, what do you deduce based on what you've observed about her?"

Miller made a show of surveying the dining car, being careful not to fix his gaze on the woman directly. "She is currently alone. She had only a small bag on her arm, but I thought I noticed a claim ticket sticking out of her pocket. If she continues to Crasherton, perhaps it is to join someone who is already there."

"The only conversation that I've heard since entering the dining car is about the spectacle," Winston said. "I am certain that our fellow passengers are taking the same journey." He caught the eye of a waiter and beckoned. The policemen ordered their meals and their talk turned to the spectacle itself, mirroring the conversations around them.

The meal passed pleasantly, and as Winston and Miller returned to their carriage, the sky had taken on the golden glow that accompanies summer evenings.

The woman had seated herself near the window of the compartment. Winston and Miller bowed slightly in her direction. She offered a small smile and short nod, then turned to gaze out the window once more. Her hands sat in her lap, folded over a book. For nearly twenty minutes they sat in a companionable silence, broken only by Miller's quiet questions spoken into Winston's ear.

*

As the steamboat slowed on its approach to the landing in Penticton, the energy of the passengers picked up. Winston stood on the deck and welcomed the breeze from the water against the heat that had kept him from spending much time outside as they'd travelled along Okanagan Lake. Beside him, Miller gaped at the scenery.

The vista from the steamboat had not disappointed. Rolling hills, backed by surrounding mountains, framed the serene waters of the lake. Homesteads and growing communities dotted the shoreline, many skirted with uniform rows of what looked to be fruit trees. It was a clear day that would remain light for a few hours yet. Away from the turbulence the steamboat stirred; the still surface of the water reflected the blue sky. Winston and Miller had agreed to walk in the town before settling into the hotel for the night. They gathered their bags and made their way to the gangplank.

Passengers were booked into three different hotels, depending on their ticket class. Winston and Miller had rooms in the first-class Lakeside Hotel. The purser gave directions as they disembarked.

The rooms were simply appointed, and Winston wondered if there was much difference between the hotels, other than the cost of the accommodation. After dropping his bag in his room, Winston met Miller in the hotel's small lobby.

"How is your room, Thomas?" Winston asked.

"It's the first hotel room I've stayed in, sir. I don't have anything to compare it to other than my own bedroom, which I shared with my brother until recently." Miller had moved from his parents' home into one next door where he was proudly living independently, apart from the meals he regularly ate with his family. The arrangement seemed to suit Miller, but Winston appreciated the distance between himself and his own family.

"If your room is like mine, then it is likely to be quite comfortable for the night. Now, where should we eat?" They had agreed that the meal on the steamboat had been satisfying but small, and both needed something more.

"I thought we might look for a pub, sir. I need a break from the finer food we've been served," Miller said, patting his stomach. "There are sure to be choices, what with all the travelers coming through to Crasherton."

"A fine idea, Thomas."

Inside the pub, only a few seats were unoccupied. Miller found two at a long table where a group of men shared a boisterous laugh. Winston ordered a glass of beer and bowl of stew for himself and the same for Miller. He carried the drinks to the table and was assured the stew would be brought out to them. As he settled into his seat, Miller leaned close to Winston. "The woman from the train is sitting alone. Should we invite her to sit with us?"

Winston looked in the direction that Miller indicated. She wore the same dress that she'd been wearing on the train, though her shawl was now wrapped around her shoulders. She sat with her back to Winston and read a newspaper. While they had exchanged pleasantries in the train's compartment the previous evening, nothing in her current situation suggested that she was seeking company. "A kind thought, Thomas. But let's leave her."

Their food arrived, as did a bowl of stew for the woman, Winston noticed. She ate quickly and left the pub before Winston and Miller had finished their meals. Miller had stiffened when the woman stood, but his attention returned to his supper quickly enough.

"What is your assessment of the crowd, Thomas?" Winston asked when they finished eating. "Many if not all of these people will be in Crasherton."

Miller cast his gaze around the room and wiped his mouth with his napkin. "From the people who were on the train with us, I sense excitement. But not agitation. More like anticipation."

Winston nodded. "I sense the same. These people are happy and looking forward to their holiday."

"There are people who weren't on the train. Local residents, I assume. They are seated in the corners and along the wall," Miller said.

Winston followed his gaze. "I see them," he said cautiously. "They don't seem to share the travelers' excitement."

"No. They aren't openly rude, but their expressions are not as welcoming as you might expect them to be."

"Do you think there will be any trouble?" Winston asked.

Miller looked at the local residents a little longer, then returned to face Winston. "No, I doubt it. They are likely just looking forward to the crash being over and the town returning to its usual peace."

"Well assessed, Miller. It must be tiresome to have great numbers of visitors descend upon their otherwise quiet town." He stood. "I'm ready to retire. Our train leaves at eight tomorrow morning."

Winston nodded at a few passengers that he recognized from the train as they left the pub. The light was fading into dusk. The men retraced their steps back to the hotel.

As they entered the lobby, Winston pointed to a table near the door. "I believe there will be a breakfast prepared for us to collect here in the morning."

"Will there not be any breakfast on the train?" Miller asked.

"My understanding is that no dining car has been made available for this leg of the journey as the route through Crasherton is so new.

The full passenger service isn't operational. Make sure you get your breakfast package."

They bid each other good night.

Inside his room, Winston sat at the small writing desk and dashed off a short note to Riley.

Dear Riley,

We have completed a long portion of our journey to Crasherton. It has been interesting to observe Miller on his first rail journey. I am reminded of how novel it is to travel in such a way and how fortunate I am to have had the opportunity to do so several times.

The light mood had Winston musing about his past more than he usually did with Riley.

I particularly enjoyed the scenery around Okanagan Lake from the steamboat. The day has been long and I'm grateful to have a proper bed to sleep in tonight. Our train leaves early in the morning, and that will allow us to arrive in Crasherton by midday. Will your journey also require an overnight stay in Penticton?

My hotel room is small but sufficient for a single night. I expect the room I have in Crasherton will be similar. It is good that I travel with few possessions, given how little space to store them is likely to be available.

He glanced toward the furnishings of the room, which, along with the writing desk, comprised the bed, narrow wardrobe, and washstand.

Although I anticipate we will be spending most of our time patrolling the community of Crasherton, I did arrange for a few supplies to be sent ahead, including tents to serve as temporary headquarters for us.

You asked for my observations. Although the main event will not happen for a few days yet, there are several activities to entertain the crowd in the days leading to it. I have observed that the mood of those who travel with us is light, and I hope it continues to be so through the coming days. For many I expect this is their first venture away from Vancouver in some time.

I will write again with more observations after I have arrived.

Warmly,

Jack

How long would this light mood last? Winston dismissed an unwelcome wave of apprehension and readied himself for bed.

*

WINSTON SETTLED INTO a window seat opposite Miller. He scanned the passengers as they climbed the steps to board the train but didn't see the woman who'd travelled with them since leaving Vancouver. He rested his head on the panel beside the window. His sleep the night before had been disturbed by a pair of men who had enjoyed themselves a little too much and broken into song beneath his window. Another hotel guest had shouted at the men, and they had eventually moved along. But it had taken Winston a long time to fall back asleep. His thoughts had been troubled with worry over final details. Before leaving for the station, he'd run through his list again to reassure himself that nothing had been forgotten.

The view of the patchwork of farms outside Penticton shifted to rolling hills. More lakes shimmered in the distance. As Winston watched the landscape change again to foothills with rocky outcrops, the train's jostling rocked him and his eyelids grew heavy.

Startled awake, suddenly, Winston wasn't sure whether his eyes had been closed for minutes or hours. He pulled his watch from his pocket. It had only been thirty minutes since they'd departed. He sighed. It would be better to arrive in Crasherton well rested. He closed his eyes again, but his thoughts swirled now. Would his father be in the town as Philpott had predicted? Since the spectacle was organized by an engine manufacturer, Ernest Matthew Montague no doubt sensed the opportunity that lay in such an event. He would want to witness it first-hand.

The fuzziness of sleep lingered as another question pierced Winston's thoughts. How likely was it that his mother would travel? Philpott's assessment had been correct. She preferred the comforts of Toronto civilization to anything else. But she might not pass up an opportunity to see Winston, especially with how their last interaction had ended. The memory pinched his heart. Her wiping away the first tears he could remember seeing her cry. Since then, she had sent several unanswered letters, including the one in his pocket. He needed a plan for how to handle seeing her while he was supposed to be working. It wouldn't deter her from pleading with him to listen. Would he, though? Too much to contemplate. He closed his eyes.

Fabric ruffled across from Winston. He straightened, shaking off the last of his sleepy state.

"Oh dear. Have I woken you?" the woman asked, her warm voice tinged with concern.

"Not at all," Winston said. "I was merely resting my eyes." He offered her a smile, careful not to let his glance linger too long on her eyes. Such small oversights could be an affront to a woman, especially one travelling alone.

Miller must have left the compartment at some point and she had taken his seat. She wore the same dress as the day before, though it showed no signs of wrinkles. How had she managed that?

A book rested on her lap. Doyle. Winston smiled at her choice of reading matter.

"Have you read it?" She pointed at the book. "I've just started it, but I hear it's quite good."

"It is. And I won't tell you which clue set me off in the wrong direction. He's quite remarkable, though, isn't he?"

"He's just a character, isn't he?" Confusion pinched her features.

Winston shook his head. "Not Sherlock Holmes. I mean Doyle. To have such a mind. One wonders if he isn't a little criminally inclined to have come up with such stories. Though he says he's written the last of Holmes."

"Surely not," she said, pushing the book toward her knees. Should he tell her that there hadn't been a new Sherlock Holmes story in years?

She tapped her finger on the book. "Perhaps this isn't suitable material for a woman to be reading?" Confusion had turned to worry. Winston was about to answer when, without warning, she snatched the book and stashed it in her handbag, the click of the bag's latch getting lost in the squeal of the train's wheels.

The compartment door opened and Miller entered. He wore his uniform, and Winston observed the woman take notice.

Miller's cheeks reddened. "Good day, ma'am," he said, bowing almost imperceptibly in her direction.

"Have I taken your seat, Constable?"

"Not at all. Please stay where you are." He sat beside Winston.

"I've walked the length of the train. Every compartment seems to have a fine view," Miller said.

"How much longer do you think the journey will take?" the woman asked, turning her attention to the scenery. "It's just that I'm rather peckish."

Winston had eaten his packaged breakfast immediately on boarding the train in Penticton. He was ready for something more to eat as well. "There may be a sandwich cart brought around."

She tilted her head toward Winston. A curl had escaped, and she removed her hat briefly to replace it. Winston marvelled at how quickly and surely her fingers moved. Inspired by their conversation, Winston considered briefly what Holmes would deduce from this. The woman likely did not have a maid to help her dress at home, he decided.

"I will wait for that, then, thank you," she said, and she returned her gaze to the window.

Miller broke the silence by clearing his throat. Winston had seen him stealing furtive glances at the woman since she had mentioned being hungry. "Shall I go look for sandwiches, sir? For all of us?" He sprang to his feet and left the compartment with purpose before Winston had a chance to reply.

"He called you sir." The woman's statement surprised Winston. "Does that mean that you are of a higher rank than police constable?"

"For the purposes of this trip, I am a constable. But ordinarily, I am a detective. I will wait until we are settled in Crasherton before changing into my uniform." Why was he explaining this?

"Are you the only policemen attending the crash?" she asked.

Winston considered how to answer her question. He didn't want to alarm her if she wasn't aware of what had happened in Texas. "There will be so many people, it seems prudent to also have police in attendance." He saw no need to tell her exactly how many would be there.

"Well, I feel safer knowing that such a detail has been seen to," she said as she looked out the window again. "Are you expecting trouble, though? What about safety? I understand that a similar crash in Texas yielded two deaths."

So she did know about Texas. "This crash will be different," he said. Why was this woman asking these questions? Before Winston could ask, Miller returned with three wrapped sandwiches. The woman opened her small coin purse to pay. Winston waved her away and handed Miller coins to cover the purchase.

They ate their sandwiches in silence. Winston retraced the contact he'd had with the woman during the long journey. Had she purposely sought them out? The tenor of her conversation had changed once she'd seen Miller in his uniform. She was a puzzle, that much was certain.

CHAPTER 7

Jack

As the train slowed into Crasherton, Winston felt a tingle of anticipation in his stomach. The situation was unique, and the event itself was bound to be exciting. He'd been so tied up with preparations, it was the first time he'd indulged a little exhilaration. He couldn't help contrasting this feeling with the apprehension that had filled him when he'd arrived in Toronto earlier in the year for George's wedding. Winston's jaw tightened. If his parents turned up in Crasherton, he would use the excuse of his work assignment to avoid spending much time with them. His mother could continue sending weekly letters after this. He was not obligated to read them.

The long blast of the train's whistle sounded, rousing Winston from his thoughts. Outside the window, a small settlement came into view. Beyond the makeshift shack that served as a station, he could see wooden structures and tents. A few people waited at the platform for friends and family. A loud hiss of steam announced the train's braking to a stop. Winston stood and gathered his belongings.

Miller rose to hold the compartment door open for their travelling companion. She bid them goodbye and moved along the corridor. He handed Winston his bag, and the two men joined the other passengers moving in slow procession. When they stepped onto the platform, nobody waited to greet them. The other constables were set to arrive the next day.

Passengers on the platform parted for Miller, dressed in his deep blue wool with shiny buttons. Winston regretted not having changed into his constable's uniform on the train.

Outside the station, the crowd's energy pulled the men forward. Vendors offered pies and ale. Others shouted names of hotels accepting visitors. Miller turned to Winston. "Where are we staying?"

Winston pulled out his notepad and flipped to the page on which he'd recorded logistical details. "I asked the event organizers to recommend a hotel." He pulled a folded paper from his pocket. "I have secured rooms at the Crasherton Inn."

"Inn?"

"According to the telegram. The directions are to look for the white building." A quick turn on his heel revealed several white buildings, none of which resembled any inns Winston was familiar with. Even he, without any experience with manual labour, could see the buildings were constructed to be temporary. "Perhaps it's best to temper your expectations," he suggested. Although planning for the crash had begun nearly two years earlier, as seemed so often the case, the required work had failed to keep up to the original schedule.

"How many people did you say would be here, sir?" Miller asked.

"The newspapers mentioned eight thousand as a figure." The midday sun had found the back of Winston's neck. Interesting that this was a much hotter sun than the one in Vancouver.

Miller whistled softly. "That's got to be nearly half the number of residents in Vancouver."

The next census wasn't due for a few years, but the city had grown substantially since the last one taken, which had declared over thirteen thousand residents in Vancouver.

"Many people will come from the surrounding area, Washington, Idaho, and perhaps other provinces in Canada. It's not every day you have the opportunity to see two locomotives crash into each other," Winston said. As an event meant to promote rail travel, it was clever—every spectator would need to purchase rail tickets to get to the crash site. But the idea of intentionally crashing two locomotives to demonstrate the safety of rail travel seemed contradictory.

Winston wondered what George thought. He was a true railwayman himself now, in his management role of their father's railway business.

As they approached the townsite, Miller said, "It's quite something, isn't it, sir?"

Winston followed Miller's gaze to the sizable number of saloons among the new structures. The tallest buildings were two storeys, and as they searched the landscape in front of them, nothing appeared to be as grand as one might expect for an inn. "I imagine we will be given little more than a bed in each room. If we're lucky, doors that close," Winston said.

To their left, frenzied sawing and hammering drowned out the noise of the crowd. As they walked, smells from the market stalls promised food, Winston's stomach grumbling in response. He hadn't eaten since the small sandwich on the train.

The men continued along the street until they found the hastily drawn sign for the Crasherton Inn, established 1898. It seemed some were betting on this becoming an annual event or even a permanent settlement. Was this why his father had allowed the townsite and crash to be set up so close to his railway line? There must be benefits to the Pacific National Railway, even with the locomotives and the event belonging to other enterprises. There were, Winston knew, mines in the area. Perhaps that was his father's interest.

A porch wrapped around the inn, with two chairs propped against the wall beside the entrance—a door split horizontally, with the bottom half shut. Someone had tried to make the space inviting with a handful of blooms cut from what Winston assumed were local plants. He tilted his head at the display. "That's promising, Miller. Someone around here cares."

"Cares?" A voice from inside the inn called out from behind the open half of the door. "Of course we care. But if you've come for a place to stay, I'm sorry to say everything has been rented."

Winston pushed the bottom half of the door. "I arranged earlier for a pair of rooms."

Behind a waist-height counter stood a bespectacled man. He looked from Winston to Miller, taking in the constable's uniform. "Ah, right." He checked the register in front of him for longer than Winston thought necessary. When he looked up, the man's ears had coloured. "There appears to have been a mix-up. I received word about only one guest, and…" He checked the register again. "We do have a single room. Whose name should I record as staying in it?" He pulled the ledger toward himself, obstructing Winston's view of it.

Beside him, Winston felt Miller tense. "You take it, sir. I imagine the other lads will be in the same boat. Unless you arranged somewhere for them too?"

Winston's ears prickled with heat. "I admit, Miller, I neglected to ask about hotel accommodation for the constables." He chided himself for the oversight as he remembered standing in the post office, dictating his reply telegram. He'd requested the two tents to serve as a temporary station but hadn't made arrangements for the extra constables. "I'm certain I requested two chambers here." Winston directed this sentence to the man, who shook his head in response.

"For my forgetfulness, I will let you have the room, Thomas."

Miller raised his hand to protest just as the innkeeper motioned for the men to follow him to the door. He pointed to a patchwork of tents set up between two buildings. "Overflow accommodation is available but looks to be filling quickly. I can rent you a tent if you haven't brought one."

Miller's face briefly brightened with a smile. "Look, sir. We are not here long, and we will hardly rest, I should think. It's no trouble for me to stay there." He jutted his chin forward. A flash of colour near the tents revealed the source of Miller's smile. A woman who looked much like their fellow train passenger stood at the entrance of one tent, smoothing the front of her dress.

"Very well, Thomas," said Winston, relieved to have avoided staying with the mess of people Miller seemed keen to mingle with.

Winston pulled his notes from his satchel and turned to the innkeeper. "Can I arrange for seven tents, please? I have a group of men arriving on the next train." He'd elected to add two extra tents to the number required to house the constables. Better to get them now than to regret the missed opportunity later. They completed the arrangements.

The policemen climbed the stairs and located Winston's room. They decided to store both bags in his room until Miller's tent was ready.

"Shall we look for something to eat, sir?" Miller asked as they exited the small room.

"A fine idea, Thomas. Let us first walk around and get a feel for the town. I'd like to get a look at the site of the planned crash, particularly the seating area for the spectators. Then we'll get a proper lunch."

The Crasherton Inn was situated close to the end of one of the streets that was lined with wooden buildings. Winston and Miller walked toward the centre of the town, passing several saloons and other small lodgings, all with hastily painted signs indicating they were full. Situated at the town's nexus was the grandest of the buildings, clearly identified as Crasherton Hall. The next building clockwise was smaller, with MAIN OFFICE painted on a sign in bold letters. Opposite the hall was a souvenir shop adorned with red and blue banners. Another large hotel faced into the square.

Most of the people wandering up and down the main streets wore either blue or red rosettes. "They must be to signify their support," Miller said after a pair of men called out to each other. One pointed to his rosette, then the rosette on the other man's lapel. The men slapped each other on the back and continued walking in separate directions.

"Well observed, Thomas," said Winston as a similar scene played out across the road. "We should remain neutral." The mood was jovial. People were in the town to enjoy themselves. The collective anticipation and enthusiasm were remarkable and would perhaps be enough to keep the crowd happy.

"It wouldn't do for us to be thought of as having favourites, sir."

The men continued on their walk, reaching what was supposed to be the crash site after an easy fifteen minutes. Along the way, groups of people exchanged friendly greetings and light banter, depending on which colours they had chosen. At one point, a small stage had been set up, and entertainers sang or danced for attendees. Winston paused to watch singers finish a rousing version of "Daisy Bell," a song that reminded him of a moment he had witnessed between Ellis and his mother. They'd been playing a duet on the piano and were both immersed in the popular song. His initial surprise that his mother was familiar with the song quickly gave way to a warm recognition of pure joy on their faces. It might have been the first and last time he'd seen such a moment between them. Winston squeezed the stone in his pocket and caught up to Miller.

The route was dotted with stalls offering all manner of goods—food, clothing, memorabilia. One stall even offered bicycles for rent during the festival days that preceded the crash, a clever idea to serve those who preferred not to walk between the town and the crash location.

At the crash site, the two locomotives were positioned opposite each other, nose to nose. The crowd here was dense where people had congregated to see the engines up close. Stanchions had been set up to prevent anyone from touching the machines, whose paint glistened in the sun. Winston scanned the site, noting the bowl shape of the terrain at the far edge that created a natural seating area. The distance of the perimeter established would keep spectators well back from the tracks. The organizers had evidently taken good lessons from the event in Texas.

On the outskirts of the crowd, they had identified a pie seller and were approaching the stall when Miller exclaimed and spun around.

"Is something wrong, Thomas?" Winston asked.

"This woman has just tugged on my sleeve."

"Please, sir. Are you with the police?" she asked. Her hat was askew and the hem of her dress dusty. A slick of perspiration glistened on her cheeks. None of these things appeared to be of importance to her. She gripped Miller's arm.

"Are you the police?" she asked again.

"We are, madam," Winston answered calmly. "How can we help you?" Miller eased his arm from her hand and straightened his uniform.

"My friend," she sobbed. "She's dead."

*

As HE FOLLOWED Miller, Winston's thoughts raced. He would need to send word to Doctor Evans, the Vancouver medical examiner. He should alert the event organizers. Would this death impact the timing of the spectacle? No, he was getting ahead of himself. He needed to see the body and assess the scene before drawing any conclusions.

The woman had now dissolved in tears. She leaned on Miller's arm as they wove through the clusters of people gathered for the pre-crash festivities. "Madam, are you certain she is dead?" Miller asked.

A muffled "I think so" was her answer amid the sobs.

If her friend was gravely injured, they would need to find the hospital tent. In his preparations, Winston had confirmed with the organizers that a space would be allocated to tend to the medical needs of the temporary town. He had been planning to visit the space tomorrow so he would know where to direct people, if required.

The woman stopped suddenly, and Winston nearly ran into her. She turned to Miller with a puzzled expression. "The way she fell…It almost seemed unnatural," she said at last. Yet a spark of hope flickered in her eyes. "We must hurry if she isn't dead!" They moved through the throng of people toward one of the locomotives sched-uled to be crashed. It had been decorated with red banners as if it were a prize animal.

Just as had happened earlier at the train platform, the sea of people parted upon seeing Miller in his uniform. When they reached its centre, they found a woman crouching beside another woman, who lay on her back. "Kitty. Good, you've brought the police," the crouching woman said, barely lifting her eyes from the body.

The woman's arms had been folded across her stomach, and her dress unfurled such that she appeared to have lain down for a rest. Winston looked at the crowd, which consisted largely of women, some of whom wore suffrage banners. It wasn't surprising that their cause had not been left behind in the city. He made a brief appeal to the cluster of onlookers. "Please move along while we attend to this woman. I know that she and her friends will appreciate the privacy and the space." A murmur passed through the gathered throng, and many nodded and averted their eyes as they moved on.

"Her name is Harmony Fenton," the woman who had found them said.

"Thank you, Miss…?"

"Simmons. Mrs. Kitty Simmons."

"Who found Mrs. Fenton, Mrs. Simmons?"

The woman kneeling beside the body stroked the dead woman's hand. "We were walking when suddenly she collapsed." The steady, warm voice triggered a tightening in Winston's stomach. He knew that voice.

"Melodia?"

She looked up, the shock of loss leaving her features limp. "We were just talking."

Winston lowered himself to Melodia's side. He began to reach for her to offer her comfort when Miller cleared his throat. Winston avoided looking at Miller but returned his hand to his side. "I'm sorry, Melodia," he said.

He turned to the woman who lay before him. The face retained its colour, but the features were slack. He removed his hat, setting it beside him. Leaning forward, he felt for a pulse on the woman's throat. Finding none, he looked for any sign of respirations. Again, none. He could see no obvious wounds on the woman.

Winston turned to Melodia and met her eyes. She brought Harmony Fenton's hand to her cheek. "I know. There is no life left in her," she said.

The dead woman wore a wedding band on her left ring finger. "Do you know where her husband is?" Miller asked.

"He works for the railway. Quite senior. He must be doing what railwaymen do," Melodia answered.

"Do you know where they are staying?" Miller asked. "We must inform him of this."

"I expect they are at the accommodation built especially for the executives of the railway. The CRC Hotel, I believe it's called."

They had passed the building as they'd left the Crasherton Inn. Winston had noticed that, as with Crasherton Hall, additional time had been spent in its construction. Not surprising, with Coastal Rail Company being the main organizer of the event. "Miller, after you clear this crowd away,"—Winston swept an arm in the direction of the additional onlookers who'd gathered—"please return to the town and find Mrs. Fenton's husband. Try to avoid panicking him. Simply tell him that he is needed urgently."

"Shall I see if Doctor Evans is at the inn, sir?"

Winston nodded. "Please. We will need his assistance."

Miller turned to Melodia. "What is her husband's first name?"

"Isaac." Melodia clutched Harmony's hand to her chest.

Miller rose, motioning to a few male bystanders. "This woman is hurt and we are attending to her. Please help me disperse the crowd so you can resume enjoying today's events."

After Miller set off on his task, Winston inched closer to Melodia. He unfurled her fingers from their clasp and lowered Harmony's hand. "You said she just collapsed? Without warning? Did she clutch at her stomach, or head, or anywhere else to indicate she was in pain?"

"Nothing. She was like a rag doll, just crumpled." She dabbed her eye. "I think I screamed."

"I'm sure it was quite a shock." Winston paused to let her collect herself, then continued. "Did you dine with her today? Do you recall what she ate?"

Melodia blanched, bringing her hand to cradle her stomach. "We shared everything today. A bun for breakfast, a pie with some ale at lunch." Was this woman more than a client that Melodia would have spent so much time with her?

"You knew her well," Winston said.

Melodia lowered her eyes. "I did." Beside her, Mrs. Simmons frowned. "She is my sister." Melodia picked up her sister's hand again. "She was murdered."

CHAPTER 8

Jack

Murdered? He hadn't yet reached that conclusion. How had she?

A new cluster of people crowded closer. The men Miller had appointed to manage the crowd had seemingly abandoned their task. Winston stood and marshalled the bystanders. He tried to keep his voice light. "Move along, please. I'm sure you'll want to give this woman her privacy. Besides, there is much to see and do. Carry on and enjoy yourselves." He pointed toward the locomotive and the stalls and other nearby amusements. Winston slipped his jacket off and draped it over the body.

Murder. He turned to ask Melodia why she had made this pronouncement, but she had slipped away. Why wouldn't she remain so she could share what she knew? Kitty Simmons had stayed behind and now crouched to take Melodia's place, crying near the body.

The onlookers had dispersed, for the most part. Only a few stragglers remained. Kitty dabbed at her eyes with the back of her hand.

"Mrs. Simmons. I am sorry for this loss you've suffered today."

"Thank you." The woman's voice cracked, and she balled her hand into a fist and brought it to her mouth to stifle a fresh sob.

Winston asked her where Melodia had gone.

She stood, her expression at first showing surprise. She turned around as if to look for her. Then she took on a knowing look. "She's an odd one" was her only response.

Winston considered the woman standing in front of him. She appeared to be younger than Melodia and the dead woman, and she was dressed more simply than either of them. She'd removed her gloves, and her fingernails were short and clean. But her hands looked to be somewhat roughened by use. Had she spent some time performing manual work? Not in the immediate past, but the evidence showed in the hands nonetheless.

He crouched again and lifted the edge of his jacket to retrieve Mrs. Fenton's hand. He removed the glove and examined the hand. For her, any manual labour she'd performed had taken place longer ago than for her friend. Her palms bore soft calluses. But she had, evidently, at some point performed tasks with these hands. Her manner of dress suggested that such labour was no longer necessary.

He turned his attention back to the sniffling friend. What more could she tell him about what had happened? He handed her his handkerchief but she waved it away, pulling her own from her reticule.

"I should have said before now. I'm Detective Jack Winston of the Vancouver Constabulary." He replaced his hat and stood. The woman's eyes widened briefly upon hearing he was a detective. "How well did you know Mrs. Fenton?" he asked, keeping his voice quiet. As he spoke, he bent down and adjusted his jacket to ensure the woman's head was entirely covered. A trio paused to see what was happening, and he sent them on their way with a sideways nod of his head.

"Harmony and I have been friends for years."

"Do you know Mrs. Spectre? Melodia?"

"Of course, sir. She is Harmony's sister."

Melodia had not mentioned her family in any of their previous encounters, Winston realized with some embarrassment. He had spoken freely about his own and had failed to ask about hers. He was prevented from considering this further when a voice called out his name. Winston looked around to see the friendly face of Doctor

Nathaniel Evans, who was approaching on a bicycle. After Evans dismounted, Winston extended his hand and forced himself to offer a grim smile.

"Doctor. I am relieved to see you. Did Constable Miller find you?"

Evans shook Winston's hand. "He did. Very good to see you, Detective." At this, he dropped his eyes to where the woman lay near Winston's feet. "Though I would prefer it was under different circumstances. Your constable found me at the Crasherton Inn. Now I see the wisdom in your choosing rooms at the same establishment as me."

"I had not expected to find death so soon upon my arrival, Doctor," Winston said, pointing at Harmony Fenton's body. "I had hoped we might avoid it completely while here."

"I've taken the liberty of dispatching Constable Miller to find one or two things I will need after we've moved the body. I hope you don't mind."

"Not at all." Winston reached to gently retrieve his jacket.

Evans lowered himself to inspect the body. "What can you tell me?"

Winston swivelled to look up at the latest group of onlookers that gathered. At its edge he spotted Melodia, colour beginning to return to her face. He returned his attention to Doctor Evans.

"This is Harmony Fenton." He indicated the body with his head. "And this is her friend, Mrs. Kitty Simmons. She summoned us shortly after Miller and I arrived in Crasherton."

Kitty nodded shyly at the doctor and took a step back from the body.

"Mrs. Simmons reports that Mrs. Fenton collapsed without a history of recent injury or illness. The dead woman doesn't look to be otherwise incapacitated, though I'll leave that assessment to you."

Winston stood and stepped closer to Kitty. "I'd like to speak to you later. Where will I be able to find you?" he asked. He wrote the information she gave him in his notepad, and she joined Melodia.

Evans rose to his full height. "I'll have to examine her. Have you a station set up somewhere?"

Winston pressed air through his lips. "Can we move her to the medical tent?"

Evans shook his head. "Best to keep her away from those we may be called upon to treat. Are your arrangements for the police station complete?" Winston had discussed his plans with Evans as part of his preparations.

"We have two tents that will serve as the temporary station. I'm reluctant to give one up for Mrs. Fenton." Winston pulled at his face. He had not considered the possibility of needing a morgue. "Perhaps a hotel room." The sun's rays seemed to focus on Winston's neck. "I imagine we should move her soon and find somewhere cool."

The energy of the gathering crowd thrummed around them. "I have rented a room. I wonder if we may be able to use it as an autopsy suite," Winston suggested. He thought of Miller agreeing so willingly to stay in a tent. He couldn't ask Evans to do the same, especially if his wife had joined him. Winston would give up his own room. He'd use one of the extra tents he'd secured for himself.

Evans shook his head. "I brought a few essentials, Detective. I may be able to secure more tools if needed." He rubbed his hands around the woman's limbs. "I don't feel any broken bones. I'd like to examine her more thoroughly before I comment on her cause of death or confirm what else I might need."

"Let's start by getting her out of the sun," said Winston. "We will need a wagon to transport her. Would you like to stay with the body, or will I?"

Evans offered to remain at the crash site.

"In that case, I will also confirm with the innkeeper his permission to use his establishment to house the body—discreetly, of course. He may have another entrance we can use. And I will ask him where to find block ice. My room will have to serve as her accommodation until we find something more suitable."

At the edge of the onlookers, Melodia huddled with Kitty in a loose embrace. As Winston walked past, Melodia slipped her arm from Kitty's and walked beside him. "I must speak to you, Jack."

"This is, as you can no doubt imagine, not a good time, Melodia. Er, Mrs. Spectre." He knew his tone was perhaps unfair, but they needed to get the body inside at once.

"I have some information," she said.

Winston steeled himself against the distraction of Melodia's urging voice. He raised his hand, counting on his fingers as he spoke. "We must move the body. Doctor Evans must examine it. We must notify her loved ones." He softened his tone and met her eyes. "I will take your statement, but not yet. Where will I find you?"

"But..." Melodia said, "she's my sister."

"I'm deeply sorry she has died, Melodia." Winston picked up the bicycle that Evans had ridden.

"I believe she was murdered."

Winston wheeled the bicycle to the side of the road so it was out of the way. "I would like to hear why you think that. And if she was murdered, I will investigate. But we must get this body...your sister's body...into the hotel." Winston stepped over the bicycle's crossbar. "Please. Wait here. Or return to the town and I'll find you later." He paused, then added, "I'm sorry."

Winston clenched his teeth. Perching on the seat, he balanced his toes on the baked earth of the road's surface. A tentative push of the pedal made the bicycle wobble dramatically. He had a couple of false starts, careening toward the boardwalk one moment, then heading for people walking in the middle of the road the next. Finally, he gained the momentum required to carry him forward. He rode into the town, grateful for the slight breeze he created for himself while pedalling. He could appreciate why Miller was so fond of his two-wheeled patrol duties. When he arrived at the inn, he rested the bicycle against the wall. The short journey and the heat had left his shirt clinging to his back. He plucked it and caught his breath before entering.

Inside, the lobby was empty save for a single elderly gentleman seated at a chair, reading a newspaper. Winston greeted the innkeeper and took him aside, away from the room's single occupant. He apprised the man of the situation and negotiated an arrangement to bring the body to his rented room.

"On a very temporary basis, you understand," the man said in a stage whisper. "I must insist that this will be for 24 hours only—until tomorrow afternoon at the very latest." He fussed with the cravat at his neck. "I have my other guests to consider."

"Of course. I understand." Winston would strategize what to do beyond that time, but for now, he was grateful to have somewhere to serve as a temporary morgue. The man was pleased to furnish Winston with blankets for a fee and directed him to use the back entrance and the back stairs to transport the body. Winston promised all costs would be covered. The hotel even had the use of a cart and horse, which he hired for another fee. The cart driver helped to load the bicycle before taking Winston back to Evans.

When he arrived, Winston found that two of the men that Miller conscripted had returned and were assisting Doctor Evans in keeping the area free of gawking spectators. He asked them to help move the body.

They laid one of the blankets on the ground. Winston and Evans moved the body to the blanket, adding a second blanket over the body for dignity. With the help of the other two men, they carried the woman between them to the cart.

As they passed her, he saw Melodia peel away from a small cluster of women to watch the procession. He wanted to reach out to her but could not while holding the blanket. With a slow nod and a pained expression, Melodia turned and walked away. Winston watched her retreat for a moment, then signalled for Evans to accompany the body.

Sweat dampened Winston's hairline as he walked, wheeling the bicycle instead of riding it. Even if he was unable to stay in his room, surely he would be able to use the inn's bathing facilities. He shook his head when he recalled the pain on Melodia's face. How insensitive for him to be wishing for his own physical comfort when she had just seen her sister die.

*

IN WINSTON'S ROOM, Harmony Fenton had been laid on a military-style camp cot close to the open window. At Evans's bidding, Miller had secured the foldable cot from the hotel operator, who had a good supply to serve the town's visitors. He was only too happy to oblige, understandably unwilling to have the deceased lay in rest on the room's bed. Although the day had felt airless, the window of the second-floor room admitted a soft breeze. Winston was thankful that the room was at the back of the hotel, fully in shade at this time of day.

He watched as Evans took a moment to smooth the hair from the woman's forehead before he began gently removing her clothing. When he felt his cheeks redden at the intimacy of Evans's movements, Winston focused his attention on a print on the wall. It showed a rural scene: cows grazing on a hillside, a farmhouse at the crest of the hill. "Now that we are away from the crowd, Doctor, have you a better sense of her condition?" Winston asked.

"Other than dead, you mean?"

As they had become more comfortable with each other, Evans had revealed a rather dark humour. Still, his comment grated on Winston. "Have you found any sign of injury?" he asked as Evans laid the dress beside the body.

"As before, nothing obvious. She could simply have a weak heart that chose today to stop. It happens, you know."

"I'm aware. My concern, and no doubt what will also concern the event organizers, is that of murder. If her death is natural, there is no cause for alarm."

"I understand. I too was hoping for a few quiet days to enjoy the spectacle."

Winston shook his head. "To be honest, I would prefer a murder. My skills would be better used." He pulled at his shirt from where it had stuck to his back. "I'm expected to wear a uniform while here. An investigation would save me from that fate." Seeing Evans's eyes widen, Winston lowered his head. "I mean no disrespect to the woman, nor do I wish to discover that she is a victim. I simply mean I'd rather be investigating than standing watch."

A hint of a smile signalled that Evans shared Winston's sentiment. "Now that I've been involved in your inquiries, I can't imagine returning to attending exclusively to the living." He worked his hands around her body, examining it with more care than when they had been on the street. After a minute, he paused and drew a sheet over the body. "Detective, you mentioned she collapsed suddenly. Do you know if she'd been in a crowd?"

Winston jutted his chin toward the window. "That's exactly what they were doing—walking amongst the crowd. One of the locomotives was on display." The noise of the street filtered through the open window. Pie and fruit sellers shouted about their wares; horse hooves clipped along the dusty side street below. If he closed his eyes, he could believe he was in Vancouver. But the snap in the air from the excitement was unlike any he'd experienced in that city. He returned his attention to Evans. "Why do you ask about the crowd?"

Evans brought a piece of the woman's dress close to his face. After a moment's inspection, he drew the fabric through his fingers. With a gentle hand, he lifted the sheet covering the body and held the dress fabric against the side of her body as if matching it against where it would be if she were wearing it. "Someone killed her, Jack."

CHAPTER 9

Riley

RILEY DODGED A conga line of laughing women in matching neon
Crashers T-shirts snaking its way through the growing crowd. Their
giddy excitement made her smile. Though music festivals weren't
really her thing, she was a people watcher, and the site was a feast of
colourful characters.

Earlier, she'd explored the VIP area, checking out the canopied
food and beverage areas and communal firepit. Ample trailer accommodations were available, and the area was slowly filling with people, most
of whom appeared to know each other.

Now, as Riley went in search of the vendors' tables, she stopped
to watch a group wearing bright colours strike poses as they snapped
pictures. The urge to capture the moments before a significant event
was a given in a smartphone world. Was there the same compulsion
in Jack's time? She wondered if Crasherton had been rife with
photographers for the spectacle. She'd found some images in her
research but hoped to discover more when she visited the ghost town.

Infrequent bursts of music drifted from the main stage area, competing with the soundtrack of tunes piped through the PA system. It
sounded like musicians were testing the equipment before the show
kicked off the next day. Riley passed the main festival entrance tent
where the people from the camping area streamed in. Beyond the gate
she spied row upon row of tents—the area she'd originally assumed
was her destination. She had to admit, even though Lucy's approach
was frustrating, she was glad to have the comfort of the trailer.

Riley spied a bunch of site maps fanned out on a table near the entrance tent and picked one up. She'd been kicking herself for forgetting to bring hers from the welcome goody bag. She traced the way to the vendors' area and checked her watch. She had time to do a quick tour before meeting up with Jules.

Aromas of different foods wafted from the food trucks and set Riley's mouth to water. She paused to scope out a menu when she heard her name.

"Riley! Hey!" Jules waved from an approaching wave of festival goers. His day pack was slung across his shoulder and the Crasher baseball cap sat low on his head. He looked lit up with excitement, like the rest of the crowd. Riley grinned at him and waved him over. "This place is great!" he said. "Did you get a look around?"

Riley told him about the areas she'd managed to check out. "I haven't made it to the vendors' area yet. I wondered if someone from the local historical society might have a table with info about the staged train crash—you know, stuff I can use to support the exhibit idea when I do a final presentation to Nick."

"Good thinking," Jules said, "but can it wait? The smell of this food is doing me in. What's the plan for dinner?" He mimed an exaggerated starving man's pose.

Riley giggled and linked her arm through his. "C'mon, you whiner. Lucy said there's a meal planned back at the VIP area."

✳

CLUSTERS OF LAUGHING people stood around tall tables. Many held mugs like the ones Riley and Jules had been handed when they'd arrived back at the VIP area. A small group had gathered off to the side to play a game and let out a cheer as a point was won.

The food trucks were arranged in a semicircle, creating a cozy, market-like atmosphere. Areas had been set up with loungers and chairs arranged in groupings. Lanterns and strings of party lights hung everywhere. It wasn't dark yet, but the effect would be stunning in a couple of hours.

The setting was picture-perfect. Lucy really had outdone herself. "Lucy is right to be proud," Riley said. "Everyone already looks like they're having a great time." She felt a swell of pride. "I hope everything goes perfectly."

"You're a good sister," Jules said, nudging her shoulder. "Let's grab a drink and get the details on dinner." Jules fetched a glass of beer for Riley, and they scouted for a tall table they could claim.

After everyone enjoyed a delicious dinner prepared by a trio of food trucks, the VIP area turned into a party. Jules had found people he knew from the city, and Riley watched as he regaled them with stories about his life in London. Lucy flitted in and out of Riley's field of vision, tending to the different needs of the guests. As darkness fell, solar-powered lamps came to life, and the scene took on a soft orange glow. Music streamed in from unseen speakers.

Riley sat at a table and nursed a now warm beer, trying not to think about how nice it would be to have Johnny sitting beside her. Feeling her energy fading, she caught Jules's eye and excused herself.

"You didn't have to leave yet," she said as Jules pulled the trailer's door shut behind him. "I just know I need to rest now so I can be Fun Riley tomorrow."

"Aren't you always Fun Riley?" Jules mimicked the air quotes she'd used around the nickname.

"That's what I said to Lucy. I don't think she bought it." She waved the comment away. "But seriously, it looked like you were enjoying yourself."

"I've had a long day. I should rest up too." Jules manoeuvred the table to transform it into his bed. "What do you have planned before the music gets going tomorrow?"

"I'd like to visit the town I was telling you about. Actually, it's more of a ghost town now, but after the original crash here, it thrived for a few years."

Jules cocked his head. "A ghost town? You're not scared?" He held his fingers out and wiggled them.

She laughed when she saw he wasn't being serious. "Of course not. It's not haunted. But it's part of the local history, and you know how I feel about history."

"Mind if I join you?"

"Tomorrow? *You* won't be scared?" she asked.

"I'd like to see what you see," he said.

"Well, that's a good thing, because I was going to ask you to drive me anyhow." Riley gave him a sheepish smile.

He opened his mouth to respond, but whatever he was going to say was interrupted by a yawn. "I should get to bed. Sleep well, Fun Riley."

She answered him by throwing her hand towel at him, only to have to wait for him to hand it back to her. "Thanks. You too."

After brushing her teeth and changing into her pyjamas, Riley heard Jules enter the trailer's tiny bathroom. She scrolled through her phone until she heard him climb onto his bed, then she pulled out her journal to see if Jack had replied.

Riley felt the usual spark of satisfaction at seeing a new entry from Jack. Even though it was by her design, Riley marvelled at being in the same location as him, only 120 years apart. Somehow, she felt closer to him than when they were both in Vancouver. She puzzled over how to reply to his question about staying in Penticton. It had made her smile. She had spent time there in the summer but didn't know much about its history. Perhaps she would be able to persuade

Johnny—or Jules, if Johnny didn't make it to the festival—to visit the town museum on their way back to Vancouver.

> *Dear Jack,*
>
> *My journey did not require me to stay in Penticton, though I know that it's a beautiful spot. I will visit Crasherton tomorrow. The festival that I am attending is a little further from the town than where the crash you are attending was staged. This is to accommodate larger attendee numbers in the twenty-first century. Still, the event is close enough that I can spend time in the town tomorrow morning before the activities here begin.*

She couldn't tell him that the town was virtually unoccupied now and decided on asking questions to help with her museum project.

> *Is there anything that surprises you about the event or the people attending? Is there any unique fashion at the event? Do the attendees accurately represent the residents of Vancouver, or do you notice that particular groups are over- or underrepresented?*
>
> *I know you'll be very busy, but (only if you find a quiet moment to yourself) please share more about what the scene is like.*
>
> *Best,*
>
> *Riley*

Snippets of music and conversation filtered in through the window, and Riley's thoughts lingered on Jack. As the gentle pull of sleep overtook her, she imagined him wandering around the same townsite she would visit in just a few hours.

*

RILEY WOKE THE next morning to sunlight filtering through the shades of the camper and silence outside. A twinge of excitement shivered through her as she thought about visiting the old ghost town. She swung out of bed when a quiet hum filtered into her small sleeping area. Jules must be awake. She pulled on some clothes and opened the pocket door to the main space of the trailer.

"Morning," she said.

Jules's unkempt hair stuck out from beneath a baseball cap for a long-defunct Montreal team. He'd started wearing a longer hairstyle since moving to the UK. "Hey, how was your sleep?" he asked as he pushed a mug of tea toward Riley. "A drop of milk and dash of honey. Unless your morning drink preference has changed since your visit."

Riley brought the steaming mug to her nose and inhaled deeply, letting the steam warm her cheeks. During her trip to London a few months earlier to visit Jules and Steve, Jules had fixed her countless cups of tea. For ten glorious days, she toured the city, visiting museums and galleries. Her time abroad was capped off with a trip to Paris with Steve and Jules.

"This is perfect." She looked at him through the steam. Not only was he awake, but he'd also been exercising, as she noted patches of sweat on his shirt. He noticed her gaze and looked down at himself. "Mike and I just went for a run, then kicked a ball. We figured it would be too hot for much activity later in the morning."

Classic Jules. Riley loved that no matter where they went, he always seemed to run into someone he knew. Turned out he'd gone to high school with the bouncer, Mike.

Jules pulled plates from a cupboard and plated muffins and breakfast wraps. "I picked these up from one of the food trucks."

As they ate, they compared notes and agreed that their respective sleeping locations had been considerably more luxurious than sleeping on the ground would have been. "It looks like the town is about ten minutes from here," Jules said. "What time are you looking to head out?"

"Maybe twenty or thirty minutes?" She looked at the list she'd started writing the night before. "Did any of the food trucks look like they served something we can bring as snacks? I have a couple of granola bars, but I'd rather save them for emergencies."

He set his mug down and leaned his back against the trailer wall, folding his arms in front of his chest. "I can check. Mind if I jump in the shower first?"

"Not at all," Riley said. "Remember to throw a hat and your water bottle into your day pack."

"I read the description of the town. We can go in a few buildings, but most of it is in the open." He tapped the hat on his head. "I'm prepared for a day outside."

"And there is some hiking nearby if we have time. Wear good shoes." Riley could hear the mom tone in her voice and cringed. She checked her list again. Snacks, water, hat, sunscreen, a notebook, her phone. "I think I have everything I need. I'll finish up eating while you shower, then I'll be quick to get ready."

Jules gathered his towel and toiletries. Before he entered the small bathroom, he turned back to Riley. "What are you looking forward to the most at Crasherton?"

Riley bit her lip. She couldn't tell him the real answer about Jack. "It will be neat to see a place that is largely untouched by time. I mean, some of the buildings are likely ruins. But it will be easier for me to imagine what life was like at the time of the crash event when I'm surrounded by the original structures. In Vancouver, it's hard because so many buildings have been replaced or renovated."

"I get that," he said. "How did it end up a ghost town?"

Riley explained how British Columbia had its fair share of abandoned towns. The stories for most of them were similar. Minerals—gold, silver, other ores—were found nearby and extracted until it was no longer profitable, either because the market fell out or the supply was exhausted. Some had been turned into tourist attractions. Others had been completely abandoned. "But the crash set this town apart. I'm hoping that while we're there, we can learn a little more about why it didn't prosper." *And see a space almost exactly the way Jack saw it.*

CHAPTER 10

Jack

"Murdered?" Winston asked Evans. Melodia was correct. "How?"

"I can't say whether the killer intended for the death of this specific woman. But I am certain that whoever inflicted the injury had the intention of killing someone."

A chill ran through Winston. Was Mrs. Fenton killed by someone she knew? Or was a madman on the loose at Crasherton?

"She was stabbed," Evans said. He lifted the sheet and motioned for Winston to see he had removed the woman's dress by cutting through the layers of fabric. A bloom of dark bruising radiated from her side. "With a thin blade. So thin she might not have felt it, if that gives you any comfort."

Winston crouched beside Evans. The bruise didn't appear to be enough to suggest murder. He was unable to make out any marks. "Are you sure?"

Evans pressed the skin beside a small red dot. "Here."

Winston peered closer. The wound could have easily been missed. Not for the first time did he appreciate Evans's commitment to finding answers. One area was slightly swollen, and a small sliver of red revealed a puncture. "What would do this? And how was it enough to be fatal?"

Evans ran his hand across his chin. "This bruising is the result of an injury she sustained a few hours ago." He pointed to a bloom of colour on the woman's side. "Someone could have bumped into her without her realizing. She might have felt a small pain." Evans pointed to the same point on his own body. "In a crowd, it's not un-usual to get a little jostled. And with the excitement of being here, any pain was likely easy to overlook."

Winston stood. "I don't see any blood." It was difficult to believe that the woman had died from such a small nick.

Evans rose to full height. "That's the clever thing about it, if I may be so crude. The incision was too small to allow much blood loss, but it was in such a place as to cause considerable damage. See how the skin has darkened around this area?" Evans again indicated the colourful bruising.

That the doctor had detected the mark against the dark patch was impressive. "I do," Winston said. "It's rather hard not to notice. But surely it isn't enough to kill."

"She bled internally. And the damage, if we were to look inside, is extensive."

"If she didn't notice the bruising while dressing today, the injury must have occurred after she dressed this morning."

Evans nodded. "Judging by this discoloration, I'd say yes. She was quite likely dealt the fatal injury this morning, though it took her a few hours to die."

Winston pulled his notepad from his pocket. "And you think she received the injury while in the crowd?"

"The crowd certainly would have helped mask the motion." Evans wiped his brow with his handkerchief. The room was growing warm, and they wouldn't be able to leave the body for very long. "Do you know how long she was at that event?"

Winston wrote down the question. "I'll find out if she had been anywhere else today." He focused on Evans. "We know how she died," Winston said as he tapped the side of the notepad with his pencil. "Now I need to know why, and at whose hand. I'll need to speak to her husband."

He surveyed the makeshift morgue Doctor Evans had fashioned out of what was supposed to be Winston's hotel room. The cot was at an awkward height, but it would do. Evans had brought with him many instruments Winston recognized from the morgue facility at the police station. The doctor had moved the writing desk away from the wall so he could place the instruments on it for easier access.

"It's not perfect, but I have the basics. I like to be prepared" was all he offered by way of explanation as he unrolled them.

"Do you need anything more?" Winston asked. "I could ask for equipment to be sent on the next train." He drew a hand over his bearded chin. "The difficulty is the time it would take to get here. Your need of it may have passed by the time it arrived."

Evans cocked his head. "I'll make do, Jack. The more critical issue is keeping the body cool. Can you get us some ice?"

In the city, Evans had been particular about ensuring the morgue was well stocked with blocks of ice. "I'll find the organizers," Winston said. "They will have some arrangement in place for block ice, I'm certain." He wasn't certain of anything, truth be told. He rubbed at the throb in his temple. They were in the heat of summer, and Winston knew from experience how foul the body would begin to smell without the ice.

"Even with ice, we will need to work quickly. I'd rather not be the cause of any illness outbreaks," Evans said.

Winston wondered whether one of the railway's refrigerated cars might be suitable for transporting the body back to Vancouver. They would have goods in them as they travelled the nearby track, but he might be able to arrange for passage given the circumstance. But all that would take time to arrange, and time was against them.

He pulled his watch from his pocket. "Miller may have already found the woman's husband. We can't use this as our interview room as well." Through the window he caught sight of the tent community.

"We're going to need the police station sooner than I'd thought. I'll check on its readiness."

"Very well, Jack. I'll continue my examination here and work as quickly as I can."

Winston looked more closely at the woman as his thoughts returned again to whether she had been targeted or attacked randomly. The colour of her hair reminded Winston of his mother when he was younger. His throat clamped. This could have been his mother. Only it couldn't be because his mother was in Toronto, and she would never be in a crowd where she had no control. He shook the thought away.

"Thank you, Doctor." Winston straightened his suit and fetched his hat from the coat rack. "I will speak to the event organizers and arrange for a block of ice to be delivered to the room at once." He'd need to officially inform them of the death, too—discreetly. It would be best to speak privately to the most senior representative of the railway.

✳

WINSTON DIDN'T HAVE to go far to arrange for the ice. As he descended the steps, the innkeeper stood at his place at the lobby desk. His eyebrows were raised in an expression of expectation, as though he'd positioned himself there hoping Winston might take him into his confidence and perhaps share details about the death.

"Hello again," Winston said. "I wonder if you could direct me to the head office for the organizers of the event. We require block ice to keep the room cool." Winston had leaned in and said this last bit in a confidential tone. The man didn't disappoint.

"Let me take care of that for you, sir." His voice betrayed a note of excitement at being key to the detective's work. "They've brought in a supply of block ice for preserving the food. Organizers dug an in-ground ice house up by the treeline. Stuffed the walls with straw for insulation." The man positively beamed with pride, as though he'd built the place himself. "I'll have one set up in the room right away."

Winston thanked him, assuring him that yes, he'd be sure to cover the fee for the ice…and the delivery, yes. He left word that he would be returning shortly, should Constable Miller return looking for him.

Winston walked behind the inn toward the sea of tents. Most were closed, their occupants off enjoying the festivities. Squeezed almost immediately behind the inn were the two large tents that Winston had hired to be the police station. A pair of men pulled work gloves from their hands as they emerged. "We're finished, sir. Would you like to take a look?" one asked, gesturing to the open canvas flap.

Winston had asked for the main tent to be furnished with two desks, four chairs, a bench, and a lockable trunk. All appeared to be in place. He was pleased with the size of the trunk. He placed the padlock key in his waistcoat pocket. Later he'd have Miller collect the things they'd sent ahead from where they were being held—the handcuffs, extra batons, the few sidearms and ammunition—and store them in the trunk. He dearly hoped they'd have no need of them.

In the second tent, a cot was set up along one side, with a wooden crate serving as a nightstand. Another bench faced the cot on the tent's other side. This would do nicely for constables to spell each other off during the night watch.

"Will you be needing anything else?" the same man asked.

"This looks quite adequate, thank you." Winston paused. "We will need lanterns or candles for both tents for use in the evening. And perhaps a small washstand?"

The second man scribbled a note in his small notepad. "Not a problem, sir."

"Are you still building accommodation tents?" Winston asked.

"As long as people are still arriving, we're still building them," the first man answered, turning to set off on a new task. Beyond the man, Winston saw the woman from the train weaving her way along the narrow pathway between tents. She walked with a purpose that he recognized as someone intent on speaking to him. She planted herself immediately in front of Winston and extended her hand.

"My name is Miss Lottie Smallwood," she said.

"Miss Smallwood. It is a pleasure to formally meet you. I trust you have spent a pleasant afternoon in Crasherton since arriving," he said.

"Detective," she said, reminding him that he'd shared his profession on the train. But even then, something about the woman's demeanour had suggested that she already knew who he was. "I think you have been detecting," she declared.

Winston didn't answer. He watched as she pulled a notepad from her bag. "I understand there has been a death," she said. "I write for the *Western Daily News*." She positioned her pencil over the page and waited for his answer.

Winston's heart sank at her words. A woman reporter was not going to help this situation. "There was an unexpected death earlier today, yes." He stepped to the side as if to walk past her. "As I mentioned earlier, although I am a detective, I was sent to Crasherton to assist with managing the crowd rather than to act in an investigative capacity." Perhaps that would be enough to prevent any further questions.

"Aren't you investigating this death, Detective?"

Winston considered how to answer this. It would not serve him to lie to this reporter, but he similarly did not want to give her any information with which she might construct an article. "I will ensure that the appropriate people—including those related to the dead—are informed." There was no need to tell this woman that Mrs. Fenton had been murdered.

"Do you have any information about the cause of death, Detective? I understand she collapsed and was attended to by a doctor. Is he the same one you work with on investigations in the city?" Miss Smallwood asked.

This reporter was well informed for having just arrived in Crasherton. "Why do you ask that, Miss Smallwood?" Winston couldn't help asking.

"I know you have worked with someone named Doctor Evans in the past. And you seemed to be comfortable with the man who helped you."

"There is really nothing for me to say at this point. You seem to know as much as I do." Winston hoped that by keeping his comments light, she would pursue a different story. One related to the upcoming crash, perhaps. "Are you here to report on the trains, Miss Smallwood?"

She lifted her chin and squared her shoulders. "I am here to report on the event. And a death is certainly a story to report on."

Winston was going to need to be careful in how he handled this. "I have nothing to say to you at present, Miss Smallwood." He stopped himself from sharing that he hadn't yet had a chance to speak with the dead woman's husband and that he was expecting to do so shortly, lest she decide to hang about, hoping to learn from the conversation. "Where are you staying? Should there be something I wish to be reported, I will ensure that you are notified." *And meantime, avoid you as much as possible.*

"As it happens, I have secured a tent nearby. It's a few rows over. Number eighteen." She gestured over Winston's shoulder.

They ended their conversation just as Miller approached with a well-dressed man at his elbow. Miller remained professional in his task, but Winston noted that his eyes briefly followed the retreating back of Miss Smallwood.

"Thomas." Winston swept his arm in an arc. "This is our new station. As I'm sure you've guessed, the room I rented is serving other needs."

"Should I see about getting a sign, sir?"

Winston tilted his head. They were only meant to be in Crasherton for a short time, but given their services were required within minutes of arriving, the townsfolk, however temporary their residence, may welcome the stability offered by this visible police presence. "A sign is a good idea, Thomas. Is this Mr. Fenton?"

The man standing beside Miller stepped forward when he heard his name. "The constable here wouldn't say what this was about. He found me as I was returning from inspecting the crash site. Will this take long? I am due to be at an event this evening and should find my wife."

Winston avoided glancing at Miller. "Come with me, sir." Winston parted the tent flaps so Fenton could enter. Miller shook his head as he met Winston's eyes, confirming that he had not told Fenton why he had been looking for him. Winston leaned close to his constable. "Wait thirty seconds before you enter. Linger a bit out here to see who passes. That woman from the train. She is a reporter, and she was just asking questions. I don't want her overhearing anything."

"I will, sir."

Winston ducked his head under the tent's flap and gestured toward the chairs, signalling for Fenton to choose one. The four chairs Winston had requested had been arranged in a semicircle with the small desks behind them.

Fenton chose the chair furthest from the entrance. "As I said, Detective, I am due to meet my wife."

"Where do you understand your wife to be at the moment, Mr. Fenton?"

"She's out enjoying the day. I believe she had arranged to spend it with some of her friends." Fenton leaned forward in his chair. "Why?" Concern crossed his face. "Why have you brought me here?" He stiffened. "Has Harmony done something?"

Interesting that Fenton would assume his wife was the cause of trouble rather than a victim of it. "When did you last see her?" Winston asked.

As he spoke, Miller entered. He shook his head at Winston. "Nothing, sir. There is too much noise outside. I circled the tent to be sure." He pulled his notepad from his pocket before he settled into the chair beside Winston.

The tension in Winston's shoulders eased slightly. They would be able to speak without any reporters listening in. "I'm sorry, Mr. Fenton. Please continue. You were about to tell me when you last saw your wife."

"This morning." Fenton dug the toe of his polished shoe into the ground. "What is this about? I'm not sure I like these questions." Fenton shifted his gaze between the policemen and settled on Winston.

"Mr. Fenton, I'm sorry to have to tell you this, but your wife is dead." There was no point being delicate with the man. His reaction to Winston's news would reveal whether it was truly a surprise.

Fenton's jaw dropped. His lips moved, but no sound came. "But . . . What do you mean?"

If the man was feigning shock, he was doing a convincing job.

"I'm very sorry, Mr. Fenton." Winston withheld any details, continuing to observe the man.

Fenton's shoulders slumped and he released a low moan. "Harmony? But I saw her only this morning. She was looking forward to enjoying herself." He seemed to remember where he was. "How? How did she die?"

Fenton's voice took on a pleading tone, as if upon hearing him, Winston would be able to take back what he'd just said. When Winston didn't answer, Fenton continued. "Where is she?" he asked, his voice softening to a whisper now.

"The medical examiner is looking at her now."

"Medical examiner?" The words caught in Fenton's throat. "What does he need to look at her for?" The veins on his hands pulsed as he clenched and unclenched his fists. "Are you sure it is Harmony?"

"She was with a friend, a woman named Kitty," Miller said. "And another woman named Melodia."

"Her sister," Fenton said. His eyes searched the room. "Was there an accident?" A sob broke through his question.

"Mr. Fenton, I'm afraid we think your wife was murdered."

Again, the man was rendered speechless. His jaw unhinged a second time.

"Doctor Evans—he's the medical examiner—is trying to determine how she died. I am trying to determine why." The hard wooden chair squeaked as Winston sat back. "This is a difficult time, but it would help if you could answer some questions now. Can you think of any reason why someone would kill her?"

"Harmony could never hurt a flea. But..." He pulled his hand down his face. "Some people took a dislike to her. There's a woman, Mrs. Chalk. She's a neighbour back in the city. Before we left, Harmony mentioned that Mrs. Chalk was awfully jealous of her. She resented that Harmony had secured a ticket to come here." He leaned toward Winston. "Harmony thought Mrs. Chalk poured hot water on the garden to kill the plants. Do you think she came here and hurt Harmony? Maybe she poisoned her."

Fenton had come up with someone to blame rather quickly, even though his assumption about the cause of death was wrong and the motive absurd. Winston wrote the name in his notepad and gave a slight shake of his head to Miller to discourage the constable from correcting Fenton. The shock of learning of a loved one's death was disruptive. "Have you seen Mrs. Chalk here in Crasherton?" Winston held his pencil over the page.

Fenton shook his head. "Perhaps I spoke too rashly. I've been here for two weeks, but Harmony only arrived the day before yesterday. I haven't seen our neighbour. One of Harmony's friends might know. They heard old woman Chalk bellowing for Harmony from our porch one day when they came for tea."

Winston made a note but had little intention of following up on it. "Anyone else?"

Fenton set his jaw. "Harmony's sister. Melodia. She was jealous of how much Harmony's life had improved. Harmony was never critical while her sister pretended to have the gift." Fenton nearly spat the final two words. "I provide more than enough to keep Harmony happy. She has no need to pretend anything."

In the chair beside him, Miller stiffened. Winston leaned forward. "You think her sister could have harmed Mrs. Fenton?"

"She said she needed to speak to Harmony this morning. That it was urgent. Harmony humoured her."

Winston noted the bitterness in the man's voice. He moved on to another line of questioning. "What about any of your associates, Mr. Fenton? Would any of them wish you harm and attack your wife to cause you grief?"

Fenton lowered his gaze. Winston tried to read his expression, but the only light in the tent was let in through the flap. He'd need to see about the lanterns he'd requested. A gnawing started in his stomach, and he realized he'd eaten nothing since arriving in Crasherton several hours ago.

Winston stayed quiet. Sometimes silence was useful. Fenton might feel pressured to fill it and fail to measure his words. Miller crossed his legs, then uncrossed them again.

Finally, Winston said, "Mr. Fenton?"

"What?" The man raised his head and his expression was almost startled, as if someone had shaken him awake. He was in a state of shock, very likely. The weight of the day's events suddenly sat heavily on Winston, and the task before him felt quite impossible. He reached in his pocket and clasped Ellis's stone. The perfect skipping stone. He'd been so proud when he'd found it for Ellis. The warmth of Ellis's voice as he'd pressed it into Winston's palm returned to him now: "Keep it for next time, Jack."

"Can I see my wife?" The question snapped the gloom of the tent back into focus. Winston sat straighter in his chair. No matter the restrictions he found himself working under, he was a detective and needed to solve a murder.

"Of course. But before we do that, can you answer my last question?"

"I can think of nobody."

Winston stood. "I will take you to see her now." The sooner the better, while her body was reasonably preserved. The ice would help, but he'd need to see about having the body moved by this time tomorrow. Another thing to discuss with the organizers.

Winston stood and lifted the flap to the tent. "This way, Mr. Fenton."

His thoughts swirled as he led Fenton and Miller around to the front of the inn. If transport to Vancouver could not be arranged, he would have to broach the subject of Fenton's burying his wife's body somewhere outside of Crasherton. He'd wait at least until after the man had seen her. There was no need to yet apprise him of the urgency of such arrangements. Let Fenton see his wife as he remembers her before he'd replace that image with the thought of her decomposing body.

CHAPTER 11

Jack

BEHIND THE DESK at the inn, a different man was stationed. He frowned when he saw Winston enter the establishment with Miller and Mr. Fenton. Winston regretted not using the staff entrance they had used with Mrs. Fenton's body.

"Are you guests?" the man asked. His tone made it clear that he thought he already knew the answer.

Winston approached the desk. "I am a detective with the Vancouver Constabulary. I am investigating a crime, and we are using the room I rented to assist in our task." He produced his warrant card. "I arranged all this with the innkeeper earlier."

Colour drained from the hotelier's face. "There's been no crime here," he stammered in a hushed tone. "You won't be disturbing other guests, will you?" His features shifted slowly, as if he was struck with an idea. "There will be an extra charge."

"I don't intend to pay more than I already have for the room, nor do I intend to disturb your guests. But it would be best if you instructed the cleaning staff to leave the room alone for now. So as not to interrupt us."

At this, the man narrowed his eyes. "I don't want any funny business."

Winston pressed his lips together. Did these people not speak to each other? "There's nothing funny about this. It's been approved by the innkeeper, who I assume is your employer?"

At this, the man blanched.

Winston caught sight of the edge of an envelope sticking out from the desk's blotter. "Might that be important?" he asked.

"One moment," the man said, withdrawing a single sheet of paper from within. Suddenly, he adopted a compliant tone. "Yes, of course," he said. He waved an arm toward the staircase. "Gentlemen, please proceed."

Winston saw him mop his forehead with a handkerchief as they mounted the stairs. *Officious nincompoop.*

Outside his room, Winston instructed Miller to wait with Fenton so he could check that Evans had prepared the body. It would do no good for the widower to think his wife was being disrespected.

Doctor Evans stood by the window, making an adjustment to the clothing now returned to the body.

"Nathaniel, I have Mr. Fenton outside the door. Are you ready for him?"

"Yes, Jack. You may bring him in."

Winston walked closer. He saw now why Evans had cut Mrs. Fenton's clothing from the back when he'd removed it. He'd carefully replaced it now and crossed her arms over her chest. Her face was paler than it had been earlier, but otherwise she appeared to be resting. For someone who spent much of his time with the dead, Evans had a remarkable grasp on how to treat the living. Winston would mention this to his uncle to reinforce how important it was to keep Evans as part of the team.

Winston opened the door to let Miller and Fenton into the room. The bed took up much of the space, bunching the four men together around the cot. Beads of sweat formed on each of their brows, and a single drop wove a trail down Winston's neck. They needed to find a better place to keep the body.

He quickly introduced Doctor Evans to Fenton and waited for the man to approach his dead wife's body. Winston positioned himself half a step behind Fenton and staggered his feet in case he needed to support the man when he confirmed the body was that of his wife. It was for this reason, Winston only realized later, that he didn't fall when, instead of collapsing, Fenton spun around and pushed Winston.

Winston was too stunned by the force he'd been struck by to react. To his right, Evans shouted a coarser expletive than Winston had ever heard him use. Miller, whom Fenton had somehow struck in the head, sat on the floor, rubbing his temple. "Sir?" he croaked. "Shall I go after him?"

"If you're able to, Thomas, by all means!" Winston replied, trying to remember the sequence of events. Miller, Fenton, and Winston had entered the chamber. Evans was standing by the cot, his hands clasped behind his back. Miller was stood beside him, and Winston was behind Fenton, who had hardly entered the room and hardly even glanced at his dead wife before rushing out. Was it simply the shock of seeing his dead wife? Or had something else driven him away so suddenly?

✳

WINSTON RETURNED TO the main crossroads of Crasherton and walked to the building that housed the office of the Coastal Rail Company. The town's position in a valley ensured the dust swept from the near continuous wind and gave the buildings a dirty appearance despite the fresh coats of paint. Although the sun was lower in the horizon, its rays had seemed to only grow stronger, and by the time Winston reached the main office, sweat had dampened his shirt.

On either side of the building were two drinking establishments where the town's temporary residents demonstrated their support for one of the two engines by frequenting either the Blue Arms or the Red Legend, representing the colours assigned to the trains. It was,

Winston had to admit, cleverly done. Both establishments were likely owned by the Coastal Rail Company, so it ultimately mattered not which one amassed more visitors.

The celebratory sound emanating from the pubs spilled onto the street. This area would become rowdy before long if people continued with their revelry. Winston squeezed past a small crowd milling outside the Blue Arms as he approached the railway office. Each man he passed bore a piece of blue cloth wrapped around his arm. He refused the offer of the fabric with a wave. "I'm a neutral party," he explained when the crowd called playfully.

Inside the railway office, Winston was greeted by a buzz of activity. Three men sat at a desk that look liked it was intended for two at best. Somehow, they managed to type without bumping their elbows. A bearded man stood behind the table, his attention alternating between the seated men and a sheet of paper he held in his hand. He looked up as Winston approached the men. "Welcome to the Coastal Rail Company. If you're looking for somewhere to sleep, I hear there is more room for tents just outside of town. Though you'll have to hurry." He looked down at the men crowded around the desk. "Space is scarce here."

"Actually, I'm looking for the person in charge. I'm with the Vancouver Constabulary."

The bearded man smiled and clasped Winston's arm. "Yes, I've been expecting you. Wonderful to have a police presence here. Not that we need one, mind. We have organized men to keep the crowd back on crash day." He looked over the shoulder of one of the seated men and made a notation on the document the man was reviewing. "I'm Abe Coulter," the man said when he was finished.

"Detective Inspector Jack Winston." Winston shook the man's hand.

"I believe we exchanged telegrams in preparation for this week," Coulter said. "I am serious about the scarcity of accommodation. Did you have any trouble with yours? I understand only tents remain." He leaned toward Winston. "We are as successful as we were hoping to be. Perhaps more."

"Yes, everything is fine," Winston said, thinking of the body in his hotel room. "We are using tents as the police station. They are set up now, and tents have been made available for the additional officers, who will arrive shortly."

"Excellent to hear. Do let me know if there is anything I can help with." He looked at Winston expectantly.

Winston considered whether to ask the man for a few additional bodies to serve as crowd control now. He could see the need after seeing the town and crash site, and especially with Mrs. Fenton's death. He wouldn't be able to supply them with uniforms because they were made in Seattle. But perhaps he could request several shirts of the same colour to be sent from Vancouver, with large buttons to identify the men as having some standing with the police.

As if he read Winston's mind, Coulter continued. "We have appointed men from the trains to act as guards during the crash to keep the crowd in hand. We even gave them uniforms, much like they wear when working on the trains. You may have wasted your time coming here. No need for the police."

Winston was reluctant to break the jovial atmosphere, but he needed to expedite things. "Actually, you do, Mr. Coulter." He lowered his voice. "A woman has died."

The clatter of the typewriters halted, and Coulter's eyes widened. Winston took the man aside to the back corner of the room. "I believe it is murder," he whispered.

"Murder?" Coulter repeated, mirroring Winston's whisper. His mouth gaped. "Surely it has nothing to do with the train or the crash?"

"Everyone is here because of the crash, sir. The motive for the crime remains unknown at present. It would be best if I could speak with whomever is in charge directly."

The entrance door opened, and a man began speaking before he was in the room. "Mr. Parker has given me a list—" He nodded to Winston, lowering the clipboard he'd been waving in the air, and directed his statement to Coulter. "Apologies. I must speak to you urgently."

The men conferred and Winston waited. Parker. He knew the name from conversations with his father. He was head of the Coastal Rail Company.

"I thought this was an event by the engine manufacturer," Winston said.

"Mr. Parker has a lot of interests," Coulter said. For a moment, his eyes lost some of their sparkle.

Winston set the statement aside. He could ask his father for information about Parker. He turned to the other man. "You've come from Mr. Parker? As it turns out, I must speak with him," Winston said. He produced his warrant card. "It's a police matter."

The man had clearly hurried to the main office. He wiped at his brow with a handkerchief. Like many in the town, he had done away with a jacket and wore only his shirt with its sleeves rolled to his elbows. A bead of sweat trickled down Winston's spine. The man blinked and dabbed again at his brow. "Daniel Craven," he said, extending his hand. "I am Mr. Parker's assistant." His voice took on a reverent tone when he mentioned his employer's name. "Mr. Parker will be dining shortly. At Crasherton Hall. Do you know where that is?" Craven tore a page from the clipboard and handed it to Coulter. "Here is the list of what we need to see to." Turning back to Winston, he said, "I'm going there shortly. I'll take you."

"It is just across the street, unless there is another?" Winston asked.

"Yes, you're right. That's it."

The man's breathless delivery of everything he uttered exhausted Winston. "Then there's no need for you to interrupt your schedule. Though I thank you for the offer."

CHAPTER 12

Jack

As Winston approached Crasherton Hall, a stern-looking man standing outside the entrance shifted his stance to block the front of the door. "Invitation only."

"I'm a detective with the Vancouver Constabulary. I've been sent here to provide police services." When the man didn't move, Winston retrieved his police identification from his pocket. "This should serve as my invitation." Reluctantly, the man stepped aside.

The hall had been decorated with bunting in the colours of the two locomotives set to crash in two days' time. Laughter from groups of men was punctuated by the tittering of women. All were dressed as if for a formal dinner. Winston paused when he recognized his father. In the activity of the day, he'd forgotten that his father was expected at Crasherton. He associated his family with his life before arriving in Vancouver. Now he was investigating a murder, and he found it difficult to accommodate the presence of his family in this picture—the darkness of the crimes he spent his days thinking about. This feeling deepened when, with a flutter in his stomach, he caught sight of his mother speaking to another woman. She hadn't noticed her son, and Winston watched her for a moment. Despite their differences, it was good to see her smiling with what appeared to be genuine pleasure. Perhaps travel suited her. His fingers glanced his pocket, patting the reassuring outline of Ellis's stone.

Winston's stare must have been too intense. His father looked away from his companions and his face broke into a broad grin, sending a pulse of warmth through Winston's chest. Ernest

Montague waved his son over. "Jack, my son. I was hoping to see you here." He offered an embrace, which Winston accepted stiffly. When he pulled away, his father's eyes glistened. "I'm glad to see you."

The emotion of his father's reaction surprised Winston. Usually, the man was reserved, unflappable. It was, Winston suspected, one of the traits that served him well in business. "Father," Winston said, "I'm here on official business to provide policing services to the event."

Montague examined his son. "Still, it is good to see you."

Beside him, Winston's mother reached out to touch her son's arm. "Jack," she whispered with a note of surprise. Had she not thought she might see him? Her squeeze snaked a shock through his body. "I've missed you."

Heat enveloped Winston. Neither of his parents had been demonstrative in their affection when he was younger. After Ellis disappeared, they seemed to push him further away. Only in his adult years did he think that it might have been to protect themselves.

"You'll dine with us tonight?" she asked. Hope shone in her eyes.

"Not tonight, Mother."

"Tomorrow, then. I will expect you for luncheon," she said. She left no room to decline.

"Very well, Mother. Tomorrow." Winston turned to his father. "But at the moment, I am conducting an investigation. I need to speak with Mr. Parker."

Montague stepped back and looked at his son with surprise. "Has something happened?"

"I need to speak to him directly, I'm afraid."

His father searched the crowd. Gentlemen dressed in evening attire mingled with women in formal dresses. "He's there, beside the lady in pink. Shall I introduce you?"

Winston considered his father's offer. He had tried to avoid relying on his association with his father, but despite his efforts had been unsuccessful. Because his father was one of the owners of the Pacific National Railway, his influence was considerable. Even though Winston avoided using his father's surname, it seemed everywhere he went, people—certainly other influential men—made the connection between Winston and his father. Perhaps it was time to give up trying to hide their relationship. And Parker may be more inclined to talk if he knew Winston was the son of another railwayman. They appeared to have a friendly enough competition, given Winston's father was at the event.

Winston nodded to his father and followed him through the crowd. When Hugh Parker saw them, he frowned, though from the twinkle in the man's eye, he could tell it was a playful reaction. "Montague. Who let you in here? This is for important people only." He guffawed at his joke—a hearty laugh that made the man instantly likeable.

"Parker, this is my son, Detective Jack Montague. He's with the Vancouver Constabulary."

"It's Detective Winston, actually." Winston winced at the pained look that flashed across his father's face. "I was just at your main office and was told I could find you here."

"Detective." Parker extended his hand. Winston appreciated the man's grace in avoiding saying either name. "You must have spoken with my assistant, Daniel. Have you come to see the crash?" As he spoke, the man from the railway office approached, still holding his clipboard. "There he is," Parker said. He showed no note of annoyance at being interrupted.

Parker spoke quickly with his assistant, giving him a warm pat on the shoulder when he'd finished talking. Craven cast a glance over his shoulder as he departed. Did he wish he, too, could be enjoying the festivities?

When Winston had Parker's attention again, he said, "I'm afraid there has been an incident." He surveyed the room. Around them, people were engaged in conversation, but Winston sensed a lowering of voices so that people might overhear their conversation. "Perhaps we could speak somewhere a little more private."

"I'll leave you two to your conversation, then, Jack." Winston's father left them, and Parker led Winston to a small room. It was furnished with a pair of leather chairs, an occasional table, and a cart set with glasses and three carafes of different shades of amber liquid.

"I wanted to have a space to conduct private business. I had rather hoped I might be able to meet with your father about some plans that might be of mutual interest." Parker closed the door behind them. "Do you know whether he has further expansion plans?"

The question surprised Winston. Did Parker think he had asked him to speak privately as an emissary of his father? "You'll have to discuss his plans directly with him. I'm here on another matter." Winston waited until the man nodded his understanding. "There has been a murder. The victim is the wife of a railway worker, and given the spectacle you are planning, I thought you should know."

Parker blanched and sank into one of the chairs. "A murder? Who did it?" He ran his hand through his hair, unsettling its waves. "Do you think it has something to do with the crash?"

Winston eased himself into the other chair. "I don't know, sir. But everyone in this town is here because of the crash, so I cannot discount the possibility."

"You said the victim is the wife of one of my employees." The man flushed, as if embarrassed he'd not asked this straight off. "Who?"

"It is Mrs. Harmony Fenton. Her husband Isaac works for you."

"Isaac?" Parker's face lost its colour. "His wife?" The knuckles on his hand gripping the chair turned white. "I was expecting to see him here this evening. With his wife, of course."

"How long has he worked for you?"

Parker pursed his lips as he searched for the answer. "My assistant, Daniel, will be able to answer that." He checked his pocket watch. "He is seeing to final arrangements. This event would be nothing without him," he said. "But if you don't need exact dates, Fenton has worked for the administration office for about a year. He worked on locomotives before that. He was observing tests earlier today. Did he tell you that?"

Winston chose not to answer Parker's question. The tests must have been completed by the time Winston had arrived, but Fenton would likely have been in proximity to his wife. "I would like to keep news of the death quiet, if possible." He nodded toward the door, through which the chatter of the crowd filtered. "I expect rumours will spread quickly." He pulled out his notepad. "Have you received any threats or do you have any reason to suspect that someone might not want the crash to proceed?"

"Threats?" Parker asked. "Nothing." He gestured at the door. "As you can hear, everyone is pleased to be here." Parker rose. "As to avoiding the rumours, you had better find some answers quickly, Detective."

Parker excused himself and left. Winston followed the man with his eyes, feeling rooted to the floor by the weight of this unending day. There was much to do to move the investigation ahead. A deep growl in his stomach reminded him he was no good to anyone if he didn't get something to eat soon. But he must catch up with Miller back at the tent. He hailed a passing waiter.

"Would you be so kind as to bring me two bread rolls? I must dash, I'm afraid. Will this be enough?" Winston held out a coin, but the waiter waved a hand to dismiss the gesture.

"Compliments of the Crasherton Hall, sir. Please come back to enjoy a meal when you aren't so rushed."

The man returned quickly with the rolls wrapped in a linen cloth.

"Much obliged," said Winston, tipping his hat. Once he was out-side the building, he tore off a large piece of the still-warm roll, devouring it as he made his way to the constabulary tent.

✳

WINSTON SMILED AT the hastily painted sign affixed to the police tent. When had Miller found the time to secure it? Muffled voices brought Winston's focus back to his task. He wiped his face to remove any errant crumbs from the rolls he'd just eaten as he entered the tent. "Thomas. Mr. Fenton. Continue, please." Winston motioned for the men to sit and took the chair beside Miller.

Fenton slouched in his seat. He had the look of a man who was nearing the end of the worst day of his life. "As I was saying, Constable, I'm sorry for running off earlier. Harmony. Her death. It's a lot." He cast his gaze around the tent. "Have you anything to drink? Something stiff, I mean."

"I'm afraid that's not something we provide, Mr. Fenton. We could fetch tea or coffee for you," Miller offered. The other man shook his head. His was a sorrow that needed a stronger remedy. "Let me know if you change your mind."

"I went back to the trains. After you told me about Harmony. I wanted to see where it happened."

"You had been there performing tests earlier, correct?"

"Observing them, yes. Mr. Parker is clear that there are to be no safety issues with the crash." Fenton's voice held a note of pride. "I hadn't been looking at the crowd. Before, I mean." He pressed his hands into the table. "Do you think I could have saved her? If I'd seen it happen, I mean?"

"It's unlikely," Winston said. Fenton's shoulders relaxed at this.

"Did you see Mrs. Fenton at all this morning?" Miller asked.

Fenton furrowed his brow. "I didn't see her after I left her early this morning."

Miller looked up from his notepad. "Not at the crash site?"

With his eyes closed, Fenton appeared to think. His eyes burst open. "We saw each other very briefly. That's true. But it was no more than a simple acknowledgement that she was there." Fenton's shoulders slumped. Miller wrote this down.

"When did the two of you arrive here in Crasherton?" Miller asked.

"I arrived almost two weeks ago. Harmony arrived two days ago," the man answered without raising his head. "Harmony had never sat in first class, and she and her sister travelled together." A note of bitterness crept into his voice. "I had to secure tickets for Melodia and Harmony's friend Kitty. Harmony would never have let me get away with putting only her in first class." He edged forward in his seat and looked to the corner of the tent. His face took on the passiveness of one being struck by a memory. "She was so happy." So far, Winston couldn't sense any malice in the man.

"It sounds like it," Miller said. "How long have you worked for the railway, if this was only her first journey in first class?"

Fenton squeezed his brow between his thumb and index finger. "I started working on the trains for Coastal Rail. In the engine, I mean. A year ago, I was offered a job in the office. At a desk." He rubbed his knuckles. "It's hard work on the trains, and Harmony was pleased to have me around with regular hours." Fenton locked eyes with Winston. "My boss said I'd won a prize of upgraded passage to Crasherton. For my good work." Fenton's chest swelled as he spoke, clearly proud of his award.

"And once you arrived here, where did you go?" Miller asked.

"The one thing that the railway didn't arrange was accommodation. We're staying in tents—" Fenton looked around—"something like this. Harmony and I are staying near the Coastal Rail

Hotel. We've never been away. She was so proud of how she kept our tent nice and tidy."

Winston pictured the dead woman arranging her belongings.

"Is this relevant?" Fenton asked with a voice that betrayed his fatigue. "It's just that..." He pulled his hand down his face. "I miss her."

Winston signalled to Miller with a wave of two fingers. They would get nothing more from the man this evening. "You may find it easier in the morning, after a night's rest," Winston said. Though he doubted how much rest the man would truly get. "Can we count on you to return tomorrow? Would ten o'clock suit?"

"Is it necessary?" Fenton asked.

"It's easier if you come to us, sir, rather than us spending time looking for you. That way, we can devote more time to searching for her killer."

Fenton considered this, then nodded. "I will see you tomorrow, then." He rose and nodded to the policemen before leaving the tent.

Winston turned to Miller, who was jotting something in his notepad. "Well handled, Thomas."

The constable looked up. "Do you think he killed his wife, sir?"

"It's too early to say yet. Now, let's find ourselves a meal."

They chose a pub located a short walk from the constabulary tent. The mood was festive and the patrons boisterous. Winston and Miller's conversation centred on plans for managing the growing population of Crasherton. Several people had spilled onto the street. The atmosphere was one of pleasant enthusiasm. Winston didn't sense any troublemakers in the group.

"I should think that only a few more people will arrive tomorrow, including our constables," Winston said. Part of him wished that he'd arranged to have them arrive on the same day as he and Miller. He couldn't change anything now, and they had managed without the extra men so far. "Shall we agree to meet back here for breakfast?

I'll bring Evans, and we can discuss what he learned. After our meal, we can interview Fenton and Kitty Simmons."

Satisfied that they had a plan, Winston left Miller to keep an eye on the crowd for another hour.

CHAPTER 13

Riley

JULES TURNED ONTO the dirt road, the tires of his rented SUV crunching as they rolled toward the abandoned mine site. After a minute, they passed a series of once-white buildings set into the mountainside. Machinery and heavy equipment were scattered around, left to rust for decades. Some were overgrown with vegetation, like nature was reclaiming the area.

Another minute later, they passed a pair of well-kept houses that looked like they might have current occupants. A third house in livable condition stood alone about two hundred metres from the other two. "This town was mostly abandoned," Riley explained. "But a few people still live here full-time. Hearty souls, given how far they are from the nearest community." She could see the appeal in the summer, but in deep winter it must feel lonely in its isolation. She pictured the mountains on either side, covered in snow. The sun must hardly rise above the peaks November through January. She shivered despite the sun-warmed vehicle.

She had two angles she wanted to pursue for the exhibit. First, to shine a light onto the town's past. As she'd said to Jules, several communities in the area sprang up as mineral deposits were discovered. Tracks for short branch lines, like the one that had serviced Crasherton, were laid to service the mines, and people settled in the area to work underground or on the rails. The crash in Jack's time made this town unique. Did something happen that caused Crasherton to fail to live up to its promise as a railway town?

She also hoped to see the current town through the eyes of its residents. What kept them there? Did they have some connection to the town? She made a mental note to ask about this as Jules slowed the vehicle in front of a sign welcoming them to Crasherton.

Another chill swept through her as she thought about the nearly five thousand people who had once occupied this valley. And before that, the even larger crowd of travelers who'd attended the crash. Riley imagined Jack stepping off a train when he arrived in the temporary town. Might the hotel he'd stayed at still be standing? She wished she'd asked him the name.

Just beyond the parking area, two women stood opposite each other near a weathered building and what looked to be a lunch place for visitors. They were obviously engaged in a heated discussion, judging by how vigorously one waved her hands as she spoke. The other kept her hands at her sides, spun on her heel, and walked away.

"Whoa," said Jules. "Unhappy campers."

"Yeah, I'll say."

The woman who had been gesturing was now walking in their direction. She stopped to straighten a sandwich board that advertised the café's daily fare.

"She must work here," Jules guessed.

"She's walking this way. Let's meet her halfway." They grabbed their day packs and scrambled out of the suv.

Dressing in period costume all summer would have been stifling. Still, it would have made the moment feel more authentic than the shorts, flip-flops, and T-shirt the woman wore. Riley shook the thought from her mind. She was probably one of the community's remaining residents. Why would she walk around in a heavy costume all day?

"I'm so glad you've made it to Crasherton," she said. Any residual anger from her earlier argument was absent from her features. She handed them each a flyer and launched into a brief overview of the community, pointing out on the flyer's map which buildings to visit. "We have a small café, if you're hungry. And be sure to visit the museum and gift shop." She nodded toward the building across from them.

Riley thanked her and took a closer look at the site map. It looked like a handful of buildings made up the main part of the tour. She did a 360 and scanned what remained of the townsite, shading her eyes from the glare of the morning sun. Remnants of buildings lined three sides of a large area, which must have served as the town square. Some looked to be in decent shape, but most were barely discernable as buildings—just bits of foundations or partial walls. A couple of recognizable staircases led nowhere. The gaps between buildings were dotted with abandoned equipment and tools, making the entire space an open-air museum. How did they protect the artifacts from the elements? Maybe they didn't care. Again, Riley dismissed the thoughts. Rusting equipment only added to the charm of the place. It's not like it needed to be operational.

As she and Jules approached the first building, he paused to take a picture. What had caught his eye? She slid beside him. "This is the former municipal hall." She read a description from the flyer. "'It was constructed in 1905 after the first municipal hall was destroyed in a tragic fire earlier that year.'" Perhaps Jack had been in the original building, but it was unlikely he'd visited this one. "'The same fire destroyed nearly three-quarters of the town's buildings. Only half were reconstructed because by then, the mine was already showing signs of declining viability. The area continued to be mined for another ten years, when the population had dropped from five thousand to five hundred as the prices of different minerals dropped. By the middle of the century the population had dwindled to thirty-five, with today's population—eight full-time residents—largely being the descendants of three original families.'" Riley gave herself a virtual pat on the back for guessing correctly.

"But isn't this where the train crash was staged?" Jules asked. "That's where the name comes from, right?"

"Exactly. This explains that originally the crash was planned here in 1898 because it would be easy to access from different train lines. The vision was that this would become a hub. Soon after the staged locomotive crash, coal was discovered in one of the nearby mountains. The town boomed for a few years. There wasn't as much coal as they thought, though, which is why the mine didn't last long." She folded the flyer and tucked it into her pocket. "Because most of the buildings were still standing and usable, the town had a brief revival when it was used as a Japanese internment camp during the Second World War. There is a beautiful museum a few hours from here that marks that dark history of the region." She looked at Jules. "Maybe we could do a detour on the way home."

"I'd like that." Jules's voice had grown quiet. "You know, my mom's mom lived in one of the camps when she was a kid. She never talks about it."

They moved through the town for a few minutes in silence, pausing in front of derelict buildings as Riley compared them with the buildings on the crude map on the back of the flyer. "Amazing," Jules whispered. "Imagine having such a connection to a place that you refuse to leave, even after nearly everyone else has gone. That is some commitment."

Faint music drifted from inside a building with its door propped open. "Should we take a look?" Riley asked.

The former municipal hall, labelled Museum of Crasherton on the map, contained as eclectic a collection of items as outside, only these were suitable for indoor use. A bored teenager sat behind the cash register near the entrance, and behind him was a faded blue banner emblazoned with the image of a train. He didn't look up from whatever he was reading when Riley and Jules entered. Further into the museum, old plates and serving sets, pictures of 1960s movie stars, costume jewellery, and a collection of records that looked like it might be worth flipping through were nestled among faded wooden children's toys and puzzles.

There didn't appear to be any specific organization, other than general groupings of similar items—kitchen utensils here, apothecary jars there, and a surprising number of sewing machines. Riley's mind whirred as she considered how she would organize the collection if given the chance.

"Let's check out another building," Jules suggested as he set down a stack of tea cozies. "I don't want to be rude, but it smells … old in here," he whispered.

"That is rude, and you're noticing the smell because in most museums, everything is climate-controlled." Riley nudged Jules gently with her shoulder. "Let's go see the power station."

They had only made it a few steps when Jules stopped. "What about here?" It bore a sign that read UNOFFICIAL CRASHERTON MUSEUM, with the first two letters painted by hand. The building was a two-storey structure with a veranda that had seen better days. Like the other building, the door was propped open to signal that visitors were allowed to enter.

Riley checked the map. "It's not listed on here." She looked over her shoulder. The woman from the café had her back to them while she watered one of the largest rhododendron bushes Riley had ever seen. "Should we ask her?"

"Why? It's open. Let's go in," Jules said. He stepped through the door, avoiding the rusted tool that propped it open. Riley followed him to find another woman sitting inside. She recognized her as the one who'd had the disagreement with Café Lady outside. The woman set down her mug when she saw the visitors. A faint, sweet aroma reached Riley's nose through the stronger, musty scent.

"Welcome to the Official Crasherton Museum," she said, rising from her seat.

This room was filled with memorabilia from the train crash—much closer to what Riley had been expecting to find. She paused in front of a collection of faded red and blue banners. "We were just in the building back there." Riley nodded toward the open door. "Is this an extension of that museum?"

A scowl crossed the woman's face. Unlike Café Lady, she seemed to have held on to her frustration. She brushed a strand of grey hair behind her ear. "Despite what the sign out front says, this is the official museum. Where you just were is no better than a junk shop."

Although the woman's tone was far from the welcoming one she would expect at any tourist attraction, Riley agreed silently with her assessment. "Are we interrupting you? Are you open?"

"The door's open." She raised her shoulder in a half-shrug. "I'm open. Just don't waste your time back there. You want the real Crasherton? I can give it to you." A cloud of hostility seemed to surround her.

Riley gestured toward the banners. "Is it okay if I take a few pictures? I work for a museum in Vancouver and am considering an exhibition about the crash."

The woman waved her arm in what Riley took to be permission. She began by taking a photo of the sashes and the small card that explained their purpose. She skirted the room, snapping more photos of promotional posters and handbills, a small replica of one of the locomotives painted a bright blue, clippings of personal accounts from spectators, a display of faded tickets, and—in a sealed glass case—a collection of metal pieces, rusted at the edges but with patches of red and blue still visible in spots. Riley took these to be remnants of debris from the crash itself. She paused to make some notes and had just moved on to capture more shots of some tableware and a menu when the woman cleared her throat. "How many pictures are you planning to take?"

Riley tucked her phone away, feeling her cheeks flush. She tried to think of a response when Jules began speaking.

"I was hoping to learn a little about the town. It sounds like you know a lot about its history. What are the highlights?" The woman's shoulders seemed to relax after she heard his soothing voice.

"That's my sister out there. She claims to be the town historian, but she's only interested in making a dollar. Can you believe she wants to turn this place into a resort? There is gold in these hills. And I have a company willing to mine. But they'd need the festival grounds. They've agreed to keep this." She swept her arm to indicate the building. "This is the real history of the town."

She led Riley and Jules through a series of rooms that had been set up to appear as if a family continued to live in the house. A child's bedroom contained an old bed and dresser, worn stuffed animals, and a set of faded clothing on the bed, as if the child were about to prepare for the day. Inside the kitchen was an old wood stove with a well-used dining table. On one side, a rusted vegetable peeler with a cracked wooden handle rested beside a large bowl, as if someone were about to prepare a meal. Riley pictured a family seated around the table using the dishes that the other side had been set with.

As they continued through the house, the woman explained how the house had once belonged to her great-great-grandfather. He'd arrived in the town for the train crash and stayed to search for gold. "He found some. He died before he told anyone where the mine was after he was cheated by his partner. Just like my sister is cheating me."

If the woman felt awkward about unloading her frustration on them, she didn't show it. Riley understood. Sometimes it was easier to have a more honest conversation with someone you were never going to see again.

"That gold is our birthright. This is our legacy." As she spoke, she picked up a hole-filled blanket from the bed in the parents' bedroom, sliding her fingers between the broken threads.

Riley gave Jules a sidelong glance. His posture was rigid, and he leaned in like he was gearing up to find a moment to interject. Before he could, the woman continued. "Mining West has agreed to preserve this building and many of the others, too." She let the blanket drop. "My sister's plan would see nothing of the town's history preserved. The mining company only wants to access the mountains and the festival area."

Jules cleared his throat. "Well, it's a lovely house, and clearly you care a lot about it. Thank you for showing it to us," he said. "I'm sorry things aren't going so well with your sister." He steered Riley toward the door.

She planted a foot to ask a last key question. "I'm only here for a couple of days, for the music festival. Can we arrange a time for me to look at your records of the crash? Like I said earlier, I'm researching the event for a potential museum exhibit."

"Right now isn't a good time." The woman's tone had picked up the hard edge she'd had at the start. Then, as if remembering her role as an ambassador of the town, she motioned toward the door. "There is more to see in town. You should check out the power station next."

Riley accepted the dismissal and stepped out into the sunlight. She'd need to find a way, maybe tomorrow, to sweet-talk this odd woman into allowing her access to her records.

"That was…unusual," she said.

"Bordering on bizarre," Jules agreed.

In the half hour they'd spent in the museum, the temperature outside had risen noticeably. "Let's grab some shade," she said, steering him toward the shade of a leafy tree next to a rundown building. Jules pulled out a water bottle and drank deeply.

Riley looked across to the few buildings that faced the square directly opposite. She and Jules were virtually the only ones there. She almost expected a tumbleweed to roll down the path in front of them, like a scene from an old-timey western movie. Closing her eyes, she imagined the town bustling with people dressed in attire from the turn of the last century, all newly arrived to view the crash. She could almost smell the freshly cut lumber used to construct the buildings, hear the footsteps of people walking along the wooden boardwalk, feel the unique energy of a crowd gathered to be entertained. She pictured Jack, leaning against the frame of a doorway leading to a saloon after having enjoyed a meal.

Jules interrupted her daydream. "Where'd you go there?"

Riley's eyes snapped open. "I was picturing the scene when this place was filled with throngs of excited people anticipating the train crash spectacle." It was easier to go with the truth than to fumble around for something plausible to explain why she'd checked out for a bit.

"Must have been quite a scene."

And it must have been quite an undertaking to manage such a scene. Riley's heart warmed at the thought of Jack as the keeper of the peace in a rowdy town.

∗

THEY WALKED IN silence for the rest of the journey toward the power station. The sound of rushing water grew louder as they approached a building situated atop a ridge that overlooked the town. The steep hill only took a minute to climb, but the friends were out of breath when they reached the station. Riley paused and looked back over the town, again picturing it during its prime. Had Jack seen the town from this vantage point?

Light reflected off the station's fresh paint, causing it to almost glow. Riley wasn't surprised this building received attention, given the machinery inside still generated electricity for the few residents of

Crasherton and for three local communities. But she was stunned to see how old the machinery was.

"We've kept as much original equipment as possible." The voice belonged to a man who'd appeared from behind a large piece of machinery. "It was all built to last, as long as you look after it." His boiler suit was covered in grease, and his boots were well worn. Riley noted a wrench poking out from his pocket.

In contrast to the rusting heaps outside, everything inside this building looked clean. Rather than a musty atmosphere, the air was heavy with the tang of oil. The man acted as a guide, showing them how the mechanisms worked to generate electricity. Riley nodded along, but the explanation was largely lost on her. She let her mind wander to the town's history. Did the first settlers exude a similar pride and enthusiasm as this guide? They must have done. They'd built the town together and shared a vision for its future. She thought of the bickering sisters. It was sad that they'd lost the solidarity that builds community.

Riley and Lucy were different people, obviously. Each was pursuing a different career. But they came together when it mattered. Like how they'd pulled together to support their mother when she was swindled. Still, Riley had trouble picturing herself and Lucy as the sole residents of an abandoned town. She shivered the thought away.

The guide paused to ask if they had any questions. Riley saw this as her opportunity to redirect the discussion. "What can you tell me about the Crasherton event?"

He cocked his head, clearly having expected a question related to what he'd just been explaining. "The music festival? It started a few years ago. We have no involvement other than renting the land to them. We do get a few more visitors when it's on. And there are some other festivals later in the summer." The guide assessed Riley and Jules. "Are you here for it? You don't look like typical festival goers."

Riley brought her hand to her mouth and masked a laugh with a cough. "Actually, I'm more interested in the train crash."

"Of course, the crash. You would have met my wife when you arrived. And her sister works in the museum. Either one can tell you all about it."

Or not, thought Riley.

He looked back at the machinery. "I'm more focused on keeping this going."

"Okay, thanks. This was a great tour." Riley looked past the guide and scanned the room. "Can you remind me again when this building was constructed? Was it after the crash?"

"It was built to support the first mining operation. When the last project was shut down, this stayed operational because it provided power for the surrounding communities. The festival and this facility are what allow us to continue to live here. Otherwise, we don't really get enough visitors. But my wife has a plan to change that." Pride had slipped into his voice with the last sentence.

Of the two sisters' plans, Riley thought his wife's was less realistic. Surely making this a thriving tourist attraction required far more work than handing the town to a mining company.

Riley expressed her thanks and headed toward the exit. Outside, she nodded toward the main town centre to let Jules know where she was heading. "I'm going to talk again with the woman who greeted us. His wife, I suppose. Now that we've seen everything in here."

Disappointment clouded Jules's face. During their tour, he had asked the guide several questions about the power station's operation. Riley had zoned out, but Jules seemed keen on the details. "Did you want to stay here?" she asked.

"I'll come. It was just surprisingly interesting in there. Did you see that some of that machinery was designed by Nikola Tesla?"

Jules hadn't expressed more than a passing interest in history before, but she didn't want to discourage him. "I don't think my conversation will take long," Riley said. "Why don't you stay up here and we can grab something to eat after?"

Jules nodded toward the power station. "The guy in there says the café serves the best sandwiches he's ever had. But I wouldn't mind asking him a few more things first."

Riley checked the time on her phone. "Do you want to meet me there in an hour? If you finish early, you could explore one of the trails." She pointed to the trailhead a few hundred metres away.

With a thumbs-up, Jules turned, and Riley headed down the path back to the town museum.

The first woman Riley had met stood outside the café, which was little more than half a dozen picnic tables arranged in front of a tiny corrugated structure. "It's a converted rail container," the woman explained. "It withstands the weather better than wood." She pointed to the forest behind her. "Not that we have a shortage of the stuff."

"I was just talking to your husband," Riley said as she pointed up the hill, "and I was hoping you could tell me a little about the crash. In 1898, I mean."

"That was the town's beginning. But we're so much more than that now."

Riley noted how clipped the woman's tone was. Odd, considering the crash gave the town its name. Why wouldn't she want to speak about that part of its history? Hadn't her sister said this woman considered herself the town historian? She tried a different approach. "I'm researching the crash for an exhibit at a museum in Vancouver. I thought you might have some resources. Do you have any old records I could look at?"

The woman's mouth remained a firm line. "We are more than a locomotive crash." She offered a brief overview, adding nothing to what Riley already knew. This was supposed to be a temporary site for the crash, but when the nearby hills were found to contain coal deposits, a permanent community stayed behind. "We have extensive information about the town's prosperous years. And I can show you the plans for the town's future." She motioned toward the container. "I'll go get them," she said with decidedly more enthusiasm.

Moments later, she had unfurled a roll of architectural drawings. "This is going to be the first phase of the Crasherton Resort and Spa. A relaxation destination."

Riley had the same feeling she'd had toward the end of the museum tour: the need to extricate herself from a conversation that was peripheral at best to what she hoped to learn. "Yes, the setting is certainly relaxing," she heard herself say.

The woman droned on for a bit, landing, at last, on the matter of how she would fund the plans. "We will find the money. I had been speaking to a potential investor, but the conversation stalled when my sister insisted that a mining company was buying the town. That simply isn't going to happen." She slammed her fist on the table. "She needs to move on from the crash, and we need the hotel."

The woman was clearly passionate, and surprisingly honest. Riley wanted to steer the conversation back to the crash. "This is an ideal setting for a spa," she began. "Until it's built, perhaps you could really lean into the crash. There are others, like me, who find the history of the town fascinating." She took a breath and kept going. "Might I look at the archival records?"

"You'll have to speak to my sister. She's the one who is stuck in the past." The woman rolled up her documents. "And that past is best forgotten," she said through clenched teeth. "It's time to move on."

The woman walked briskly back to the café trailer. Riley stared after her, feeling like she needed to give her head a shake. What an odd interaction. This woman relied on the town's history to survive. Why did she want to distance herself from it?

Riley took a seat at one of the picnic tables that was in partial shade. She wondered if there'd been some scandal associated with the crash event. Thinking back to the newspaper articles that she'd read, she recalled the brief mention of two deaths. Is that what the woman was referring to? Riley needed to get a look at the town's documents.

CHAPTER 14

Jack

WINSTON SAT IN his tent at the end of a day that had been filled with unexpected events. Both of his parents were here and wanted to spend time with him. Melodia was here and involved in a murder. Evans, thankfully, was here to help with the investigation.

Despite not being in Vancouver, he was surrounded by people and crimes he was familiar with. Was he comforted by this? Puzzled? Did he follow crime here, or did it follow him? He wasn't so foolish as to believe that he actually had any impact on whether a crime occurred, but he'd hardly stepped foot in Crasherton before he'd learned about Harmony Fenton's death. And then, just now, he'd left Isaac Fenton, mourning his wife. Death and grief. Such was the life of a detective.

The prospect of crash day loomed in his mind as well. Provided the safety measures were followed, he trusted the crash would occur without any loss of life. Well, without any more loss of life. He thought again of Isaac Fenton. Hadn't he been checking on the crash's safety when she died? Was her death a ploy to distract him? To sabotage the crash? Who would do that? Why? By the soft glow of a lantern that had been dropped off earlier, Winston wrote the questions in his notepad.

The rough-hewn wood of the chair provided little comfort for his exhausted frame, and the cot didn't look to hold much greater promise. He pulled his journal toward him and captured a few thoughts for Riley, hoping that writing to her would lift his spirits.

Dear Riley,

Shortly after I arrived in Crasherton, I learned that a woman had been killed. She collapsed while in a crowd, though Doctor Evans (who is here expecting solely to enjoy the festivities and unfortunately has been called upon to work) believes that she was stabbed with a long, thin blade some time before she died.

We have decided to keep news about her death as quiet as possible. I would not like to cause a panic amongst the people who are attending the crash. However, the violence has not put a mark on the otherwise celebratory mood of the people who have come here to enjoy what will likely be a once-in-a-lifetime spectacle.

Describing those in attendance triggered a thought about his parents. Winston lifted his pencil from the page. Was that their chief reason for being here—simply to enjoy the spectacle? Or did they have another agenda? He shook his head to dismiss the thought and continued.

To my surprise, my parents are here—though that my father is here to witness the crash is perhaps expected. The need to solve this murder will mean that I will be unable to spend much time with them.

I am struggling to put into words how animated the people here are, and I anticipate their enthusiasm will only grow as we approach the event, which is scheduled for the day after tomorrow. I feel some pressure to solve the murder before then, as the crowds are sure to disappear as soon as the trains have crashed.

There. He had articulated his concern. It would be nearly impossible to solve this crime after the crash. In this light, the investigation provided him with an excuse not to spend much time with his parents. He had agreed to see them the next day, and his need to interview others related to Mrs. Fenton's death would allow him to keep their engagement brief.

I trust that you are well.

Warmly,

Jack

Outside the tent, he could hear the sounds of other people retiring for the evening. The celebratory mood meant that many were drunk, though nobody sounded out of control. Anyone who got too rowdy could be handled by the constables. He'd have to watch them, especially the younger men, who would need reminding—again—that they were there to work, not to join in the festivities. Though it would be unfair of him to prevent them from watching the crash.

The crash. Such a rare opportunity to see destruction first-hand. And while attendees were assured that organizers had strategized to reduce the risks they would be exposed to, Winston had observed many people swagger down the newly carved streets of the town with a daredevil attitude, as if they'd just embarked on some reckless adventure.

The crowds attested to the draw such an experience held. That this event had drawn his mother, pulling her from her beloved Toronto, surprised him. He longed to ask her about her reasoning for attending the event but could not think of a way to do so without causing offence. Could it be simply that she wanted to see her son? Perhaps a night of rest would allow him to think of an appropriate question for her when they met. With that thought, he turned down his lamp and settled into his bed.

*

AFTER A FEW hours of fitful dozing, Winston sat up. The noises outside his tent had been largely reduced to a low murmur of others preparing to retire for the night, save for the occasional whoop of cheer. SHe slipped his feet into his shoes. Perhaps a short walk around the town would help quiet the questions still swimming through his head. The names of those he'd need to find the next day—Melodia, Kitty, and Fenton—took turns as top priority. The puzzle of how he would interact with his parents after all he'd learned about Ellis and his death loomed in his mind. The hour was small and few others were stirring. As he picked his way between the tents, he decided his first stop would be to check whether Melodia had left a message for him with the clerk at the Crasherton Inn.

The night man now stood behind the desk, visibly tired from passing the night standing up. He apologized to Winston, explaining they still had no additional available rooms. "I understand," Winston said. "But perhaps someone has left a note for me here? Mrs. Spectre for Jack Winston?"

The clerk shook his head. "I'm afraid there is nothing here for you. She isn't a guest, is she?"

"No, but I am paying for a room here."

The man cocked his head. Winston had just come in from outside rather than from the staircase to the inn's rooms. "Shall I show her to it if she arrives?" the clerk asked.

"No, please don't. In fact, I've left word about this already, but please ensure that nobody disturbs room 203." Winston waited as the man wrote the instruction. "No housekeeping required." Winston slid a few coins across the desk.

"The cleaning girls will appreciate that, sir. It's busy and they're running off their feet."

Winston left the hotel and found a bench positioned in front of a store selling banners and other souvenirs. A chorus of birds chirped at his arrival but quieted after he had been sitting for a minute. He settled into the seat and leaned his head against the exterior of the shop, closing his eyes. He fell asleep until a hand brushed his.

"Jack?"

The voice was soft and low. Winston peeled his eyes open. Melodia Spectre sat beside him, her gloved hands now folded in her lap. He straightened. "Mrs. Spectre . . . I'm sorry . . . Your sister." His words escaped him and were lost to the sounds of the town as it came to life.

She stared forward and pushed air through her lips. "I know. And now you know. She was murdered."

"Have you spoken with Doctor Evans?" As soon as the question was out of his mouth, Winston realized how absurd it was. The man was very circumspect with privileged information.

"I haven't. No need to be concerned that he betrayed a confidence."

"How did you know? You told me before that you thought Harmony was murdered."

The fabric of her gloves stiffened as she clasped her hands tighter. "I didn't think it. I knew it."

"But how?"

"My sister had a secret. Someone killed her for it." She swallowed carefully. "Have you spoken with Isaac?"

Winston almost answered the confounding woman, then remembered that Melodia was more involved in this case than she had been in previous ones. "I cannot share any details about the investigation. But I do need to speak with you. To understand what happened."

"We were together. Just as Kitty told you. Harmony collapsed. Crumpled."

"How do you know she was murdered?" He searched her features, but Melodia held her emotions behind an impassive stare. He tried another question. "What did your sister know that may have made someone want to kill her?"

Melodia closed her eyes. "I only recently reconnected with Harmony. She does not—did not—support how I live my life." She opened her eyes slowly. "I was surprised when she invited me to join her here."

Winston waited for her to continue. After a few breaths, she squared her shoulders. "We passed a lovely morning. After breakfast, we walked around the townsite. It is, I'm sure you will agree, quite a remarkable feat that has been accomplished here in such a short time." She turned to look at him, and he nodded his agreement.

"She wanted to see the engines. Both were on display. She and Kitty went ahead to see them before the larger crowd began to build. I met them there a little later after stopping to visit a friend who is a vendor here." Melodia paused and tilted her head. "Harmony favoured the red one. I hadn't made a choice, but I will support red now to honour her." She tugged a red handkerchief from her bag.

Winston stayed quiet to let her elaborate on her recollections.

"I saw Isaac there, doing his tests. Harmony told me later that she'd spoken to him briefly."

"Melodia, you said you'd only recently reconnected with your sister. What was the reason for your estrangement, and what prompted this reconciliation?"

Melodia focused her gaze on the handkerchief now resting in her lap. "Harmony's husband forced her to cut me from her life. He said I was a drag on Harmony. Despite his instructions, she sought me out."

Winston noted that Melodia's interpretation of the sisters' disagreement was different from the one Isaac Fenton had shared. What did Fenton gain by misleading Winston? Winston breathed deeply. For that matter, what did Melodia? He didn't have time to consider the answers as Melodia continued.

"She was with child, and we have no other relations. She was excited, looking forward to motherhood and passing the wisdom of womanhood to her daughter."

Fenton had not mentioned any children. Did he know about the pregnancy? Winston noted that Melodia identified the expected child as a daughter. He chose not to pursue this in his questioning but to stay on the critical line of inquiry. "Had she told her husband? Was he also excited?"

At this, Melodia simply lowered her gaze. "He didn't know," she said.

Winston couldn't help his sharp inhale. A passing group of festival goers turned their heads at his sudden gasp. "She told you this?"

"As the pregnancy ran its course, he would have learned of it soon enough. It was still very early. Too early to announce it. Though I could see it in her face, her shape. Those clues would be easy for a man to miss." She scrunched the red cloth. "She was planning to tell him here, at the festival."

If Harmony had already told her husband of their expanding family, could it be that the news upset him? Could he have harmed her? Why wouldn't a husband celebrate such joyous news? Suddenly, it dawned on him. "It wasn't her husband's."

Melodia nodded once. "Which is why she came to me. She thought I might be able to persuade him to accept the child."

"How, if he isn't fond of you?" A cheer erupted from a nearby group.

"By speaking to him. She asked me to explain that she intended for the child to be theirs."

"And what did you tell her?"

"That was a conversation to be had between her and her husband. I could not help her. She intended to tell him yesterday morning."

So Fenton did know, and he chose not to mention the pregnancy to the police. "Do you know who the father is?" Winston asked. If the father is also here and Fenton knows, he may also be in danger.

"I believe he is a man of some importance. She did not name him, but she did say he is here."

Perhaps Harmony had told someone else. "Did your sister have any papers? A diary, perhaps?"

Melodia considered this question. "Many women do, but Harmony never spoke of one."

Winston would need to ask Fenton for his wife's belongings and why he didn't admit to knowing about her condition.

Melodia returned the handkerchief to her bag and stood. "Please find who killed my sister, Jack." She set off down the main street without looking back at Winston. He watched her disappear around a corner and considered his next step. Soon he would meet Miller and Evans for breakfast before meeting again with Fenton. He returned to his tent, hoping for a few hours' sleep before then.

CHAPTER 15

Riley

At the next table, Café Lady took an order from an older couple. Riley overheard snippets of their conversation—a light and pleasant exchange. Nothing about the interaction was laced with the tension she had felt when she'd spoken with the woman. Perhaps she had started on the wrong foot.

Riley checked her watch. Jules would meet her in twenty-five minutes. She'd give this woman some space and try again with her sister.

The grey-haired woman from the museum sat at the same desk. She raised her eyes as Riley approached, her expression unreadable.

"I'm just waiting for my friend to return from his hike," Riley said, hoping that her prickliness had passed. "I'd love to hear more about the town and its history—if you have a moment."

The woman settled into her chair, and a slow grin spread across her face. "You mentioned that earlier. Well, you've come to the right place." She pointed to a second chair, inviting Riley to sit across from her. "I don't think I introduced myself earlier." She splayed her fingers across her chest. "My name is Sonya. Shall I start with the crash?" she asked. She seemed to have forgotten her earlier refusal to help.

"Please," said Riley, rolling with this more friendly attitude. "I'm Riley." She pulled a notebook from her day pack. "Is it okay if I take notes?" A frisson of excitement shivered through her. She was finally getting somewhere.

The woman nodded and began. "Of course." Sonya's voice held none of its previous irritation. "My family has lived in the area for

120

over one hundred years. My great-great-grandfather helped build many of the buildings still standing here, and he worked at the power station for most of his life."

At this, Riley looked up from her notebook. "He wasn't a miner?"

"No, though I don't know why. So many of the men of his time would have been." She shrugged. "I suppose someone needed to maintain things above ground." Sonya looked in the direction of the mine. "Someone from my family has lived here since 1898."

"Your great-great-grandfather. I understand he came here for the crash?"

"Yes. And he saw what this place could be." She puffed out her chest, yet her eyes bore a pained expression.

"It must be difficult to compare his dreams to how things turned out for the town," Riley said.

Sonya straightened a stack of brochures, adding in a wistful voice, "People left to chase other mines. And without the trains..."

Riley nodded. Often the only connection between communities, trains were vital to a town's existence. "But your family stayed," she said. She kept her voice soft and her words few, not wanting to lose this woman's thread now that she was being more forthcoming.

"We did."

"And now?"

She adjusted the brochure stack again. "Now my sister has plans to turn the town around, but I think it's time to let go. We don't need this town dragging us down."

Not for the first time, this woman's words struck Riley as ironic, out of sync with her observed values. She had cared enough about the town to preserve the artifacts and maintain the museum.

Sonya straightened in her chair. "But enough about my family. Let me tell you about the crash. At the time, two different lines competed to control the movement of people and goods in the area. The

Pacific National Railway had started work on a second line from Vancouver through to Alberta—the same route the Crowsnest Highway follows today. You probably took it to get here."

Riley nodded. She knew this bit of history but let the woman continue.

"The Coastal Rail Company was willing to create a third route that would travel partway through the US, and it was contingent on using some of the PNR line. After the crash, their friendly rivalry fell apart. I think the mine owners played the two companies off each other, but ultimately, PNR won out and the Coastal Rail line was never built."

Riley knew CRC organized the crash. The company no longer existed, but she couldn't remember when it had been absorbed by PNR. She made a note to read up on rail history in the region. Which line was it that Jack's family had had an interest in?

"My mom used to run the museum." A look of sadness crossed Sonya's face. "When it became too much for Mom, my sister suggested that we split the collection." She leaned in. "Minnie sold everything she could. She's kept all the kitschy tat, which isn't going to fund her vision."

This explained the distinction between the collections of items on display at the museum and the unofficial museum. Sonya's effort, despite the unofficial moniker, was better at preserving the town's story. "What is Minnie's vision?" Riley had seen the plans but was curious to hear Sonya's view.

Sonya pressed her hands into the desk. "She wants Crasherton to become a resort. A destination for people seeking outdoor experiences and relaxation."

The setting was perfect, no doubt. "But you don't want this?"

"No. It's time for our family to move on. A mining company is interested in taking over the town for its operations. I think my great-

great-grandfather was right and more minerals are in those mountains."

Minnie's emphatic words rang in Riley's head. *That simply isn't going to happen.*

"We would have to leave the town, but we'd have enough money to settle almost anywhere. And the mining company has promised to create a proper museum to honour Crasherton's history."

Riley set down her pen. It was a difficult decision, and she didn't envy the sisters for having to make it. A narrative was starting to form for her exhibit idea—the life cycle of a town and its impact on the fragility of dreams. She made a quick note and met Sonya's eyes. The woman's eyebrows were raised, as if waiting for the next question. A deep rumble in Riley's stomach brought an immediate flush of heat to her cheeks. "Pardon me," she said.

Sonya laughed. "Minnie makes the best sandwiches for miles."

Surely she makes the only sandwiches available for miles, thought Riley.

As if reading her mind, Sonya continued. "Even in Grand Forks, you won't find a better lunch. Minnie uses bread from the Doukhobors. There are several enclaves in the area." She pushed forward a small pot of honey. "And put this in your tea. We make it here using our own hives. This one is a new recipe."

Local bread, local honey. Minnie's resort idea might have legs. Riley picked up the jar and read the purple label. She'd noticed the same little bee on a few of the less kitschy items in the "official" museum. "Does Minnie use it in skin care products?"

"Yes. And she's very good at it. She could run a spa. I just don't think it needs to be here."

Riley took that as her cue to leave. God forbid the woman should get wound up on that topic again. She thanked Sonya for her time and paid for the honey. It was time to meet Jules.

*

OUTSIDE THE MUSEUM, Riley fished in her bag for her sunglasses and made for the shade of the same tree they'd found earlier. She pulled out her notebook to reread the hasty scribbles she'd made about a theme for the exhibit. While Sonya hadn't revealed any new information about the crash, she'd at least inspired a trail of thoughts Riley could use to shape the exhibit's flow. She'd ask Jack for details to flesh out her ideas.

She adjusted her cap and began walking toward the café just as Jules called her name. In a gap between buildings, he emerged from the trees that formed the backdrop of the town. "I found a great trail," he called as he jogged toward her. "It passed by what looked like some ruins." His eyes twinkled like those of a little boy who had found a treasure.

"Should we have something to eat, then you can show me?" Riley found a picnic table and shimmied over to let him sit down.

"Sure. It's a short walk. Looks like the café isn't busy yet."

There were three other cars parked beside theirs now. The other visitors must be exploring, as she hadn't seen any other sign of them. "I think they can squeeze us in," she whispered.

Sonya was correct. Minnie's towering sandwiches, accompanied by a mountain of fries, were delicious. She'd asked Jules to place the order and the woman had been all sweetness and light, apparently.

After lunch, they walked toward the path Jules had emerged from earlier. Inside the forest, with the tall green canopy overhead, the air felt cooler, cleaner. Riley inhaled and let the forest air fill her lungs. She could picture herself really unplugging here and appreciated Minnie's vision for the setting.

They walked for about ten minutes, picking their way along a lightly used trail. Riley wondered if Jack had followed the same path during his time in the town. Had he needed to get away from the activity?

When they reached a clearing, Jules stopped and held her arm. "Listen."

She listened to him breathing, only slightly faster than usual. After a minute, she turned to him. "What, exactly, are we listening for?" She could only hear the hum of forest insects.

"That's it. We can't hear anything. Just the wind rustling the leaves, the birds, the bugs, and the ghosts." He wiggled his fingers as he'd done in the trailer earlier.

Despite herself, a chill snaked down Riley's spine. "Ghosts?"

"Crasherton is a ghost town. Don't you think the former residents haunt the buildings they used to live in?"

"What are you talking about? I didn't think you were a big paranormal believer." She longed to reach for the journal in her bag, but she couldn't think of a good reason to pull it out without having to answer any questions. Instead, she fidgeted with the cap of her water bottle, throwing droplets onto herself as she flicked it open and shut.

He grinned. "I'm just playing with you. But if there were ever somewhere to find a ghost—if you believed in such things—this would be it."

Riley rolled her eyes. "What did you want to show me?"

He pulled her toward an overgrown path. A few steps in, she saw two gravestones. They lay abandoned on their backs, their condition showing years of neglect. Tendrils of moss wove a pattern over the fronts of the stones. They were darkened with age, and combined with the effect of the moss web, it was impossible to see whether anything was written on them. Riley crouched in front of the first stone. As she reached for it, the hair on her arm stood up.

"Why are these here, just the two of them?" Riley asked. "I wonder where the graveyard for the rest of Crasherton is." She stood, searching for other grave markers. "The dead have to be buried some-where."

"I hadn't thought of that," Jules said. "Now that you mention it, it's a good question. This place seems a little out of the way. And there must be more than two people who have died here."

"It doesn't seem like a typical location. We'll have to ask. Sonya at the museum said her family has lived here for years. I'm sure she'll know." Riley pulled out her phone and snapped pictures of both graves. "Look at this," she said, handing her phone to Jules. "It's hard to make out when you look at them in person, but the camera catches the shadows of something written on them."

Jules held the phone close to his face. "I think it's numbers. Maybe a year? One … eight … nine … is that a three or an eight, do you think?"

"It's probably an eight. The first mining started nearby in 1894 or so. But the crash happened in 1898, and that's when the area was really settled." She took the phone from him. "Maybe it's a zero? Either way, it's from the 1890s." She knelt beside the stones again and tried to clear away more of the dirt and weeds, but she was still unable to make out the date. "Whenever they were buried, it's a beautiful spot to be nestled in—among the trees forever." Another chill reached her fingertips, and she pulled them from the dirt. "Do you mind if we head back, though?"

Jules nodded. "We should probably get to the festival soon, anyway."

Riley gasped. "Oh no! I forgot. Lucy will flip out if we miss the opening." She turned back to the graves. "I feel like this is something I need to look into, though. Let's ask in the town before we leave for the festival."

Back at the townsite, Minnie waved to a car as it drove away. "Did you make it to the waterfall?" she asked when she saw Riley and Jules.

"No, actually. We didn't get very far down the path," Riley said.

"I found a couple of gravestones," Jules said.

"Gravestones?" Minnie shook her head. "Are you sure? The cemetery is that way." She pointed in the direction the car had just taken. "You probably didn't see it because most of the stones are overgrown with weeds. I try to tidy it up once a year, but with everything else that needs attention here…"

"I'm pretty sure they were gravestones. They had engravings. But they were set back from the path," Riley said.

Minnie's face lit up with recognition. "I know where you mean. They've been there forever. They mark the resting place of the people who died during the crash. Actually, not in the crash, but as part of the festival."

Riley's pulse quickened. These were likely the deaths she had read about in the articles.

"After they died and were buried there, the town council of the time decided to leave those graves and choose a site a little further out of town for the town cemetery. There wasn't enough space up the trail there to accommodate many graves." She looked toward the treeline. "It's a pretty special spot they're in."

"Definitely." Riley pulled her phone from her pocket to show her the photo. She took a chance that Minnie was more prepared for a question now that her mood had improved. "Do you know anything more about them?"

"Not really. Not many people find it, and I haven't been up there in ages."

"Thanks," Riley said. She checked the time on her watch. "We should get going. It was nice to meet you." She would have liked to ask her a few more targeted questions about the crash, but they needed to get back. And as for asking Sonya, Riley wasn't sure what kind of reaction she'd face if she returned to the unofficial museum a third time.

They exchanged goodbyes and walked back to Jules's rental.

Mobile connectivity had been spotty in the ghost town, but as soon as they entered an area of better reception, Riley's phone started to buzz. Lucy had sent a series of texts. Riley's hands grew clammier as she read each one.

2:02 p.m.

> When are you back here?

2:08 p.m.

> Something happened.

2:09 p.m.

> It's not good.

2:09 p.m.

> It's very bad.

2:10 p.m.

> Where are you?

2:11 p.m.

> HELP!!

CHAPTER 16

Riley

COMPETING CHORUSES OF music streamed from the open windows of the cars that snaked along the dirt road leading to the music festival site. Because of Riley's VIP status, they rolled past them to the exclusive parking lot set up close to the VIP area. Riley shook her head again at Lucy having made her trudge from the general parking area the afternoon before.

Riley glanced at her phone again. Since the onslaught of messages had landed, she had tried to reach Lucy, dialling her number every thirty seconds. After another unsuccessful attempt, she dropped the phone in her lap. "I'm worried, Jules. She is usually glued to her phone. And after these messages, I assumed she'd be quick to pick up." Her leg bounced while she waited for Jules to park the vehicle.

He hadn't turned off the engine before she was racing toward the VIP entrance. Mike was shaking his head as he spoke to two men and a woman. His face was set in a firm but friendly expression. What kinds of excuses were they trying to give him so they could gain access? Mike gave her a wave. She caught a nasty look from the woman in the group. She probably wondered how such a mousy-looking person had access to the area while she, tanned and beautiful, did not. Riley pushed the thought away. She needed to find Lucy.

She would be able to move more easily without her day pack and approached her trailer to drop it off. Lucy stood to the side of the trailers. "Riley. Where have you been?" Her sister's voice was pitched higher than usual. Though she didn't display it physically, she was feeling the stress of the occasion.

Riley tucked a strand of hair under her baseball cap. "At the ghost town. I told you." She held out her phone. "You sent me a bunch of texts. What's the emergency?" Riley took a quick scan of the VIP area. Nothing seemed amiss. "What's up? I was really concerned."

"Right. It's just that I thought you'd be back earlier. I didn't want you to miss the first act. Plus, one of the bands had an instrument go missing."

"What was I going to do about a misplaced instrument?" Riley looked over her shoulder toward the VIP entrance, where Mike and Jules were chatting. "Don't you have security? Why didn't Mike stop someone from walking out with an instrument?"

"Mike doesn't know who plays what instruments. Besides, he's responsible for who gets admitted here, not who walks out." Lucy sounded exasperated. "But never mind." She waved her hand through the air. "It's over now. The musician realized later he'd left it in his trailer, not behind the stage like he'd thought. Not a big deal."

Riley couldn't let her frustration with her sister go. "Aren't these people professionals?"

Lucy scrunched her nose. "Of course they're professionals." Just as she spoke, someone wearing a gig bag strapped across his back raced past them with his arms raised skyward, clapping in time with the music. "Though perhaps that guy's having a little too much fun." Lucy giggled. "Anyway, it doesn't matter. You're here." She reached for Riley's hand and squeezed it.

Riley pulled her hand away. "I need a few minutes. I'm dusty and tired." *And you're super annoying*, Riley kept herself from saying aloud. "I'll get to the music when I can," she said, turning her back on Lucy.

Inside the trailer, the water ran as Jules took a shower. When he emerged and saw that she wasn't ready, he paused. "Mike assured me there wasn't an emergency."

"There wasn't. Lucy was being Lucy. I just need some time."

Jules looked torn. "Do you want me to stay?"

"No. I'll be there. You go. You can still get there before the music starts."

"Mike says there's a great listening space for us. I'll save you a spot."

Riley closed the door to her sleeping area and set out clothes to wear to the concert while the kettle boiled. While the outfit was not something Riley typically wore, she had pulled together something she thought would be suitable—a flowy shirt and embroidered gaucho pants, tied at the waist. The kettle whistled. Despite the heat, a cup of tea would refresh her.

She looked through the accessories she'd brought and chose the floral clips her sister had given her one Christmas. At the time, she had wondered what occasion her sister thought she would ever wear them for. Flowers were not really Riley's style. But she had to admit that Lucy had a good eye and the colours of the petals complemented her hair. Would Lucy recognize them?

Jules called out, "Bye!" Riley waited until the trailer door shut, then headed for the shower, where she let the water rinse away her frustration. When she exited, she wrapped herself in a towel and plunked down on the bed, pulling the journal toward her.

Her heart briefly leaped to her throat when she read Jack's message. One person has died—murdered. She had found the grave markers for the two deaths at the crash. She couldn't warn him about the second. The graves she and Jules had found might have been for the two people who died during the Crasherton event, but that didn't mean both were police matters. Eight thousand people in a space over a few days. Perhaps one had a bad heart and had suffered too much excitement. Or perhaps there had been an accident.

She fixed her tea, then opened her laptop. Could she find the names in the digital death certificates available online? The names hadn't been legible in the photographs she'd taken of the gravestones, but they might be mentioned in articles online. Riley limited her search to the week of the crash and entered "Crasherton Crash, 1898" and "deaths" into her browser's search field.

She scanned the results until she found the article she'd read earlier that spoke about the event being a great success, despite two deaths shortly before the crash—Mrs. Fenton and Mr. Montague. Next, she entered the names, month, and year into the search fields for the province's online death records. Both certificates had been signed by Doctor N. Evans. She recognized his name from Jack's messages. Jack had said that the doctor was attending the event and had examined the first body.

Harmony Fenton and Ernest Montague were both listed as having died from wounds. Jack's message had said that Evans believed Mrs. Fenton was stabbed. Murdered. Reading between the lines of the death certificate, Mr. Montague was about to meet the same fate. As much as she might want to, she couldn't alert Jack. It was a rule she was unwilling to break, as she didn't know what the impact of doing so might be.

Her curiosity piqued, she entered the name into the search engine. Ernest Montague was head of the Pacific National Railway. Was that the one Jack's family was involved in? She found the man's obituary. Her stomach sank when she got to the section about his family. Three sons. Ellis, Jack, and George. Montague was Jack's father. She pulled out her journal. She and Jack had moved on to a new book after filling the first one they'd shared, so she didn't have all the earlier messages that they'd exchanged. But she was certain that he had previously shared that when he moved to Vancouver, he had elected not to use his father's surname because of his influence, even thousands of kilometres away.

Her chest tightened as she considered what to do next. She couldn't tell Jack that his father was about to die. But to possess this knowledge, to know his future . . . nothing she'd learned up to this point had been anywhere near as significant as this information. Could she break the rules they'd established? What would he do with the information? What could he do with it? What if she only told him there would be a second death but not who it was?

She placed her palms on the book, as if doing so grounded her thoughts. For a moment, it did. She realized that if she told Jack that his father was about to die, he would forever associate her with that awful event. It was better that she said nothing and supported him when he told her of the news. She would have to simply accept that Mr. Montague, like Mrs. Fenton, was dead and had a beautiful resting spot. When she picked up her pen, it shook in her fingers.

Dear Jack,

I am sorry to learn that you've been plunged into a murder investigation during your time at Crasherton. I can imagine how critical it must be to keep this event...

Riley was poised to write *under the radar,* then realized that would have no meaning for Jack.

...out of the public eye. The concern that visitors will have if they think that there is someone at large attacking people would cause chaos.

Do you believe the murder was random? Or was the victim targeted? I will continue to search for information about the crimes.

She didn't know yet who the culprit was, so there was no risk that she might reveal that person's identity. But she did know who was going to die. She reread his earlier messages to her. He had mentioned that his parents were in Crasherton. Should she tell him to cherish this visit with his father? Had she known her father would die shortly afterwards, she might not have enjoyed what ended up being the last time she spent time with him. Those memories were not tainted by worry that he was enjoying himself. Perhaps it was better that she didn't warn him. Instead, she settled on a gentle suggestion.

> *I hope that you get an opportunity to spend time with your parents. Are they planning to visit Vancouver after the crash?*
>
> *I have found little information about crowd unruliness at the festival, so I hope I am not revealing too much by sharing that your plan to restrict details appears to have been successful. However, it does seem to limit how much information is available to me to help you.*
>
> *I will see if I can find anything more when I return to Crasherton tomorrow or the next day.*
>
> *Riley*

When she finished her note to Jack, Riley downloaded the death certificates and the obituary and saved them to a folder on her laptop. With a sigh, she closed her computer and tidied the journal away. The time she'd spent researching had been long enough to soften her emotions, and in the warm air, her hair was nearly dry.

Someone knocked on the door of a neighbouring trailer and shouted, "Hustle, Danielle! It's starting!" Riley jumped to her feet and checked one last time in the mirror. She was here to support Lucy and shouldn't miss the opening of the festival. The crowd cheered as she closed the trailer door, and she hurried to the festival grounds.

*

RILEY FOUND JULES in the VIP listening area, sharing a table with a couple who seemed to be enjoying themselves. They exchanged greetings over the din of the call-and-response chants the emcee exchanged with the crowd. Jules brought her a drink of the festival's special cocktail, sweetened with a syrup using Crasherton honey, and Riley settled in to enjoy herself. The next band was due to take the stage in ten minutes, and the general crowd slowly filtered past them on their way toward the stage.

As she sipped her drink, she let her mind wander to the event Jack was attending. More than an event—surely it was a spectacle. There were about ten thousand attendees at the music festival, which Lucy had described as a manageable number. When Jack had first mentioned the scheduled train crash, she'd looked it up and confirmed that fewer people had attended. In contrast, crashes in the United States a few years before the Crasherton Crash had drawn crowds of over forty thousand. At the Texas event, the one she found the most information about, an entire city had sprung up around the event, much like Crasherton. To some degree, the music festival was not unlike this, with the temporary accommodation and eating facilities set up. She shuddered at the idea of sharing a washroom with thousands of others. Any guilt she'd felt about not having earned a VIP space had evaporated.

The area near the stage had a luxuriously rustic feel, a juxtaposition only Lucy could dream up. Most of the guests held designer cocktails and perched at tables made from reclaimed wood. For anyone interested in getting closer to the music, an area immediately in front of the stage had been roped off, and Jules pulled Riley toward it.

"Won't it be too loud?" Riley asked. The crowd roared behind her as the band walked onto the stage.

"Probably," Jules shouted. "But that's the point, isn't it?"

As soon as the band struck its first chords, Riley realized Jules was right. She was caught up in the exhilaration of the crowd. The music was great. She abandoned her inhibitions, cheering and moving with the crowd. The second act was equally good, and Riley was swept up by the music's rhythm and by the crowd's infectious energy.

As the third band was preparing to go on, Jules touched her arm. "Are you hungry? I could go for something to eat." She nodded and followed him to a table that had been laid with festival-friendly finger foods. They were fixing their plates with artisanal sliders and locally grown vegetables when Riley noticed the trio she'd seen earlier. Somehow they'd managed to get into the VIP area. She spotted Lucy leaning in to say something to a glittering threesome of women at another table. The annoyance she had felt earlier with her sister had faded. Lucy threw her head back and laughed at a shared joke. It was good to see her glow with the success of the event.

Riley returned to the dancing throng and joined in. As Lucy had promised, the music was consistently great—loud, but great. Between each band, music was pumped through the speakers, and Riley swayed to the sound. She turned to say something to Jules, but he was no longer beside her. The crowd had grown larger, even in the VIP area. How could that be? Hadn't Lucy said that they had a limited number of guests, and Mike would be keeping their entry controlled? Riley scanned the faces that surrounded her. In the dim light, she didn't recognize any of the people standing near her, and she'd thought she had met nearly everyone staying in the area earlier. She checked the wrist of the person nearest to her. No band. Someone nudged her from behind, and another person filled the space as soon as she turned. There was no sign of Lucy or Jules. Or Mike, for that matter, which was very odd. She fumbled for her phone, but what she really wanted was another one of those yummy drinks. Through all the undulating people, she couldn't spot the area with the tables.

She turned back and let herself be carried along by the swell of the crowd. *Oh, big deal.* Did it really matter if a few extra people were in the VIP area?

Riley shook her head. She felt muddled. The music, the drink, the heat of the day. She needed to sit down. But the relentless thumping of the bass was making it hard for her to quiet her limbs. They seemed to move on their own. She pinched the back of her hand but felt nothing. What was going on? Why was she suddenly feeling so woozy?

CHAPTER 17

Riley

As RILEY STUMBLED back to her trailer alone, her fingers prickled. She fumbled with the key, but now her fingers were thick. So slow. She finally gave the door a shove and slid to the trailer floor. She dangled her legs out the door and leaned her head against the cool wall. The prickles had moved to her mouth. Something was wrong.

But she needed to rest. She closed her eyes and tried to think. A row of perfectly ripe strawberries danced in her vision. Strawberries? She reached for one, unable to close her fingers around it. How wonderful—strawberries floating around just waiting to be plucked from the air. She dropped her hand when it came back empty. Perhaps Jules would bring her a strawberry. She found her phone in her pocket and typed a message to him, then closed her eyes and waited for him to arrive.

Something pinched Riley's shoulder. She tried to swat it away, but her arms were heavy. Instead, she opened her eyes and saw Jules leaning over her. "She's coming around," he said.

"Around where?" Riley asked, the words rolling around her mouth.

"You. You scared me."

"And me," said Lucy from behind Jules. "What happened?"

"I don't know. I was listening to the music." Riley pulled a heavy arm up over her head and onto a pillow. When she closed her eyes, she saw fragments of the night, but everything was mixed up. When she closed her eyes to reorder them, the jumble remained. "Then I couldn't see anyone. The crowd was suddenly very different." Riley looked around. "Where am I?" Everything in her trailer had moved around.

"You're in my trailer," Lucy said.

"How did you know to look for me?" Flashes of memory started returning. and Riley had a strong craving for strawberries.

"You texted Johnny a string of nonsense. Just letters and numbers. He phoned me," Jules said. "He was really worried."

Heat flooded Riley. "I think I was trying to text you."

"Well, he's getting into his car first thing tomorrow to drive up here."

"He doesn't need to do that," Riley protested weakly. "I'm fine. Just need a little sleep. And some strawberries."

"Is that what you were asking for?" Jules asked. "I thought the last part might be berries, based on the letters." Jules read them out. "*a-r-e-q-m-4-5-5-p-4-s*."

"You got *berries* from that?" Lucy asked.

Jules shrugged. "I like puzzles. I looked at my phone keyboard to see what letters were close to what Riley had sent. Anyway, Johnny was certain something was wrong and asked me to look for you. What happened?"

Riley felt tears welling in her eyes. "I don't know. One minute I was fine, the next I could hardly stand up." She traced her eyebrows with her index fingers as if to clear her head. "I had a couple of those Crasherton cocktails. Did anyone else have a reaction?"

"Allergic, you mean?" Lucy asked. She checked her phone. "I don't see any incident reports. And we would, I'm sure."

"This doesn't seem like allergies," Jules said. "Are you sure you didn't take anything?"

"Drugs?" Lucy asked. "Not Riley."

"What about in the drink?" Riley asked.

Jules placed the back of his hand on Riley's forehead. "I don't think so. Anyone who had a drink with the same ingredients would be feeling the same. Lucy's right. We'd know."

Riley thought back to what else she'd consumed that day. "The sandwich in Crasherton. But you had one too, Jules."

"I'm fine. And I had more than one of the cocktails. They're handed out when you get to the music area." He helped Riley stand. "Let's get you back to your trailer, and we can try to figure it out tomorrow. Maybe it was just having the drinks after being in the heat." He opened a water bottle and offered it to her. "Here we go," he said as he eased Riley down Lucy's trailer's steps and guided her the short distance to their own.

Riley didn't protest as her sister helped her undress and slide into her bed. Within minutes, she let herself drift toward the warm embrace of sleep.

CHAPTER 18

Jack

THE SMELL OF bacon roused Winston from his sleep. Rustling from nearby tents suggested others were equally drawn by it. Before looking into its source, he opened his journal to see if Riley had responded. A shiver travelled his spine as he read her note. Crimes. She referred to multiple crimes in Crasherton.

Could she have made a mistake? She was, he had found, typically deliberate in her messages to him, particularly because she did not want to influence his decisions without understanding what the impact of that influence might be. However, like him, she was away from her home and her routine may be disrupted. Enough to cause her to mistakenly add an *s* to her message?

He considered writing to ask but decided against it. If she referred to multiple crimes—presumably multiple deaths—intentionally, it was to prepare him. Another death would add to demands, but he had investigated multiple murders in the past. He would just need to be careful not to mention to Miller or Evans that he was waiting for another death.

Evans had kindly offered to let Winston use his room to wash and dress. Hoping it was not too early, Winston gathered his belongings and made his way to the hotel. Along the way, he noted the enterprising chefs who had set up several grills, each with strips of meat sizzling on top. At the end of the line, a pair of women prepared bacon sandwiches for eager customers. Winston nodded at one of the men behind the grill as he passed. A crown of sweat framed the man's head, but he appeared to be in his element, singing as he worked. How nice to see someone enjoying his work.

At the lobby desk, Winston was relieved to see the innkeeper back at his post. He stopped to make tentative arrangements for moving Mrs. Fenton's body to a more suitable location. Once more, he conducted himself as though he took the man into his confidence with the request. The innkeeper was keen to oblige, though not without the usual reminders about related costs.

"There is a barn at the edge of the forest." The man pointed over his shoulder. "It's used to store construction equipment. It's in the shade, well ventilated, and away from the town centre. You'll need to obtain permission from the main office to use the space, but I'm sure they'll agree, given the situation." He gave Winston a conspiratorial wink. "I will speak to the cart driver and have him standing by for your instruction."

Winston thanked the innkeeper, leaving him looking very self-important behind his desk. The man was becoming quite indispensable.

The doctor was already dressed and waiting for Winston when the detective knocked. "Good morning, Evans. I hope I am not disturbing your wife."

"Not at all, Jack. She's in line for one of those bacon sandwiches. Someone told her about them yesterday. In Vancouver, she would never eat such a thing, but being out of the city and away from our routine seems to have freed her from her usual practices." Evans leaned toward Winston. "I think she rather enjoys it, but she won't admit it if you ask."

After Winston had prepared for the day, they headed to the pub where they had arranged to meet with Miller. They engaged in easy conversation as they walked and found the quietest corner to sit in. Despite the early hour, revellers were already cheering and taunting each other as they enjoyed their breakfasts. A few played darts or card games. The space was considerably louder than Winston had hoped it would be. Still, they would be able to speak without worrying that anyone was paying them any attention. The constabulary's other policemen would be arriving in about an hour, and he wanted to discuss what they knew with the others before they arrived.

After they settled into the wooden chairs, Winston began. "Harmony Fenton was enjoying the pre-crash festival when, according to Doctor Evans, she was jostled and stabbed deeply enough to fatally injure her, but with a blade thin enough that she hardly noticed. It may be difficult to determine the exact hour the injury occurred." Winston read the final note he'd jotted in his notepad the night before. "Thomas, I want you to lead the conversation when we interview her friend Kitty. We need to find out where they went and when. Find out who they encountered and the details of each environment. Be as precise as you can."

Miller nodded and wrote a few words in his notepad.

"I will assign most of the men who are arriving to provide a visible presence. We don't want the community of Crasherton, as temporary as it might be, to forget that they are meant to be law-abiding citizens. Seeing uniformed constables will remind them of this."

His colleagues nodded their agreement. "I've prepared a rotation for officers to man the police tent at all times." He turned to Doctor Evans. "Have you checked on Mrs. Fenton?"

"I have. The ice is intact for now, and it's set above a trough to collect the drainage, but it won't last much longer than today. We'll need to move the body by this afternoon, Jack."

Winston swallowed. "Yes, I understand." He didn't want Evans to go into the details of how the body decomposes after the first twenty-four hours following death. "I've made that commitment to the innkeeper as well, and he's already making arrangements."

Winston related the details about the barn. "Beyond that, if we can't transport the body by train, could we bury her here?"

Evans pursed his lips. "I suppose. It would eliminate the issue of the body's . . . rapid decline, in light of these less-than-ideal conditions."

Winston's thoughts about a bacon sandwich fled. He cleared his throat. "Thomas, will you speak with Mr. Fenton later today, please? I mean, after our scheduled interview with him this morning. Extend, again, our sympathies and talk about the practicalities—the need to make prompt arrangements. I trust your sensitivity. Find out if he's amenable to the idea of burying his wife near here, if it comes to that."

Miller blinked rapidly for a moment, as if absorbing all Winston had said. "I will, sir," he said at last, scribbling more notes on his pad.

Winston returned his attention to Evans. "Doctor, have you determined anything new after examining Mrs. Fenton's body again?"

"As you say, a small, thin blade inflicted the wound. It must have been at least two and a half, three inches long to have reached her organs."

Winston considered this. "Surely someone would notice a madman walking around with a blade. It would cause panic."

"What if it was concealed, in a sleeve, say, or in something like an umbrella?" Miller asked.

"Even so, there is no need for an umbrella, and there hasn't been for some time. Look at the dust outside. It hasn't rained here in days." He signalled for Miller to stand. "And someone walking by and jabbing her with an umbrella would be remarked upon." As he spoke, he made a forceful stabbing motion, as if he were attacking Miller.

Miller nodded his acceptance. Before they returned to their seats, Evans rose. "It was more like this," he said as he adjusted the angle at which Winston approached Miller. "Up. And in." The demonstration made it easier to imagine the quick motions the killer would have used.

"What about her corset? Wouldn't it have prevented the blade from causing any damage?" Miller asked as he shielded his torso with his hands.

Their movements had caught the attention of nearby patrons. Winston's cheeks started to burn. "Perhaps this isn't the right place to be discussing this, men." He returned to his seat. "We can continue our re-enactment another time. Evans, would her attacker need some knowledge of anatomy?"

"That, and likely an understanding of women's clothing and where the fabric was more likely to be free of barriers such as corsets."

Melodia's revelation echoed for Winston. "I've spoken with her sister, Melodia." Evans and Miller raised their eyebrows upon hearing Winston's use of her given name. "I mean … Mrs. Spectre. She was with Mrs. Fenton when she collapsed." Winston cleared his throat. "Mrs. Spectre said that her sister was pregnant."

Miller took in a breath sharply. "Doctor, is that something you can confirm?"

Evans nodded. "Actually, this was the other finding I wanted to mention. Yes, she was with child."

Miller exchanged a significant look with Winston. The implications were clear. Did Fenton know? Had he suspected the child was not his? That would certainly point to motive.

"Thank you, Nathaniel. I don't know how we would manage without you. Are you satisfied you've learned everything you need from examining Mrs. Fenton's body?"

"Yes, Jack. You may confirm the arrangements to have the body moved." Evans rose to leave, brushing at the crumbs on his trousers. "Do you think you'll find her killer?" he asked in a hushed voice. "Here, I mean?"

Winston pushed a breath through his lips. "Honestly, it will be challenging. It's a transient population. We're all vagrants, really." He gave voice to the pressure he felt. "Time is not on our side. Many will leave town before they might be questioned, and then how would we ever track them down?" He waved the question away. "Nevertheless, I'd like to have something to share with Chief Constable Philpott when he arrives. If not the murderer, then perhaps the motive. Thomas and I will spend the day following the most pressing questions."

"Very good." Evans clasped his hands together. "Do let me know if you need me, but—and I'm not being rude when I say this—I hope you do not."

Winston chuckled. "I understand the sentiment. Go. Enjoy the town. I'll be at the constabulary tent later this afternoon, should you change your mind about wanting to see me." He offered Evans a wink.

After the doctor had left them, Winston turned his attention to Miller. "Thomas, when we speak with Kitty, let's find out her impressions of Harmony's marriage. Did she and her husband get along?"

"What about the Chalk woman that Isaac Fenton spoke of?" Miller asked.

"Does she feel like a likely suspect to you?" Winston asked.

Miller shook his head. "Not really. But should we rule her out without speaking to her?"

"If we find her somehow in the throng of people, we can talk with the woman. But she isn't the priority. A secret pregnancy is a more likely motive than some disagreement between neighbours," Winston said. "Especially if the father is not her husband. We will learn more when we meet with Fenton this morning. His wife was pregnant, and the child might not have been his."

A loud cheer erupted from a nearby table.

Miller leaned in toward Winston. "He is here now, sir."

"Who?"

"Fenton. He doesn't look like a man who recently lost his wife." Miller indicated with his head.

Slowly, Winston scanned the room. There, seated at a table surrounded by several men, Fenton cheered on a man engaged in an arm wrestle. He raised his head and stared directly at him, the expression in his eyes sending a chill through Winston.

*

FENTON EXCUSED HIMSELF and approached the exit. Winston could accept that grief impacts everyone differently, yet something about the look on the man's face didn't sit well, and the detective rose from his seat to follow Fenton.

Outside, the cooler morning air made Winston realize how stifling the pub had been. While he filled his lungs deeply, he observed Fenton. The man had stepped only a few feet from the entrance. His posture was that of a confident man, his shoulders square and back straight. Fenton turned to face Winston, his arms crossed over his chest. "Detective. Fine morning, isn't it?"

The calmness with which the question was asked surprised Winston. As Miller had suggested, Fenton had recovered remarkably well for a man who had only the night before seen his dead wife. Would it be better for Winston to pretend like he didn't notice? Best to hold off any surprise until he had more information about the woman's death. Winston closed the distance between them. "Yes. Though the morning temperature is cooler than what I've grown accustomed to on the coast." As if to emphasize the point, a gust of wind blew past them, bouncing a scrap of paper past Winston's feet. "Mr. Fenton, it is a little earlier than we had arranged, but perhaps now I can ask my questions about your wife." Winston kept his voice calm as he spoke.

The cacophony of the revellers grew louder briefly as the doors to the pub opened and closed. Winston sensed someone standing behind him. He didn't look to confirm, but he assumed Miller had slipped outside. Winston didn't expect Fenton to run, but Miller would best him if he did.

Satisfied that Miller was ready to act if needed, Winston continued. "Mr. Fenton, we have some questions for you. Would you be so kind as to come to the"—The tent wasn't a station. And referring to a tent didn't give it sufficient gravitas—"to the temporary constabulary."

Fenton arched his eyebrows. "You questioned me yesterday. I've told you all I know." He opened his palms in a mute appeal. "Can we not do this tomorrow? I had a lot to drink last night. I'm in mourning." Fenton swayed as if to demonstrate he was still intoxicated, but his words were clear and unencumbered.

With another tentative step, Winston reached out his arm to prevent Fenton from moving forward. "I understand, Mr. Fenton. However, we did agree to speak today at ten. Since we have encountered each other early, I'd rather do so now. Please take a seat for a moment while I speak with my constable." The man obliged, meek as a kitten now, it seemed.

Winston took Miller to one side and dispatched him to the main office to obtain permission to use the barn to store Mrs. Fenton's body until the practicalities were sorted. From there, he'd need to go to the inn to confirm with the innkeeper that he may proceed with the arrangements to move the body. After that, it would be time for Miller to meet the other constables soon to arrive by train. It was a good thing he'd fortified himself with a substantial breakfast.

"Let's move to the constabulary tent, Mr. Fenton." Fenton stood, and Winston grasped him by the elbow, guiding him for the short distance. He offered no resistance.

When they had settled in, Winston positioned himself across from Fenton. The desk sat between them, and Fenton leaned his forearms on it, his head in his hands. He smelled of drink but, as when they had been standing outside the saloon, showed no ill effects of over-consumption. Winston pulled his notepad from his pocket and set it on the desk, keeping his pencil in his hand.

"Now, Mr. Fenton. I'm sorry that it's necessary to continue our conversation today. Unexpected loss is difficult. What you say to me, though, will help me to uncover what happened to your wife."

Fenton wet his lips before he began. "That first night, we met up with the others and had a nice meal in one of the pubs. We decided on supporting the red train. Though it doesn't matter much, does it?"

"I suppose not," Winston agreed.

"Anyway, that night, Mr. Parker held a reception. Invited us. Harmony loved it—the fancy food, the wine. I'd just as soon eat at the pub myself."

Winston could picture the man preferring to stand on the sidelines of such an event. He shared the same preference and had attended too many of them to count. "When was that?"

"Night before last. We were supposed to be at a dinner last night. I couldn't bring myself to attend." The one Winston had found Parker at. "We were supposed to attend another event tonight. And tomorrow there's a grand ball. Harmony made herself a dress for it." At this, the man's eyes glistened. "I'll not attend that. It wouldn't be right to go without her. I'd rather return to Vancouver."

"I need you to stay for at least a few days, sir," Winston said. He leaned back in his chair. "How did you and Harmony spend the rest of your time here?" Winston was most interested in what had happened immediately before Harmony's death, but perhaps they had seen someone or something without realizing it was important.

"I had some work to do here. I was sent to check the safety protocols yesterday. That's what I do in the head office—safety. Harmony was spending the day with her friend Kitty and her sister. Melodia."

Winston noted the beat before Melodia's name. "You said the sisters had recently become reacquainted."

"Melodia holds herself out to be a wise woman. She certainly knows how to part a man and his money. If that's wise .."

"What was the reason for their falling-out?" Winston leaned toward the man. He justified the question by telling himself the answer might have some relevance to the investigation, but there was an element of his own curiosity that prompted it.

"Sisters. They're hot and cold. They'd been cold for a few years, then just within the last month or so became reconnected. Harmony pleaded for me to cover Melodia's passage. Which I did." He puffed his chest.

"What about the woman who argued with your wife?" Winston checked his notes, although he had no need to. "Mrs. Chalk. Do you really think she was angry enough that she would come here and harm your wife?"

Fenton passed his hand over his mouth. Was he embarrassed at having suggested the motive? "I hardly know the woman. It's just that Harmony seemed to think she was out for her. They had such a row once that afterwards, Harmony told me, Mrs. Chalk gave her a hat. To apologize."

Winston stopped writing. "What was the argument about?"

Fenton shook his head. "I don't know. It seemed unlikely to me, if I'm honest. I never heard Mrs. Chalk say a word about anyone." He wrung his hands. "You see, Harmony. . . Well, she could be . . . dramatic."

"When was this?" Winston asked.

"About a month ago. The hat just appeared at our house."

Winston reviewed his notes. The dead woman had had an argument with a neighbour, apparently serious enough that the neighbour felt obliged to give Mrs. Fenton a hat to apologize. He scratched at his temple. This line of questioning was not worth pursuing. He crossed off the name in his notepad, then looked across at Fenton. He saw pain, sadness. Not guilt. And he was about to bring the man more sadness. "Mr. Fenton, I have a delicate question to ask. Did you know that your wife was pregnant?"

Fenton's mouth fell open. Such shock is hard to feign. "A baby? She never said." His eyes glistened, and he fumbled for a handkerchief. "You're certain?"

Winston lowered his gaze. "The medical examiner has confirmed it. I'm very sorry." This was, for Winston, one of the worst parts of his job, to have to deliver such dreadful news, compounding the sorrow of someone who was already grieving. He felt for Ellis's stone in his pocket. The pocket was empty. Winston caught his breath as a wave of heat washed through him. He met Fenton's eyes briefly—the man knit his brows in a puzzled expression. "Forgive me, Mr. Fenton. I've misplaced something."

Winston stood and patted down the other pockets in his jacket. He checked his trousers and the small pocket of his waistcoat. He glanced again at Fenton, who now held his head in his hands, overcome again at the depth of his losses. Winston made a cursory search of the chair and the earthen floor at his feet. Nothing. His pulse pounded in his ears. He sat again, suppressing a sigh. This man needed his attention.

"Mr. Fenton, I'm sure you would appreciate some time to take in this news. Do you have a friend here that we could summon to sit with you?"

Fenton raised his red-rimmed eyes and pressed his back into the chair. "No. There's no one." He twisted his fingers in his lap.

Winston let a moment pass, and when Fenton appeared to have nothing further to say, he broke the silence. "Please remain in Crasherton, Mr. Fenton. If I need to find you, I'll seek you out."

"I'll need to be back in the city in a few days. After the crash is over, I'll be expected at work."

"I understand," Winston answered. He stood and held the tent flap open for Fenton, who kept his head low as he walked away. Everyone would return to their homes after the spectacle. Would Winston have answers for this man before then?

CHAPTER 19

Jack

WINSTON REPOSITIONED THE newspaper in the last corner of the constabulary tent he'd not yet searched. He dropped to his knees on this makeshift kneeling pad and scanned the area, lowering his head to ground level and turning to look in all directions across the dirt floor. He moved to get out of his own shadow and looked again. It was no use. The stone wasn't here.

He heard Miller's voice and the approach of many footsteps. Winston got to his feet and brushed the front of his trousers. He reached for his jacket, readying himself to speak with the newly arrived constables.

On the boardwalk path outside the constabulary tent, Winston reviewed the appointed duties with the assembled constables and gave them a first assignment to patrol the town after they had settled in. Winston reminded the men that they were officially on duty and were not to get too caught up in the festivities. He suspected it was a reminder that would need to be repeated.

After the constables set out on their tasks, Winston briefed Miller on what he'd learned from Fenton. "Our next key priority is to speak to Harmony Fenton's friend, Mrs. Kitty Simmons, as soon as possible. She and her husband have a tent behind the Coastal Rail Hotel, and it's still early enough in the day that we might find her there. I want to understand exactly who Mrs. Simmons and Mrs. Fenton had contact with yesterday morning."

As they walked to the hotel, Winston mentally retraced the steps he'd taken this morning—his tent, Evans's room and the shared bathroom, the pub, the constabulary tent—and all the pathways between. Where had he misplaced Ellis's stone? He swallowed against the dryness in his throat.

"There she is, sir." Miller pointed to a group of women standing outside the tents behind the hotel. The women appeared to be consoling each other. When she saw the police officers, Harmony Fenton's friend stood up from a small circle of chairs that had been arranged outside a tent. Similar circles dotted other tents. An entire community had sprung up among these Crasherton visitors. Mrs. Simmons wiped her red eyes. She looked to have been crying since she'd left Winston the previous day. Understandably. It was unlikely she had ever seen a dead body, and to have a friend die in front of her would have been unthinkable.

Winston approached the woman slowly. "Mrs. Simmons. I realize this is a difficult time. But we would like to ask you a few questions." Miller guided her to a distance beyond the hearing of the other women.

With a quiet voice, he began. "Would you prefer we spoke elsewhere? I saw a tea house facing the square where you would be comfortable."

The corners of her mouth relaxed ever so slightly. "Thank you. That would be lovely."

As the three made their way to the tea shop, Winston admired how Miller built up a rapport with Kitty. A thoughtful way to put her at ease and encourage honest answers to their questions. Winston let Miller begin the interview once they had settled around a small round table.

"Can you remind me, Mrs. Simmons? What day did you arrive?" Miller asked. They knew this detail from Fenton, but starting with a simple question would help ease the woman into the interview.

"The day before yesterday. Harmony was so pleased to be here. We went to a welcome reception the night before last, and we were set to go to a tea today." She pointed at the tea service in front of her. "Not like this. 'Meet the Ladies of Crasherton', it was called." She sniffed. "I guess this will have to do." Was her disappointment at missing her friend or the event? Or both?

"Have you seen anyone while you've been here? By that, I mean have you bumped into anyone that you know from the city?" Miller leaned forward as he asked his questions.

She looked puzzled at the question. "Bumped into? Nearly everyone here is from the city. I've seen many acquaintances." Kitty assumed a defensive stance. "In Vancouver, Harmony and I would never be considered proper ladies. Though Harmony's life has…had taken a better turn. Her husband was recently awarded a raise." A better salary to accompany the shift in his work location. "I work, but the work I do is necessary. I would do it even if I didn't need to."

"What work is that, Mrs. Simmons?" Miller asked.

"I work in a home for fallen women." It was noble work, and she knew it. Her voice strengthened with pride.

Miller flushed but nodded his approval.

"The women who stay there contribute to the house in their own ways—laundering, cooking, cleaning. But as they come closer to their times, they can do less. I help when they cannot, but otherwise I spend most of my time seeking appropriate homes for their children."

Winston's mother had been involved in a similar organization, though her responsibility was less active than he imagined Kitty's role to be. She traced the pattern of the lace tablecloth with her finger. Her hands were callused with years of hard work. He suppressed a smile at the idea of his mother with her elbows deep in laundry water or scrubbing on her hands and knees.

Miller continued with his gentle questioning. "But Mrs. Fenton didn't work with you?"

She pulled in a deep breath. "Not yet. I was hoping to persuade her to help. She had a wonderful way with people. She could speak with anyone, no matter their background, and make them feel as if she cared about them."

Miller captured a thought in his notepad. "Can you tell us about your time here with Mrs. Fenton? What happened at the welcome reception?"

Kitty's eyes widened with excitement. "It was a wonderful event. Everyone was dressed up beautifully, and we met Mr. Parker and his wife. They spoke with each of the guests." She cocked her head. "Actually, Harmony introduced me to them. She must know them because of her husband."

"And you were invited because of Mrs. Fenton?" Miller asked.

"Her husband. He was given the tickets. The reception, the tea we were supposed to attend today, and a grand ball tomorrow were part of being here."

"Did Mrs. Fenton have contact with anyone else at the reception?" Winston asked. Perhaps the baby's father is in Crasherton and she spoke to him there.

"She must have spoken with everyone there. I think only about fifty guests attended. The ball is meant to be a much grander affair." Kitty's gaze became wistful. Winston wondered if she would attend, even though her friend would not be joining her for the event.

"And what about yesterday? Did you and Mrs. Fenton encounter anyone?" Miller's question returned them to the hours before Mrs. Fenton's death.

Kitty closed her eyes, considering the question. When she opened them, her face had taken on a look of concern. "We went to look at the engines. We had planned to arrive early enough that we might avoid the larger crowds, but many people had already gathered there." She tilted her head. "Harmony seemed to thrive in the atmosphere. Everyone was excited."

"Go on, please." Miller encouraged her with a warm smile.

"The crowd by the locomotive grew. Soon there were more people than I've ever seen, and we seemed to be right in the middle of them. I became nervous, and Harmony walked with me to the edge of the crowd." Her face flushed, as if the memory revived the stress of being pressed on all sides in a crowd. "As we moved, people pushed us and we started moving in the opposite direction. But Harmony was a strong woman. She took the lead." Kitty dropped her chin and paused. "Then Harmony said we should go see some of the booths, particularly the handicrafts—you know, jewellery, lacework, that sort of thing. And we stopped to listen to some of the music. We had a lovely morning, really." Her voice took on a wistful note.

Winston stayed quiet. The woman was speaking freely now, as if a faucet had been turned on. He didn't want to interrupt the flow. Across from him, Miller took steady notes.

"I know that Harmony was doing all this to distract me. She wanted me to recover my nerve so that we might return to the trains." She smiled. "And it worked. After we'd explored for about an hour, or maybe ninety minutes, we made our way back to where the locomotive was."

Here the woman's countenance darkened, and she dropped her gaze again.

"Are you able to tell us what happened after this, Mrs. Simmons?" Miller asked.

She swallowed. "Yes, I am." She raised a hand to decline Miller's offer of more tea. "Harmony led us through the crowd. She'd told me to look up and keep my eyes on the hats everyone wore so that I wouldn't feel anxious. And to take full breaths." She demonstrated a deep breath, her face brightening. "She was hoping to get to the fellow who was giving out the rosettes. She wanted to pick up a blue one for Isaac, although I expect he'd have found his own by that point."

"You said Harmony led 'us,'" Miller said. "Had someone joined you at this point? Mrs. Spectre, perhaps?"

"Melodia?" Mrs. Simmons waited for Miller to nod before she continued. "Yes, I should have said. We found her earlier in the morning. She joined us to listen to some of the music. They're sisters, you know. Harmony and Melodia." She stared off at something over Winston's shoulder. "I have never heard them utter a strong word against each other, even though they didn't always agree."

Miller cleared his throat.

"I noticed that Harmony had slowed down. She seemed to be carried by the crowd more than making her own way through it. We linked arms with her and carried on, but after a few steps, she stopped. 'It doesn't matter,' she said."

"What didn't matter?" Winston asked.

"About the rosettes, she meant. She said, 'Now it's me who needs more air,' so we walked with her back to the edge. It was shortly after we were free of the crowd—" Her breath hitched. "When we'd moved free of the crowd to the spot I brought you to yesterday, she . . . collapsed." Kitty pressed her lips together.

Miller exchanged a glance with Winston. Then he gently continued his questions. "Did you experience any unusually aggressive shoving? Anything that might have been targeted at you or Mrs. Fenton specifically?"

Kitty brought her hand to her mouth, the horror of the suggestion reflecting in her eyes. "Everyone was being bumped. We were in tight quarters. But it didn't seem like anyone was intentionally after us, no." She looked away, as if trying to recall the scene.

"Do you remember any individuals in the crowd, anyone that you recognized?" Miller asked.

"I recognized several people. Mr. and Mrs. Parker were there, of course. That was earlier, when we first went to see the trains. They arrived early, like us. One of the organizers cleared them a path through the crowd, and they passed us as they went to stand in front of the engine. This was before I felt the crowd really press in on me."

She furrowed her eyebrows. "I remember thinking the Parkers wouldn't likely recognize me from the night before. I didn't try to speak to them."

Winston nodded for her to continue.

"Some of the other girls from back home, they were there too, but not dressed as finely as me or Harmony." Her cheeks coloured. "We didn't talk with them either, what with the noise of the crowd."

Winston sensed some shame creeping into her voice. Had she and Harmony deliberately ignored their friends because they weren't dressed finely? Would such a slight be enough to provoke someone to cause injury? "These friends, did they see you?"

"I don't think so. Which is good. I wouldn't want them to think we were being rude." She looked down at her hands, then her head snapped up. "You know, there was someone who knocked into Harmony. Were it not so crowded she surely would have fallen down, but as it was, the people around us were enough to right her."

"When was this?"

"Shortly after we had first arrived to see the trains. It was thinking of the Parkers passing us that brought it to mind."

"Did you recognize who it was that knocked into her? Was it a man? A woman?" Miller asked.

"No, I'm sorry." Kitty shook her head. "It all happened so quickly. Whoever did it must have moved through the people while I was making sure Harmony was all right. We were all getting jostled, but this one was a good shove." She closed her eyes as if recalling the scene. "I'm sorry, Constable. It's a blur. The crowd…and we wanted to see the train. People were waiting to take a photograph in front of it. The photographer had two cameras set up. One was always taking a picture while the other was being prepared." She paused, meeting Winston's eyes. "I'm sorry. That's all I can recall."

Miller assured her she'd been most helpful. He began to read back a few specifics from his notes, asking Kitty to confirm he had the details correct.

What had they just learned? Someone bumped into Mrs. Fenton when they'd first arrived to view the trains. Ninety minutes, or possibly two hours later, she collapsed. Winston would have to confirm whether the timing made sense to Evans. How quickly could such a small wound cause death? And photographers were in attendance. Could they have captured an image of Harmony's killer with one of their devices? Winston wrote the word *photograph* in his notepad. He checked his pocket watch discreetly. His appointment with his parents was approaching. He weighed being on time for them against remaining to finish this interview. He'd prefer to avoid a scolding from his mother. How, as an adult, did avoiding unpleasantness with her continue to influence his actions? But Miller was conducting the interview well. If Winton needed to excuse himself, his constable could finish.

Kitty sipped from her tea, which must have now grown cold. "I don't know anything more," she said as she replaced her teacup on its saucer.

"That's quite all right, Mrs. Simmons," Winston said. "Though if anything more occurs to you, please report it to us. We'll need to know how long you will be staying in Crasherton. Miller, please make sure to also take down Mrs. Simmons's address in the city." Miller reopened his notepad to write her details.

"One more thing," Miller said. Winston sighed. He couldn't leave until he'd heard Miller's question. "Did you and Mrs. Fenton stand for one of the photographs?"

"Yes. I was told it would be ready tomorrow."

"I should very much like to see it when you have it," Miller said. Winston underlined the word he had just written.

Kitty Simmons rose and thanked them for the tea. Winston checked his watch again. "Thomas, I need to meet my parents. I will see you this afternoon."

"Shall I see if I can find the photographers from yesterday, sir?" Miller asked.

"Yes. An excellent idea. Ask for copies from all their plates from the rally at the train." Winston clapped a hand on his shoulder. "You conducted yourself very well in this interview, Thomas."

Miller beamed, then turned and took his leave.

Winston picked up his hat and settled the bill with the woman at the front. His step had a little more energy as he left to meet his parents for luncheon. Finally, it felt as though they had a direction for their inquiries. What might they find in the photographs? He would soon know.

CHAPTER 20

Riley

THE NEXT MORNING, Riley was up before Jules. Still groggy from the night before, she tried to piece together what had happened. She pulled her notebook toward her and started a list, writing down everything she'd consumed the day before and its source.

Breakfast: food from the nearby food trucks. Jules had brought it after his morning run. He ate the same food and didn't have any issues.

Lunch: sandwich from the café in Crasherton. Again, Jules had the same thing without any effect.

They had returned to the festival site in a panic because of the messages from Lucy, which turned out to be nothing. Then she and Jules had gone to the show. Snacks and drinks there. Once more, nobody else had taken ill.

She nibbled the top of her pen as she reviewed her list. She hadn't left her drink unattended at the festival. And why would her drink, specifically, be targeted? She pushed her notebook away in frustration. Maybe she would never know the source. The thought chilled her.

Her next thought was what to do about Johnny arriving later in the day. He would need somewhere to sleep. Maybe Lucy had another trailer that Johnny could stay in. Or maybe she could move in with Lucy so Jules and Johnny could stay in this trailer. She wrote out both options on a fresh page in her notebook.

There were still no sounds out of Jules, but she assumed he would be up soon. She pulled her journal from the bedside drawer. Maybe Jack had found a chance to write. No, there was still no answer to her latest entry. She sighed. Was he overwhelmed with policing? In Vancouver, when that was the case, he usually found a moment to dash off a quick note, even if just to say that he was busy. She didn't have any updates for him, and she certainly wasn't going to share about the night before. Jack would be worried. Like Johnny.

Just then, her phone buzzed with a message.

> I hope I'm not waking you. I'm leaving now for Crasherton. I'll be there early afternoon.

Her chest tingled as she reread the message. Were they over whatever bump they'd encountered? If so, what did that mean? She typed the first response she thought of and sent it without letting herself reconsider.

> Drive safe. XO.

✳

AT BREAKFAST IN the VIP food area, Riley made sure to choose the same items as Jules. "Strawberry?" he offered with a playful grin. She accepted the fruit but waited until he popped one into his own mouth before she ate hers. "Did you sleep okay after last night?" he asked, this time without the playfulness.

"I slept really well, actually. No more dreams about strawberries. I can't think of what I ate that would have made me react like that." Her head was beginning to ache, and she pulled her baseball cap lower to shield her eyes from the morning sun. "Could it have been the heat?"

"Maybe, but I saw you drink a lot of water yesterday. And we didn't spend too much time in direct sunlight," Jules said, spearing another strawberry with his fork.

He was right. Despite the sun and heat, there was ample shade on the festival grounds, and they had spent time indoors or in the woods in the ghost town. To be safe, she'd already slathered on sunscreen. She looked at her arm, still glistening as the cream absorbed into her skin. "Do you think it could be from the cream?"

Jules shook his head. "Maybe if you squeezed some of it into your drink." He snickered playfully. "No, I think it's something you ingested."

"What, then? I made a list of everything I ate or drank yesterday. Nobody else was sick, so what was it?" Her voice had taken on an edge.

Jules put his hand on Riley's arm. "Let's stick around here today. Take it easy."

Riley had hoped to return to Crasherton to find anything that might help Jack, but she was feeling increasingly like she wouldn't find answers. Besides, Johnny was arriving today, and she wanted to be here to greet him. And her head hurt. "Can we go back to the ghost town tomorrow?"

"You didn't get enough yesterday?" Jules asked.

"I'd like to see if Sonya, the sister who was working at the museum, will let me do a little more research there. We didn't really get into the history with all her talk about the town's future." Riley bit into her breakfast sandwich after watching Jules do the same.

"If you're feeling up for it, we can go back. Now, do you want another strawberry?"

Riley gave him a swat.

∗

RILEY STARTED PREPARING her trailer in anticipation of Johnny's arrival. She still hadn't figured out what the sleeping arrangements were going to be. To occupy her mind, she tidied. The trailer didn't have a broom or any other cleaning supplies, so she asked Lucy where to find them. Her sister had rolled her eyes but directed Riley to a trailer being used for storage. As she made her way through the rows of trailers, Riley turned the previous night over in her mind. Maybe focusing on cleaning would let her do a little subconscious processing. She might remember something.

Most of the items scattered haphazardly in the trailer looked to be extras from the welcome goody bag that had been left in her trailer, though they'd been strewn about in this one. Baseball caps spilled out of a box. Sample-size and full-sized bottles of different creams and lotions had been dumped into different piles, though there wasn't any obvious order to them, as they mingled with the packages of snack foods. Even the bags that the items had been in were stacked among the goodies. Lucy would never be able to find anything else in the storage trailer if Riley didn't straighten up for her. And organizing helped clear her head.

The last of the goody bag items were almost returned to their boxes and bags when she came across little pots of honey, like the one she'd bought in Crasherton. As she picked one up, she was struck by a memory of having tea after returning from Crasherton the day before. Had Jules had any? No, he was more inclined to drink coffee. And she'd made herself a cup to calm down after Lucy had been so frustrating. What had Sonya said when Riley had purchased it? *A new recipe.* She remembered the label being purple. She checked the box. The labels on all of these jars were orange. With a shiver, she closed the door to the trailer and hurried back to her own. She needed to get back to Crasherton.

CHAPTER 21

Jack

WINSTON ARRIVED AT the restaurant at the appointed hour only to receive a message that his parents were delayed by twenty minutes. He asked to be shown to the table to wait for them. The dining room was largely empty, with the wait staff preparing for the meal to come. Winston cleared his space of utensils and crockery, ignoring the look of disapproval on the face of the waiter who had seated him. He pulled out his journal. He could use the time to review the case and update Riley. The surrounding sounds died away as he held his pencil between his fingers.

Dear Riley,

I shared in my last message that my parents are also in Crasherton. What I didn't share is how remarkable this fact is, as my mother so rarely ventures beyond Toronto, finding her previous forays to have been lacking. This unexpected encounter may require me to confront her about her past behaviour, though I find myself preferring a murder investigation instead of what will surely be an unpleasant conversation. Thankfully, I have found a few minutes before I meet with my parents. I have spent the morning uncovering information relating to this case.

First, I met with Doctor Evans.

Winston shared what Evans had told him about the wound.

I also met with a friend of the victim. They spent most of the morning of Mrs. Fenton's death together, and I believe the friend was with her when the fatal wound was struck. She has suggested that there may be photographs taken of visitors to the train rally, and I have asked Constable Miller to secure the images so we might review them. I must admit that I have not previously found photographs to be of much use as they are often blurry and one must be still for so long before the image is captured, but I have asked to see them as the images may be of use.

Winston scratched his head. He kept returning to the idea that Mrs. Fenton's pregnancy was the reason for her death. He needed to determine who knew about the baby. He continued his note to Riley.

Mrs. Fenton was with child. However, I believe the father was not her husband. This presents a strong motive for her death and suggests either her husband or the father as her murderer. My task is now to determine who that man is.

The sound of conversation around him increased, and Winston expected his parents would arrive shortly.

I will write more later. I hope you're enjoying your event.

Jack

*

WINSTON TUGGED AT the cuffs of his jacket. The dining room was full now and buzzed with an almost palpable energy. Guests were cheerful and relaxed. They were on holiday, and wine flowed freely, although it was early in the day. Laughter erupted from a group at a nearby table. Snippets of conversation filtered through about the upcoming event. This crowd was just as excited as the one that had gathered in front of the engines the day before.

Winston stood when his mother entered the room. He noticed that he was not alone in being caught in her aura. She wore a day dress of muted colours, the fabric of lighter weight for the summer temperatures. Before she kissed him, she held him away from her as if to inspect him. "I didn't really get a chance to look at you last night with that lighting. Hasn't electric light made its way this far west? I thought it would have accompanied the railroad." She cast her gaze from his head to his feet. "You're too skinny. But you look happy."

Winston tried to stop himself from bristling against her criticism. He resisted an impulse to reach for his jacket pocket and tugged to straighten his waistcoat instead. "Actually, Vancouver has had electric lights for nearly a decade. Here in Crasherton, they're making do with gas lamps, given this was recently little more than a mining community with a few hundred residents." He knew he should have left her comment alone as soon as he spoke.

Winston's mother sniffed. "Still, they could have made an effort."

Beside her, Winston's father gripped his son's arm. "I'm happy to see you, son. You look well, though your mother is correct. It appears as though you could stand to eat slightly more."

"My landlady does her best. My work prevents me from keeping regular hours, so I don't always get to enjoy her meals."

Winston noticed people's eyes on their table as he held the chair for his mother. He had known his entire life that his mother was a beautiful woman. However, he had had few occasions to see just how much her beauty was admired by those around her. She seemed oblivious to their attention, though her face lit up when she saw Clarissa Philpott enter the room on the arm of her husband.

His parents' presence in the middle of an investigation was a distraction, but he could not fault them for wishing to see him, especially when so much remained unspoken between them. As they settled into their seats, his mother continued with her unwelcome observations. "You should really have your own home, Jack. A wife. Children, even." She smoothed the skirt of her dress. "George and his wife are expecting a child."

Winston reached for his glass and savoured some of the freshest water he had ever tasted. George had failed to mention anything about a child in his last letter. He and George had corresponded a few times since his return from an extended honeymoon. Their letters centred largely on their family's deception about the cause of Ellis's death. George, though younger, seemed more patient than Winston was about the betrayal. He seemed to have a quiet confidence that it would all be sorted in time. This latest news must be fresh.

"That's wonderful to hear. I hope he finds joy in starting a family. In time, I expect I will find a wife, but my focus since arriving in the city has been to solve crimes. Uncle Larry has his hands full with such a small constabulary and a growing population."

Winston's father set his hand on his wife's arm. "Dear," he said, "just enjoy his company." For the first time that Jack could ever recall, she nodded rather than offering a sharp reply. Was she softening with age, or was it the prospect of her pending role as grandmother?

"I must admit, I was surprised to find you both here. In Crasherton, I mean." Winston caught his father's gaze drop to the tablecloth, and a realization took shape in his mind. "Did Uncle Larry alert you that I was going to be here?"

The look on Ernest Montague's face revealed the truth. "I wrote to him about this event and indicated that I was planning to attend. Parker had actually suggested that I put an engine against his in the crash as a way of drawing business for both of us." He flicked his hand at the idea. "I see no value in destroying a perfectly good piece of machinery for the pure spectacle of it." He nodded at another guest who had entered the room, but the man continued on to his own table rather than stopping. It didn't surprise Winston at all that his father knew most of the men in attendance, at least in this establishment. None of these guests were sleeping in tents.

His father returned his attention to Winston. "Even though we are not participating, there is business to be done here. That Lawrence arranged to have you sent here is a pleasant outcome."

Winston had often wondered if his father didn't realize the influence he had, or if he deliberately wielded it with subtlety. Either way, his parents' presence in Crasherton was clearly put in motion long ago, and without Winston's knowledge. Though he appreciated the opportunity to see his father, he found he appreciated the thinly veiled manipulation—even if well intended—less and less. Still, Winston had no doubt his father would continue to guide his son's life until he died.

They exchanged news of mutual acquaintances for a course. When the waiter removed his father's plate, Winston noticed that the plate remained nearly full. "Are you unwell, Father?" Winston asked.

Some discomfort flickered behind his father's eyes. "My stomach is bothering me, son. I'm sure it will pass."

Winston's mother took on a look of concern and she leaned toward her son. "He complained about it earlier, when we were looking at the trains."

Heat rose in Winston's cheeks. He couldn't recall his parents speaking of such intimate things in front of him before. Something about being outside Toronto seemed to be relieving them of their inhibitions. "Well, that's a shame. This meal is rather delicious." He listened as they described the private tour they'd been given of the trains that morning.

"How many people were with you?" Winston asked, finding comfort in this neutral topic.

His mother set down her fork. "Well, Mr. Parker led the tour, and there were a few other men and their wives. Not many." She turned her nose up. "But there was quite a crowd of people who gathered in the area hoping to also gain access to the trains. I couldn't believe their impatience. It's quite something to manage, I expect."

Winston's father nodded. "Yes, the crowd seemed rather excited. I imagine that excitement will only continue to grow as the event approaches."

Winston's mother continued speaking about people that he knew in Toronto and updating him on news from their lives. She returned to the topic of George. He was doing well, learning how to run their father's company, with the railway being one of his father's chief business interests. "Why didn't George come too?" Winston asked.

"We needed someone reliable to manage the business while we are here," his father said. Winston noted the strain in his voice, and his face was starting to lose colour. He was about to say something when his mother set down her fork.

"Jack, will you think about returning to Toronto? You are missed."

Winston could not entertain the idea of living in the same city as his parents. Not after their betrayal. Still, he chose to answer their question as honestly as he could. "I haven't considered returning. At least not yet. I enjoy working with Uncle Larry. I find the work fulfilling."

"But you must have to deal with some awful people," his mother said. "Wouldn't you like to return to society?"

"Would you prefer I became a police officer in Toronto?"

The look on his mother's face indicated that was not something that would satisfy her. She opened her mouth to respond when suddenly Winston's father stood, knocking a piece of cutlery to the floor. His face was a mask of pain. "I must lie down. There is an event this evening I need to attend. But I don't think I will take part in the plans for this afternoon."

Mrs. Montague stood. "I will come with you, dear." She turned to her son. "Jack, please think about what I asked. It would be lovely to have you nearby again."

Winston rose with his mother. "I will see you to your rooms," he said. He offered his arm to his father, who leaned on him heavily. "I know a doctor here. Shall I ask him to see you, Father?"

"Perhaps you could, Jack. Just to make sure it isn't anything too serious," Winston's mother said.

"I will send him as soon as I see him, Mother," Winston promised.

✳

WINSTON LEFT HIS parents' hotel rooms and walked directly to the Crasherton Inn to leave a message for Doctor Evans. His father's sudden pain had been troubling, but his condition appeared to improve once he lay down.

As he walked down Crasherton's main street, Winston reflected that the meal with his parents had been surprisingly pleasant. Perhaps because they were in public, they had avoided any tense words about Ellis's death. That was a conversation for another day.

A steady stream of people moving toward the crash site reminded Winston that an event was scheduled for that afternoon. Was it the tug-of-war between supporters? Many members of the crowd held picnic baskets in their arms. He envied their relaxed, happy demeanour.

Scraps of blue and red fabric dotted the street, effectively marking a path toward the trains. How might he describe the scene to Riley? He paused for a moment at the edge of the moving crowd. A palpable energy pulsed around him as people swapped playful taunts. The mood was positive, though he could sense an edge to it. Any inkling of an act of violence in the town would spark shock and alarm. He needed to solve Harmony Fenton's murder quickly. He rejoined the moving mass of people.

Within minutes, Winston found himself again at the site being prepared for the crash. The area had been selected for the gently sloping hills that created a natural amphitheatre for spectators to sit and view the crash. Behind him, a couple discussed staking out the best spot tonight so they could have the best viewing angle. The man wanted to remain in town, likely thinking of the drink he would miss by spending the night trying to protect their spot.

Winston noticed a woman standing alone at the edge of the throng. She caught his attention because unlike everyone else, she was not moving. He recognized her as Miss Smallwood, the reporter. His stomach tightened. Because of the distance it needed to travel, the newspaper arriving on today's train would be yesterday's edition. He wouldn't know until later whether she'd written anything about Mrs. Fenton's death. She waved to him and headed in his direction. He steeled himself against additional questions.

"Detective," she said when she was beside him.

"Miss Smallwood." He tipped his hat to greet her. "Have you decided on an angle for today's story? Perhaps how the participants are selected for the tug-of-war? I'm unsure of the process myself."

"The teams volunteer. I'm sure one could accommodate you if you were to inquire. You'd have to select a team to support." She gestured at his arm, which bore no band. "I assume you're finished with yesterday's investigation."

This exchange allowed Winston to make two observations. First, she had well-honed deduction skills. Second, she spoke in a light, playful tone that likely made it easy to dismiss her as a simple young woman with no particular agenda. He didn't underestimate her cleverness, and he knew he'd need to be especially careful about what he revealed to her. She was ambitious, and a slip-up could appear in tomorrow's newspaper. If he shared Evans's conclusions with her and she printed them, the residents of Crasherton would panic. He settled on a half-truth. "Miss Smallwood, the investigation continues. As you might expect, the medical examiner is out of his usual element. He does not have his full set of equipment with which to conduct his examination. His conclusions are delayed."

"Will you save me from having to inquire with a crew member on the next train to learn whether it carried additional supplies?"

He prepared to tell her another half-truth when he spotted Miller and another constable firmly, but amiably, separating a pair of men who appeared to be taking their red and blue rivalries too seriously. "That's enough, now," Miller said as the second constable led the two away from the crowd.

Winston returned to face Miss Smallwood. "I'm afraid I am required. Enjoy the festivities." She accepted her dismissal without complaint, and Winston watched as she disappeared into the crowd.

"Has there been much of that?" Winston asked Miller as the other constable released the men who had been arguing. He waved at Winston before returning to his post.

"Not much at all, thankfully. Most of the crowd is well behaved. I hope that continues through the crash tomorrow." He looked past Winston in the direction that Miss Smallwood had left. "Was that the woman from the train? The reporter?" he asked.

"It was. And if you encounter her, please be careful with what you say. She is observant. I don't want her to learn of details of the investigation until we are ready to share them."

"I understand, sir."

Winston spotted three other constables' hats mixed in the crowd. When a loud cheer sounded, he shifted his focus to the stage. Parker had emerged from the crowd wearing a brightly coloured conductor's uniform of both red and blue, and the crowd cheered in excitement. He tried to imagine his father wearing such an outfit. The thought made him smile. It was absurd, as was the notion that his mother would permit him to wear the bold colours.

Parker's assistant, Craven, stood behind his boss, looking as officious as ever. This time, however, he didn't carry the clipboard that was usually tucked under his arm. Perhaps his work was complete and he could now enjoy the event.

Parker held his arms in the air until the crowd quieted. Were he asked to describe the effect, Winston would say that Parker was a gentleman showman. When he began to speak, he kept his voice firm but not overly loud. The crowd became even more hushed so they could hear him. A clever tactic that Winston tucked away for future use.

The railway official began by thanking everyone for gathering. He hoped that they were enjoying their time in Crasherton and that they would consider riding on one of his trains regardless of the outcome of the crash. This elicited a loud cheer. Winston wondered how many members of the crowd were employees of the Coastal Rail Company, like Isaac Fenton.

While Parker spoke, Winston scanned the crowd again. Was Fenton among the crowd? All faces were focused on the stage. Winston saw Kitty Simmons standing near the centre of the mass, and she raised her hand in greeting. Beside her was that infuriating reporter. Mrs. Simmons then pointed a finger to the sky, signalling that she wanted to speak to him. Winston nodded and watched as she edged her way toward him with Miss Smallwood close behind. When the women reached him, Mrs. Simmons stood on her toes and aimed her mouth toward his ear so he could hear her above the noise.

"I've thought of something. About Harmony."

He gestured toward a clearing behind them. He caught Miller's eye and signalled that he was to keep Miss Smallwood from following. Miller nodded, a little too enthusiastically, that he understood. "Hello again, Mrs. Simmons," Winston said when they were out of the throng. "Did I understand you correctly? What is it you've remembered?"

"Yes, and I thought I should tell you right away. You asked me to find you if anything occurred to me. It isn't from yesterday but from in the city. I was going to visit Harmony one afternoon after being at the women's home. Just as I arrived, a man passed me and got into a fancy carriage. He came from Harmony's house. Only her husband wasn't there. Isaac was working."

Winston immediately understood Kitty's implication but wanted to hear her confirm her thoughts. "Did you see the man's face?"

"Not directly. Harmony didn't say anything, and when I asked who the man was, she refused to tell me. That's when she invited me to join her here." She clasped her hands. "I think she had a lover." She whispered the words to avoid tarnishing her friend's reputation.

Winston captured her words in his notepad. "Can you describe him at all? What colour was his hair?" he asked.

"I don't know. He was wearing a hat and kept his head down." She closed her eyes to recall the memory. "He was polite. He said 'ma'am' when he passed me."

The description didn't help to identify who the visitor might be, other than the mention of the fancy carriage. He must have been a man of some means. "Did his voice sound old or young? Deep or higher pitched?"

"He didn't sound old. He had a deep voice. But then, he only said the one word to me." She cocked her head, indicating her wish to return to the crowd.

"Thank you, Mrs. Simmons. I appreciate your sharing this."

"Will it help you?" Kitty looked at Winston with hope in her eyes. "Find who killed Harmony, I mean."

"We never know when something might be useful, Mrs. Simmons. That's why we try to gather as much information as we can."

She disappeared into the crowd again. Winston was turning to locate Miller again when he overheard his name being called. "Detective Winston!" A messenger boy ran toward him. "You must come. Your father. Doctor Evans says he is gravely ill."

CHAPTER 22

Riley

RILEY SAT ON the steps of her trailer, typing a text to Jules.

"Riley, you're okay."

Had she been standing, her knees might have buckled at the sound of Johnny's voice, tinged with genuine concern. As it was, she had to lean on the trailer when she stood, warmth radiating through her body. "You're here! I wasn't expecting to see you for another hour." She nuzzled into his neck as they embraced. The familiar scent of his soap was overlaid with a hint of perspiration. She inhaled it again.

"Good," Riley said. "You can take me back to Crasherton."

He pushed her away to look at her, confusion clouding his face. "I thought we were in Crasherton? Are you sure you're okay?"

"The ghost town. The actual town, I mean. This is just the festival site. The town is a short drive away." She tried to guess at his thoughts. "Unless you're tired. I was just going to text Jules to ask him to take me."

"Take you where?" Jules asked, rounding the corner of the trailer as if she had summoned him by saying his name.

"I think I know what happened," Riley said, placing a hand on her chest. "To me, I mean. I need to go to Crasherton to confirm it." Her words tumbled out in a breathless rush, and Jules and Johnny reached out to steady her. She shrugged away. "I'm fine. Just excited. Please. Can we go now?"

Jules extended his arm and dangled a set of keys between his finger and thumb. "I'll drive. Johnny, you're probably tired. Do you want to stay here or join us?"

"I'm coming," he said. He removed his ball cap and wiped his brow. "Is it just me, or is it beyond hot here?"

"It is. I'll get you a snack and a drink, and you can use the trailer if you need to change or anything," Riley said. "I've got sunscreen in my bag, too."

"No need. Let's go find out what's going on," Johnny said. "Can you fill us in on the ride?"

*

"I was poisoned," Riley said from the back seat as Jules pulled out of the festival parking lot. "By someone in Crasherton."

Johnny turned around from the front passenger seat to lock eyes with her. "What? You mean … Wait. Why are we going back there?"

"I want to know if it was intentional," she said.

"And if it was, give them another opportunity?" Jules asked.

"I won't eat or drink anything while we're there. At least, not anything from Crasherton." She pointed to her backpack that contained the granola bars she had packed.

"Back up." Jules held his right hand in the air like a stop signal. "Why do you think you were poisoned?"

"I wrote down everything that I ate or drank yesterday." Riley was still speaking quickly. "Like you said earlier, we had spent most of the day together, including all meals we ate. You didn't have a reaction. But I forgot about tea. I made a cup of it after we got back from the town." She pulled the tiny jar of honey from the front pocket of her backpack. "I used this honey, which I bought in Crasherton."

"Didn't everyone get some of that honey in their welcome bags? I thought I saw a little pot like that in the one you gave me when I arrived," Jules said.

"Yes." Riley produced the orange-labelled pot from her bag. "They're not the same." She stuck her hands into the space between the front seats. "It's orange. See?"

Johnny took the jars from Riley's hands. "This one is purple."

"When I bought it, Sonya—the lady running the unofficial museum—said that they had used a new recipe for this."

"Do you think she knew it was different? That it would make you sick?" Johnny asked. He passed the honey back to Riley and pulled his phone from his pocket. "Should I get the police involved?"

"I don't know what she knew." She put her hand on his arm. "I don't think there's any need for the police yet. There is a thing called 'mad honey.' It's made from the nectar of rhododendron plants, and the symptoms match mine. Jules, did you notice the rhodo bushes while we were there?"

Through the rear-view mirror, Jules raised his eyebrow at Riley's question. "I can't say that I did."

"It doesn't matter. They're there. I recognized them because my dad grew them. Don't you remember our garden growing up?" she asked.

"Not really. I didn't know you had a green thumb," Jules said.

"I don't. But the flowers make me think of him."

Jules shook his head. "I don't remember seeing any flowers."

"They're not flowering now. But if the honey was made from bees that collected nectar from the rhododendron blossoms…"

"Why would someone intentionally poison you?" Johnny asked.

"That's why I want to go back. I don't know if it was intentional." Riley said.

"Well, you're about to find out," Jules said. He pulled the car into the same spot in front of the café as he had the day before.

CHAPTER 23

Riley

As Johnny and Jules swung open their car doors, Riley felt the dampness under her arms intensify. What if her theory was wrong and it wasn't the honey? *That's why you're here, girl,* she reminded herself. She drew a deep breath and opened her door.

"You're back," Minnie said. "With another visitor. I'm so glad you enjoyed your time here yesterday." She handed a brochure to Johnny.

"Yes, it was great," Riley said.

Minnie offered her a stack of brochures. "Is there anyone else at the festival you want to give these to?"

"I don't think so," Riley said. She looked around, unsure how to broach the subject.

"We really like the honey," Jules said, and Riley gave him a quick nod of thanks. "Riley picked some up yesterday, and we were hoping to get more."

"Our honey is very popular. I have some here I can get you." Minnie disappeared into the café trailer.

"Sorry. I could see you thinking about how to bring up the honey," Jules said.

"I guess we didn't talk about strategy. But let me take it from here. Why don't you show Johnny the power plant?"

"We're not leaving you here alone," Johnny said. "We can look at the rest of the town later."

Minnie emerged from the café with a larger jar of honey. "Here. Is this what you're looking for?"

Riley accepted the jar and rolled it between her hands. The label was orange, like the smaller jar that had come in her goody bag. "I picked up some with a purple label yesterday."

Minnie's brows knit in confusion. "Purple? We only have this. Are you sure you got it here?"

Riley gave the jar to Johnny and produced the purple-labelled pot from her backpack. "It's got the train on it. I bought it here."

Minnie extended her hand. "Can I see that? I don't think it's ours. If someone is trying to copy our honey..." She took the pot from Riley and her mouth formed an *O* as she read the label. "I need to talk to my sister."

"So do I," Riley said. They followed Minnie to the museum.

Sonya sat at her desk near the museum entrance. "Hello again," she said when she saw Riley behind her sister. When she saw Jules and Johnny, she frowned. "What's going on?"

"Did you sell this yesterday?" Minnie held the purple pot of honey between her index finger and thumb. "To her?" She indicated Riley with her head.

Sonya reached for the honey as Minnie pulled her hand away. "Let me see it," Sonya said.

"Did you sell this yesterday?" Minnie repeated her question.

Sonya's cheeks coloured. "Maybe."

"Yes," Riley said. "I bought it from you. Here. And it made me sick."

"What?" Sonya asked. The hint of a smile teased the corners of her mouth. "How sick?"

Riley felt Johnny stiffen beside her. She squeezed his arm. "I think it's mad honey. I think the bees had access to your rhododendrons." She looked at the sisters. "I recognized the bush yesterday. My father loved his rhodos."

Minnie pointed at Sonya. "You said it was an experiment. You weren't going to sell it." She shook the small pot of honey. "How could you?"

Sonya, still seated at the desk, squared her shoulders. "It was an experiment." She turned her focus to Riley. "What happened, exactly?"

"I was dizzy. My fingers and tongue became tingly." Riley remembered the strawberries. "And I hallucinated."

Sonya seemed pleased to hear this. "I wasn't sure it would work."

"And you tested it on me?" Riley asked.

"You sold it to her?" Johnny asked. "And you knew that it might harm her." He raised his voice, and it hitched as he spoke. "What if it had been worse?" He pulled out his phone. "I'm calling the police."

Riley wrapped her two hands around his, pushing the phone back toward his pocket. "Not yet," she said. Johnny complied, but he planted his feet wide apart, like he was bracing for a fight.

"But you're fine now," Minnie said. She looked fearful and kept shooting sidelong glances at her sister.

"That doesn't matter," Johnny said.

"Please," Riley said. "I want to hear what she says." She turned to Johnny. "There's no cell service here, anyway. Let's listen to her. Then you can call the police or whatever you need to do on our way back to the festival."

"Police?" Sonya asked. "Why?" She cast furtive glances between Riley and Minnie. "Has something happened?"

Minnie inhaled sharply and edged closer to her sister. "What Sonya means is that she's sorry, and she is glad that nothing serious happened."

"I'm sorry for what?" Sonya's voice was weaker now, and she hesitated, waving her hand as if swatting at an idea. "Yes, I am glad to hear that you weren't hurt."

Minnie moved to get her sister to stand. "Come, Sonya. Let's get you something to eat."

Sonya obeyed and walked toward the museum entrance. Minnie watched her sister until she was at the door and turned to the others. When she spoke, she had lowered her voice so that her sister couldn't hear. "She's not well. This was my fault."

Through the door, they could hear Sonya greeting some other visitors. "Do check out the museum. But not the honey. Someone poisoned it."

Minnie raced to follow Sonya, and Riley's little group trailed behind. Sonya sat at a picnic table with two men across from her. One held a guidebook.

"What my sister means is that you're welcome here in Crasherton. The café will open shortly, and I'd be happy to serve you lunch or even a late breakfast," Minnie said.

One of the men rose. "We heard the food was quite good. What's been poisoned?"

"Nothing," Minnie said lightly. "My sister must have misheard me. Have a wander around." She pulled a paper from the front of her apron. "This is a map of the town." She pointed to the top section of the map. "I suggest you start here, at the power station. Then make your way back here." She traced a route with her finger.

The men exchanged skeptical looks but accepted the map and set out in the direction Minnie had suggested.

When they were out of earshot, Riley turned to Minnie. "What did you mean that this was your fault?"

Minnie walked alongside Sonya, who made her way toward the café door, unfurling the umbrella shades positioned over the tables as she passed them. Minnie gestured at the now empty table and the friends sat opposite her. After everyone had settled in, she began. "My sister is not well." Minnie braced herself by pushing her palms into the tabletop. "I didn't think she'd reached this point yet." She leaned toward Riley. "I'm so sorry about all of this."

"What do you mean by 'not well'?" Johnny asked. Riley noted his protective tone.

"The mining deal. It's not real. The company doesn't exist."

"Just turning on the coffee, Min," Sonya called from the café's container kitchen.

Riley was seated between Jules and Johnny. Both men had stiffened at Minnie's statement. Jules spoke first. "You are defrauding her?"

Minnie pursed her lips and shook her head. "More like deluding her. It's easier to let her believe a mining company is buying the town, and that's why she needs to leave. It was a dream our father had, that mining would resume. He died believing it was going to happen. He'd drafted plans and convinced himself of it. When she started talking about it, I realized that, like him, she was in the early stages of mental decline." Minnie dropped her eyes to her hands, which were folded on the table. "I didn't think it hurt to let her believe it might happen."

"She's living in a fantasy and you're letting her prepare food?" Incredulity had seeped into Johnny's voice.

"Not anymore. I make all the food." She cocked her head to listen to the noises coming from the café building. "We'd made the honey for her. To see if it helped. I'd been looking into the use of 'mad honey'." Minnie curled her fingers in the universal air-quotes gesture. "In controlled doses, it's been useful for its medicinal properties. I thought it might help Sonya."

"Why did you package it like the honey you sell?" Riley asked. "If your sister's mind wasn't clear, surely you knew that she might get confused."

Minnie looked down and dug a fingernail into the wood grain. "I thought using a different colour label would help to avoid confusion." She reached out for Riley's arm. "And I kept it separated from the other stock. Sonya must have… I'm so sorry," she said again.

"What about your resort plan? Was it for real?" Riley asked.

"The deal is signed. Work begins next month. I haven't figured out a way to tell Sonya."

"Tell me what?" Sonya stood a short distance from the table, her approach unnoticed by any of them.

"About the resort," Minnie said.

"Min, we're not getting a resort here. It would take years to restore the town the way you're dreaming of. And we would run out of money long before then. Mining West's offer is a good one. They'll keep the museum. We can put whatever we want in it."

"And they'll destroy everything else around here," Minnie said, her voice catching. She looked with pleading eyes at Riley for her not to say anything.

If she was asked, Riley would agree with Minnie. The archivist in her hated the idea of losing the town. And now it seemed that wasn't going to happen. But she didn't approve of lying to Sonya about it.

"Let's get back to the honey," Johnny said. "Have you sold more of it? I just need to know for sure."

Minnie shook her head. "No more."

"Where's the rest of it?" Jules asked.

Minnie pushed herself from the table. "I'll show you."

✳

SONYA LOCKED THE door to the museum and turned the sign to CLOSED at Minnie's bidding. After everything was shut, she led the way into the museum's back rooms.

The first room they entered had the kind of stainless steel tables and shelves Riley expected to see in a restaurant kitchen. Two cardboard boxes sat on a shelf. "Sweet Crasherton" was stamped on both boxes. Minnie opened a closet along the wall. On a shelf above various supplies was another box with the same stamp, but "purple" had been scrawled across it with a marker. Sonya lifted the box down from the shelf. "Here. It's all the purple honey that we collected."

Riley counted twenty-three little jars, twenty-four with the one she'd bought.

"We have to destroy this," Johnny said, reaching for the box. "We can't let anyone else get sick."

Sonya began to make a whimpering protest, but Minnie put an arm around her and pulled her close.

"What happens now?" Riley asked. "Johnny, do you have to report Sonya?" At hearing her name, Sonya raised her head. She had a fearful expression, and Riley felt compassion for her.

Johnny raked his hand through his hair. "Honestly, I don't know if we could build a case against her."

"Are you a police officer?" Minnie asked. Her voice came out in a higher pitch, and she cleared her throat.

"Crown prosecutor," he said. "If Riley had been seriously hurt. . ." He ran his hand through his hair again. "I don't know what we would gain by prosecuting Sonya."

The muscles around Minnie's eyes relaxed when she heard Johnny's words.

"But…" Johnny raised his finger.

The two sisters seemed to hold their breath, their eyes wide.

"But I'll be watching. And if there is even a hint of someone sneezing after they visit here, I'll personally make sure that you're investigated." He glanced at Riley. "Okay?"

Riley nodded. She gave him a warm smile and squeezed his hand.

Johnny closed up the box of purple-labelled honey. "Jules, let's get this locked up in your trunk."

Riley turned to Sonya. "Since we're down here, may I look at the records from the train crash?" She'd seen the filing cabinet with a drawer labelled CRASH. "Are they in there?" She pointed at the cabinet.

Sonya still hadn't spoken, but she nodded.

Riley pulled the top drawer open, and what appeared to be several years' worth of dust puffed off the top of the cabinet.

Sonya slid beside her. She pulled a folder from the drawer and began thumbing through the contents. Behind this first folder were a few others.

"I haven't looked through any of these in a while." Sonya had found her voice. "You're welcome to search through them." She turned to Johnny. "Are you okay with me reopening now?" Her hand trembled as she placed the folder on one of the stainless steel tables.

"Sure," he said, shifting the box of tainted honey from one arm to the other.

"Johnny and I can take a look at the town for a bit. How long do you want, Riley?" Jules asked.

"Hmmm?" Riley had opened the folder and was already mentally cataloguing its contents.

Jules repeated the question.

"As long as you'll give me," she said.

Johnny and Jules exchanged glances, then followed Minnie and Sonya to the main part of the museum.

Riley spread the contents of the folder on the table. The first item was a yellowed and crumbling newspaper article. She shook her head. The page should have been stored flat and kept in an acid-free folder. She set the page to one side. The headline looked familiar. It was a hard copy of a digital version she'd read, written just after the crash. Next was a copy of a menu, though it was only of passing interest to Riley.

Underneath the menu was an envelope containing a stack of photographs. Riley paused. Jack had mentioned photographs. She tugged the envelope open. Most of the images were of individuals standing in front of a locomotive. These must have been taken before the crash. She turned each one over, but none of the photos were labelled. She flipped them back and took a picture of each with her phone.

Three photos stood out from the others. The first was a picture of the crowd, but most of the people were blurry. Riley assumed this was because of the long exposure required to capture an image. The next photo was of four people. A tall man stood far enough away from the other three to appear as if he wasn't a member of their party. His hand was on the train the way a horse trainer might hold the side of his animal. Perhaps he was one of the train engineers.

She focused now on the three men. Their features were too small and indistinct to decipher any of their expressions, but they looked to be smartly dressed. Their posture suggested they considered themselves important. She looked at the version on her phone, expanding it, but the faces became too pixelated to be useful. She set aside her phone again and brought the photo closer to the window for better light. One man held a newspaper under his arm, and another held a walking stick. They seemed to be conversing. Neither man appeared to know that they were being photographed.

The final photo was another of the three men, this time without the one she thought was an engineer. She couldn't tell in which order the photos had been taken, and after glancing at each one again, she slid the photographs back into the envelope.

The remainder of the folder contained documents outlining the plans for the crash.

Riley continued through the drawer, following the same process of emptying items and cataloguing them. Twice she returned to the photos, which were the most interesting of the items she'd found. Jack would have seen many of these people. Spoken to them. She enlarged the images on her phone but was unable to pick Jack out from the crowd photos or the individuals standing in front of the train. This didn't surprise her. With a murder investigation, he was unlikely to have posed for a picture. But he might have been nearby.

There was no way to know what date the photos were taken. Was it before Harmony Fenton died? Or maybe after her death but before Montague's? They may have been taken the morning of the crash. If Jack had eyes on these photos during his investigation in Crasherton, what would he make of them?

CHAPTER 24

Jack

AS HE RUSHED to his parents' hotel, Winston considered what he knew. Evans had called for him. He must have received the message Winston had left at the Crasherton Inn. And something dire must be wrong with his father. Anything more was speculation.

He was not surprised to find his parents' rooms were considerably more luxurious than the one he had booked. His mother paced the anteroom, biting her lip. Her hair, usually perfectly in place, had fallen as if she'd been pulling at it. Creases crumpled her dress, and it looked somehow as if she had been wearing it for days. He couldn't recall ever seeing his mother so distraught.

"Mother, what happened?" Winston asked. He couldn't keep the panic from his voice.

She opened her mouth to answer, but instead of words, she let out a sob. As she tried to regain her composure, she led Winston into the bedchamber. He hardly recognized the man lying in the bed. His father could barely open his eyes. Beads of sweat crowned his pale forehead.

Winston lowered himself to his father's side, bringing his face close. "Father. It's Jack. What happened?"

His father's eyes fluttered. He moved his mouth as if speaking, but no sound came out.

Evans stood to the side, allowing the family access to the bedside. Winston did what little he could to help his mother comfort his father. Beside the bed was a bowl with soaked cloths. Winston wrung one out and placed it across his father's forehead. His mother moistened his lips by dropping water from her finger onto them. Feeling useless and wanting to give her space, Winston rose to step away from the bed. In a burst of energy, his father grasped Winston's wrist with surprising strength. "Your brother," he croaked.

Winston froze. "George?" he asked. George was in line to take over his father's position, though considerably earlier than they had expected.

"Ellis."

Instinctively, Winston's hand went to his pocket. In its empty folds, he balled his fist and dug it into his leg. Beside him, Winston's mother finally let a word escape from her mouth. "No."

"Your brother. When he died…"

Winston put his ear next to his father's mouth. An overwhelming surge of emotion flooded him. "What? What is it, Father?" he pleaded.

Winston's mother eased her husband's fingers from Winston's wrist. "Let him rest. He doesn't know what he's saying."

Evans checked Winston's father's pulse. "He hasn't long, Jack," he said quietly.

Winston lifted his face to meet the doctor's eyes. Evans shook his head and dropped his gaze. His mother let out a choking gasp, and Winston grasped her hands in his. "Mother," was all he said, tears spilling over his cheeks.

"Take me out of here, Jack," she said. "I can't be here."

Winston rose, bending once more to kiss his father's pale and clammy forehead, then escorted his mother into the anteroom and settled her into a chair. He closed the adjoining door and returned to sit next to her.

Evans's words replayed in Winston's mind. His father was going to die. Now. Here. But something else. He looked at his mother, then he remembered. "What was he trying to tell me?" Winston's tone was measured.

Tears welled in her eyes. "This isn't the time."

Frustration wrenched at his gut. He fought the urge to slam his fist on the wall, taking in the anguish on his mother's face. "When, Mother? When is the time?" His voice came out in a croak. When would she speak about what they had done?

The scene was interrupted by Evans's appearance in the doorway to the bedroom. Winston's mother rushed to him. "Mrs. Montague, dear lady," he said. Then he turned to Winston. "I can do nothing more. Jack, I'm so sorry but your father… He's gone, Jack."

Winston stared at Evans. "What do you mean?" The knot in his gut tightened and reached his chest. "Dead?" Beside him, his mother started to wail, and she pushed her way into the bedroom. Winston reached for her but stopped to swing back to Evans. "Are you certain?" He felt for Ellis's stone, fumbling instead with the flap of his pocket. Emotion constricted his voice when he repeated the question, searching Evans's face for the answer he already knew.

*

"JACK, TAKE SOME time at the bedside with your mother. I'll wait here until you've paid your respects." Evans opened the door to the bedroom a little wider and stepped back. As Winston passed in front of him, the doctor placed a hand on his shoulder. "I wish with all my heart I could do something for you, Jack."

Winston's voice caught in his throat. He drew a ragged breath and said, "I'd like to be there when you examine him . . . his body."

"Are you sure, Jack?"

"Yes." Winston gazed at his feet, not trusting himself to meet the doctor's eyes.

His mother's sobs drew Winston further into the bedroom. She sat on one side of the body, a hand resting on her husband's hand. He stepped closer. His father's face was pale, but he looked settled, relaxed. So unlike the strain his face had shown as he'd struggled to share a last word with him. "What was Father going to say?" Winston heard himself ask. "Was he going to apologize for the secret you kept? The lie you told me?" His words stung his own mouth as he spoke.

She flinched. "Jack. I'll thank you never to speak of your brother again," she said through her tears. "There is nothing more to say beyond what I've already shared with you."

"Mother, you have shared nothing!" His voice was louder than he'd intended. He flushed, aware suddenly of the proximity of Evans outside the door.

He circled the bed to the side opposite the one where his mother wept and knelt beside his father's body, grasping his hand. "I'm sorry. I'm sorry you never heard those words from me." His breath hitched harshly in his throat as he struggled to continue. "I'm sorry you felt you needed to hide the truth. And I'm sorry you're dead." He squeezed the hand for a final time and stood.

His stomach twisted when he turned to see that his mother had not moved since his outburst. She stared ahead, unseeing, without acknowledging him. Then her shoulders rose and fell in a shuddering sob. Were this a case, he would offer unreserved comfort to any grieving family member. He moved quickly to her side, at once setting aside the anger that had so gripped him since he'd learned the truth about Ellis. "I'm sorry," he said. "I'm sorry, Mother."

Instead of looking up, she extended her hand. The gesture, seeking affection, was so uncharacteristic of her that Winston understood how much pain she must feel. He extended his own hand tentatively and set it atop hers. She leaned into her son, and he accepted her weight. Who else could support her? Who else would support her now?

They sat in silence for several minutes. Winston squeezed his mother's hand, and she squeezed back. "Mother, Doctor Evans will want to return to complete his work here."

"May I have a few more minutes with him? Alone?"

Winston stood. "Of course. I will be in the other room." He closed the door softly behind him and turned to see that Evans must have arranged for a tea service to be brought in. Winston hadn't heard it being dropped off. How thoughtful. He poured a cup now for himself and one for his mother. He brought hers to her, which she accepted wordlessly, though her gaze remained locked on Winston's father.

When he'd settled himself again in the anteroom, he leaned forward to drop his head in his hands. He had so many questions. A thought rose above the others swirling in his mind. His father's body would likely have to join that of Harmony Fenton in a burial site nearby, as the likelihood of arranging for a refrigerated car was slim. The thought left a sour taste. He would rather not rely on his father's name to organize a final journey for his body.

Was there a family plot where Ellis was buried? Why didn't he know these things? Would his father and brother be reunited in death? With a shiver, Winston realized he'd never had the opportunity to visit Ellis's grave. His parents' lie had cost him dearly.

Winston straightened in his chair. He needed to get someone to sit with his mother so he could let Evans begin his examination and so that he could get back to his responsibilities—investigating Harmony Fenton's murder. The chief constable and his wife had rented rooms in the same hotel as Winston's parents. Winston heard footsteps in the hallway and leaped to his feet, lunging for the door. He met a hotel employee with an arm full of fresh towels and asked him to let his aunt and uncle know about his father. He instructed him to ask that they attend at once. Winston underscored that discretion was paramount.

Time seemed to pass incredibly slowly as he waited for Uncle Larry and Aunt Clarissa to arrive. His mother emerged stiffly from the bedroom, and Winston settled her into an overstuffed chair. He sat with her in silence, and he used the time to force himself to consider his next steps for the case. Winston was unable to voice any more words of comfort, which he expected was the same for his mother. He was staring at a fleck of dirt on his shoe when a swish of fabrics signalled the arrival of his aunt and uncle, followed by the uniformed hotel employee.

Aunt Clarissa swept him into her arms. "What happened?" she asked. "We just saw your father earlier this morning." She brought her hand to her mouth to stifle a sob. "And now he's dead?"

Uncle Larry comforted Winston's mother. She looked like a deflated bird in his arms. Over her head, Uncle Larry looked at Winston. "Jack." His eyes searched the room.

Winston guided his aunt to a chair. "He didn't eat much at lunch. Then he and Mother returned to the room when he complained of a pain in his stomach. And then he…" A sudden realization dawned on Winston. "Evans," he said. His aunt looked up at him, her eyebrows knit in a quizzical expression. As if on cue, Evans entered the anteroom, hat in hand, and nodded courteously to the family members who'd gathered since he'd left. "My deepest condolences for your loss," he said. "Jack?" His eyes said "Are you sure about this?"

"Please excuse us," Winston said and led the doctor back into the bedchamber.

As he closed the door behind him, Winston shared his suspicion with the doctor.

"I'll have a look, Jack."

Winston moved to stand at the foot of the bed as the doctor readied his instruments. His father's face was so restful, it was difficult to believe he wasn't simply napping. Doctor Evans began his examination, and though he tried to steel himself, Winston's stomach roiled. Despite his discomfort, he needed to remain to confirm his suspicions.

After exploring the head, Evans covered the face, gently draping a cloth over it. Winston recognized Evans's gesture as an attempt to ease the detective's discomfort. With each palpation, Winston fought the urge to push Evans away to prevent any further insult to his father. *No.* He must not think of this as his father. It is a body. Simply a body.

Winston took a seat on the stool in front of his mother's dressing table, sliding his hands beneath his legs so he wouldn't be tempted to cover his eyes with them.

After he'd completed his examination, Evans cleared his throat. He pointed to a spot on the left side of the body. "Here. It's the same as with Mrs. Fenton."

Winston rose and forced himself to step closer to the body. "Show me."

Bruising had already begun to form around the puncture site. As with Mrs. Fenton, there was some dried blood crusted around the puncture. "He was pierced here. A sharp, thin blade. He bled internally for a few hours."

"Can you give me a more specific time frame?" Winston asked.

"Three, perhaps four hours. Certainly no more than six." Evans pulled his watch from his pocket. "This morning, shortly after breakfast." He looked up from his watch and locked his gaze on Winston's. "You are correct. Your father was murdered."

At this, Winston could no longer stand to be in the room. He fled, deaf to the pleas of his mother and aunt as he passed through the anteroom and out into the hall.

*

WINSTON SAT ALONE in the constabulary tent. Miller and the other constables were patrolling the temporary town, though he could hear none of the sounds of Crasherton outside. Instead, he heard Doctor Evans's words repeat in his head. "He's gone, Jack."

Sometimes the words were whispered. If he couldn't really hear them, it was almost as if they were untrue. Other times, he heard them shouted, drowning out all other thoughts. Winston recognized his responses as similar to those he'd witnessed when he had to convey this same message to the families of the deceased. Did they experience the same pain as the one he now felt in his chest?

He knew he should be with his mother, though he took comfort knowing that his Aunt Clarissa and Uncle Lawrence were with her presently. His uncle's kindness of not pursuing him when he'd fled his parents' hotel room would forever remain with him. He would check on his mother soon, once he'd had time to think and work out what, exactly, had happened.

He only had a few hours. With the crash scheduled for the next day, the temporary residents of the town of Crasherton would begin returning to their homes and their regular lives. It would be difficult, if not impossible, to find them again if necessary.

He pulled the journal closer to him. Before he began writing, he closed his eyes and placed his hand on the blank page. He imagined Riley's hand on the same page and drew strength from the connection.

Dear Riley,

I am about to share something I never imagined writing.

"He's gone, Jack."

Certainly not at this stage in my life. My father is dead. Murdered. By the same person who killed Harmony Fenton yesterday. Is there a madman in Crasherton? Or was my father targeted? Why? By whom?

"Murdered."

Winston closed his eyes again. "You failed to save him" started to insert itself into the voices that swirled in his mind.

Evans confirmed that Mrs. Fenton was stabbed a few hours before her collapse. His findings suggest that the killer used a weapon with a long, narrow shaft and a sharp point. It penetrated deeply enough to cause internal bleeding and damage to her organs, yet its entry was swift. The effect was so subtle as to not even register with her, likely because of the clothing she was wearing. Evans assured the woman's husband that she suffered little. However, after seeing my father, I'm less convinced this is the case. Like Mrs. Fenton, he had a seemingly minor wound on his side—though the doctor only found it after he died. Why didn't I insist that he be examined more thoroughly? Earlier?

Winston recalled the final meal he shared with his father. As soon as he said he was unwell, he should have sought Evans. "You failed to save him." He squeezed his temples.

The wound could have been administered by almost anyone within the last few hours, according to Evans. My father took to his bed with what he had assumed was stomach trouble.

"He's gone, Jack."

Likewise, Mrs. Fenton had been in the company of large numbers of people attending an event in anticipation of the crash. Her companions said she did not complain of physical ailments up until the moment of her collapse. Now I have the unwelcome task of having to ask my mother about her activities with my father over the last few hours. Whom did they see? Whom did they engage with? And that assumes she can remember and identify everyone.

"Murdered."

At the same time, as her son, I must comfort her. To lose one's spouse in such a sudden way is unimaginable.

"He's gone, Jack."
"You failed to save him."

I must investigate my father's murder.

Jack

"Murdered."
"Your father was murdered."
Winston pulled his hand from the page. As he did, a frisson of anger forked its way from his fingers through the rest of his body. He made a grab for a baton perched at the edge of the desk and pitched it across the tent. Clutching a fistful of his hair, he dropped his head,

then threw it back to fix his eyes at the peak of the centre ridgepole. His own voice echoed in his aching head. *Your father was murdered under your watch.* What kind of policeman allows his own father to die in front of him? Fighting an impulse to feel for Ellis's stone, he pounded the desk—he'd be damned if he'd let his father's death go unsolved! Winston closed the journal when Miller entered the tent. Seeing Winston's face, Miller paused. "Sir, is everything…?"

"He's gone, Miller. And now we have another murder to solve."

"Surely you need to mourn." Miller pulled out a chair to sit. "Do you want me to fetch you a cup of tea?"

"I want to find who killed my father. And who killed Harmony Fenton. It's the same person, Miller." Winston explained what Evans had told him. "I cannot bring him back, but I can get him justice. I will mourn later."

CHAPTER 25

Riley

LUCY STOOD WITH her hands on her hips outside the door to Riley's trailer. "Where have you been?" She dropped her gaze to the box of honey Riley carried. "Did you go back to that town? You said you were going to take it easy today."

"I believe you 'suggested' I take it easy. I made no such declaration," Riley said. "But yes, we went to the town. I was with Jules and Johnny, and everything is fine." She didn't dare tell Lucy that she'd been intentionally poisoned. She'd lose it. "I need to check your supply trailer again, though."

"What for?"

Riley hated lying. It made her stomach cramp. The faintest hint of a lie was forming, and all she'd done was omit information so far. "There was a mix-up with the honey. A batch might have been sent here that isn't suitable for consumption. It's how I got sick last night." That was close enough to the truth that her stomach relaxed.

"Why aren't the people from Crasherton checking? How do you know if they sent the right batch?"

"They told me what to look for on the label."

"Like the lot number? I can help."

The enthusiastic voice of the festival emcee rose suddenly as another act was introduced on the festival stage. Lucy tilted her head to listen.

"It's fine. I'll go check and then meet you later." She squeezed Lucy's arm. "I still have the key from before. And I'll make sure Jules and Johnny know where I am."

"Have you eaten anything?" Lucy asked. "I could get you something…"

Riley placed her hands on Lucy's shoulders and turned her toward the music. "Johnny and Jules are picking up some food right now. We'll join you later." She gave her sister a gentle nudge. "Go. Make sure everyone is having a good time. I'll be fine. Seriously." Lucy's genuine concern touched her. She watched her catch up to a couple of VIP attendees. They exchanged hugs and squealed, stopping to pose for selfies. It warmed Riley's heart to see Lucy in her element.

Johnny and Jules appeared with bags of food. Everything been delicious all weekend. What a treat to have so many options just outside her door that she didn't have to prepare. She felt spoiled.

After they ate, Johnny announced that he wanted to grab a shower after the hot and dusty Crasherton visit and Jules said he wanted to call his boyfriend in London. While they were busy, Riley headed to the storage trailer. Opening the door to find everything neatly organized made her smile. There was something so satisfying about order. It calmed her.

She opened the box of honey jars and inspected each one to confirm that the label was orange, not purple. Sonya had told the truth. There was no mad honey at the festival. She pulled a packing-tape dispenser from a drawer of supplies and sealed the box with the mad honey, labelling it clearly—"Poison. Do not open." A smaller key on the set Lucy had given her fit the trailer's supply cupboard. Riley placed the sealed box on the top shelf and relocked the cupboard. She would tell Lucy about it later to make sure it was destroyed.

Satisfied, Riley cleared a space on the table. Jules and Johnny were bound to be a while longer, and her trailer really wasn't built for three. They'd need to figure out the sleeping arrangements soon. She pulled her journal from her bag. Jack had found time to write again. Her pleasure quickly turned to alarm as she read.

Jack's usually neat writing was pinched and the page dotted with extra ink. His hands must have been shaking as he wrote. His pain came through the page as strongly as if he sat next to her, bent in grief.

She thought back to when her father had died—unexpectedly, like Jack's, but from natural causes. Riley had felt raw for days afterwards. Weeks, even. Grieving the murder of one's father must be next-level grief. And how could Jack investigate a murder, let alone his own father's, in the storm of his pain? She'd had to take time away from her summer job to grieve. How would Jack push aside his pain? She hugged the book to her chest. His situation was unimaginable. And she would help him however she could.

CHAPTER 26

Jack

"It's a short list, Thomas." Winston looked at the names of those they'd need to speak to.

"Are you okay, sir?" Miller paused to clear his throat. "I mean, with your father … it would be understandable if you didn't pursue this investigation yourself." Miller kept his voice soft.

Winston balled his fists. "There is nobody else to investigate." He ignored the flicker of disappointment on Miller's face. "I must do this." He returned to the list. "Let's start with Parker," Winston said. "We'll begin at the Crasherton offices."

As they exited the constabulary tent, Winston recognized Miss Smallwood standing to the side with her hands clasped in front of her waist. Beside him, Miller coughed a subtle warning. Winston stole a glance at the constable, whose cheeks had flared.

"Miss Smallwood. Is there something I can help you with?" Winston asked.

She stepped forward but kept her head bowed slightly. "I heard that there has been another death."

The words sent a pulse of pain through Winston. And he was sure that his facial expression had not masked his surprise. *Where did this woman get her information?*

At the hotel, Evans had spoken with the desk attendant to inform him of the death and to set arrangements in motion. He supposed it would be optimistic to think that the story would not begin circulating. As a reporter, Miss Smallwood would make it her business to get to know the people who seemed invisible to most.

Winston focused on procedure. How would he answer to avoid compromising his own family's privacy? "You have heard correctly. However, I cannot share any details about it yet."

A flash of disappointment crossed her face. Before she could say anything, he continued. "May I ask you to keep the information to yourself?" He didn't want to draw her attention to similarities between the deaths or suggest to her that Mrs. Fenton and his father were murdered. "At least until I have had an opportunity to speak with a few people."

"Is that because you're concerned there is a madman on the loose?" she asked.

"I have no such concerns, Miss Smallwood." He paused. This wasn't entirely true. He had nothing to connect his father with Mrs. Fenton. Were their deaths the result of a madman? "We must be going. Perhaps Constable Miller can speak with you later."

Winston caught the smile shared by Miller and Miss Smallwood. It would seem that the pair were content with the prospect of spending time together.

Winston and Miller made their way down Crasherton's main street. As they walked, Winston looked at his feet. He'd passed this way earlier on his way from his pub breakfast. There were many rocks scattered on the path. It would be a nearly impossible task to find Ellis's stone if he'd dropped it there. But it would stand out to him, he felt sure, despite the odds.

"When you speak to Miss Smallwood, Thomas, I must underscore again that you must be particularly careful not to reveal any details about the investigation. She's clever. She knows how to make people drop their guard."

"Understood, sir."

They entered the Crasherton offices, where Abe Coulter sat at the main desk. He looked surprised to see the policemen.

"I'm looking for Mr. Parker," Winston said after they'd exchanged greetings.

"He was here earlier. He is doing a final check of the locomotives now, before they're taken to their starting locations tomorrow." The excitement in the man's voice matched that of the people outside. Everyone seemed to sense they were shortly going to see something remarkable.

"Do you have a favourite?" Winston asked, allowing himself to set aside his grief and share in the man's flush of anticipation. "Red or blue?"

The man held up his hands, his grin wide. "Oh no! I can't have favourites. It wouldn't be right."

Like Winston, the man was a neutral observer. "Do you have a moment to tell me again about the crash?"

The man puffed his chest. As Winston had anticipated, this was clearly a topic he was comfortable with. Proud of, even. "The engines are identical in all aspects and will be starting from a distance of one mile from the crash site, which you know is just outside of town."

It took, Winston knew from experience, just over ten minutes to walk to the crash site. He pictured the scene, the natural amphitheatre of the viewing area packed with excited spectators.

"Each engine will be piloted by an engineer. He and a coal man will be the only ones on the train and will, of course, jump off at a designated spot before the crash to ensure their safety." He spoke with such authority and confidence.

Miller took his cue from Winston's line of questioning and asked, "How will you ensure that the men have enough time to get off the trains?"

"Smarter men than I have worked out the speed at which the trains will be travelling and the distance that they will cover. They have calculated exactly where the men need to be off, and we've planted a red flag at each location." He traced his finger along a map that had been hung on a wall. "There are warning flags at intervals leading to the final flag. The men will be ready. And they have practised the manoeuvre many times."

A heaviness in Winston's limbs could no longer be ignored. He shared a final note of encouragement with the enthusiastic man. "I see the crowd outside is certainly looking forward to it."

The conversation had been so reasonable in a completely unreasonable moment. Now the pain threatened to overwhelm him once more. He had to keep moving. Winston straightened his jacket. "We really must speak with Mr. Parker. If you'll excuse us, we'll go find him now."

As promised, Mr. Parker was still at the crash location. Barriers were being set up at what Winston guessed had been calculated to be a safe distance from the crash so that the crowd avoided being injured by any resulting airborne debris. Winston passed through the barriers with Miller at his heels.

Mr. Parker and his assistant, Craven, were speaking with men Winston assumed must be the train engineers. He paused when he saw the policemen, then exchanged a handshake with each of the engineers, clasping their elbows as he shook. This friendly gesture earned him shoulder claps, and Winston saw in Mr. Parker the kind of care that he knew his father also felt for his employees.

"Detective!" The man greeted Winston warmly. "Are you here to observe our final preparations?"

Unlike Miss Smallwood, Parker evidently had not yet heard news of his father's death. Winston had hoped he would not have to be the one to deliver it. He opened his mouth to speak just as Craven stepped between him and Parker.

"We're on a tight schedule. I'm afraid that Mr. Parker has limited time to speak with you." He pointed Parker away with his arm.

Winston held up his hand. "Mr. Parker will want to hear this." Parker motioned for Winston to continue. "I'm afraid I have some difficult news." Winston's throat constricted as he spoke so that the final word was little more than a rasp.

"Oh?" Concern washed over Parker. "What is it?" The man's voice had taken on an air of genuine concern, Winston noted. "It's. . ." Winston started "It's. . ." His throat had closed entirely.

Constable Miller stepped forward. "There's been a death, sir. It's Mr. Montague." Miller indicated Winston with his head.

What had been concern was rapidly replaced by shock on Mr. Parker's face. "Dead?" His expression was aghast. "When?"

"A few hours ago. I was with him." Winston pushed the words out, the memory of the event still raw. "He's been murdered. Stabbed." Winston swallowed. "In a similar manner to the woman—Mrs. Fenton—yesterday."

Parker lost his footing and nearly collapsed into his assistant, who stretched out an arm to support him. When Parker recovered, he focused his gaze on Winston. "Are you saying the same person killed Mrs. Fenton and your father? Who would do such a thing? Who would know to do such a thing?"

Behind the barriers, the crowd of onlookers chanted teasing rhymes, taunting each other about their loyalties to their respective trains. The absurdity of it all made Winston feel for a moment like he was outside his body observing the scene. He blinked and answered, "That is what I will find out. I know you and my father were on tense terms with each other for many years, and your relationship has not always been friendly. Why did you invite him to this event?" Winston asked.

Parker pressed his lips together and considered Winston's question. "As you say, I have known your father for a long time. We are no longer the young men we once were, and I thought it was time to put our rivalries aside. I had hoped there would be an opportunity to work together. I invited your father here to show him the value of such co-operation."

"And did you have a chance to speak to my father about this?" Although Winston was not formally involved in his father's business, the elder man had regularly shared news of the business and decisions he was considering. He had not mentioned anything relating to working with Parker. Parker shook his head.

"Can you think of any reason why someone would want to harm my father?"

Parker considered this. "Your father has many business interests. The railway is but one of them. Perhaps it was someone related to one of the others."

Craven checked his pocket watch. "I don't mean to be rude, but Mr. Parker needs to be going."

"Just a few more questions, please." Winston did not temper the irritation in his voice. Parker nodded and Winston continued.

"And are any of those people from my father's other business interests likely to be here?" Winston regretted the tone of his question as soon as he asked it.

If Parker received it as a hostile challenge, he did not show it. "Look, Jack. I'm appalled at this news about your father, but I do need to get on with planning for tomorrow." He gripped Winston's hand. "Let your mother know that she must tell me if there's anything I can do. I'll send my wife around to check on her." Parker released Winston's hand but locked eyes with him. "I'm so deeply sorry about your father." His eyes glistened as he spoke. "My resources, my people are at your disposal. As I will be too once I attend to these pressing matters."

"Thank you." Winston turned to leave when Parker called after him.

"Look for Charles Howell. He and your father had harsh words yesterday. He is staying at the same hotel as your father," Parker said as Craven ushered him away.

*

As Winston and Miller approached the hotel, several revellers passed them, walking toward the far end of the makeshift town. Their light mood felt obscene considering the day's events.

Winston braced himself to re-enter the hotel. He clenched his fists as a flash of anger coursed through him afresh. It was quickly followed by a wave of nausea. He needed to gain control of these swings of emotions hindering his investigation. Winston cast a glance at Miller, who was seemingly unaware of his emotional storm. He closed his eyes and counted. Slowly, his internal chaos began to quiet.

"Sir?" Miller's voice drew Winston back to the task at hand. "Should you be leading this?"

"I have already answered that question, Thomas. Please do not ask again." Winston's reply was gruff. His cheeks warmed with shame when Miller looked away. "There's no one else to do it, Thomas." He searched for the words. "I wouldn't feel right with anyone else doing it, and I'm the only detective here," he said, softening his tone.

Miller's expression revealed nothing of what he thought of Winston's situation.

"Please wait for me here. I need to check on my mother. And I will interview her about my father's activities this morning before…"

Miller looked at his feet.

"I need to meet with her alone, Thomas." Seeing a flash of confusion on the constable's face, he continued. "She is a. . ." Winston couldn't find the words. "I will find you afterwards and we'll continue together." Miller nodded, and Winston set off.

He found his mother sitting alone in the anteroom of her hotel room. He sat beside her for a few minutes in silence. She stayed perfectly still, saying nothing. "Where is everyone?" he asked.

"I sent them away after your doctor friend removed your father's body." She stared vacantly at the wall.

Winston appreciated Evans's efficiency. The temporary arrangements made for the body of Mrs. Fenton were well suited for the unwelcome addition of his father's body. "That's for the best, Mother. With the heat, we need to keep him cool. Constables are on watch to guard the building."

"The doctor said the same thing." She brought her attention to her son. "What are you doing here, Jack?"

"Mother," he said, "I know this is difficult, but I need to ask you some questions. About Father's last day."

She clenched her fists. "Is this something that must be done today? Am I not to have a moment with my grief?"

"I assure you, Mother, I understand this is not what you want to do right now. This is not what I want to do right now." Winston kept his voice steady. "But for me to find answers, I must ask questions. And I must speak to everyone who was with him in the last twenty-four hours." He reached for her hand, unsure how she would respond to the gesture. "Please."

She pulled her hand away and gripped it in the other one, staring down at her lap. "Very well." Her voice had become stronger. "As you know, we arrived here the day before yesterday. I had developed a headache on the journey, and we came up to the room immediately so that I might rest. In the evening, I joined your father at an event." She tilted her head as if picturing the scene. "A dinner with about fifty guests. Your father knew most of the men there. It has been some time since I have had to attend an engagement with him. At home in Toronto, he has attended fewer events recently." She returned to the question at hand. "As far as I know, your father slept soundly that night." She met Winston's gaze.

"This is good, Mother. Do you recall anyone in particular that he spoke with at the event?" While she had been speaking, he had pulled his notepad and pencil from his pocket.

"I only recognized a few men. Mr. Parker, of course. This whole thing is his invention." She closed her eyes to recall the other faces. "I saw Charles Howell, though your father has not had any dealings with him for some time, I believe. I'm unsure whether they spoke that evening." She shared the names of two other men that Winston wrote down.

"Howell. What business did he have with Father?"

Winston's mother waved the question away. "I don't know what any of them do. They meet. They shake hands. They exchange money. Does it matter?"

"Can you think of anyone else he might have encountered?" Winston kept his voice soft. "Did he say anything to you about the event?"

"Only that the occasion confirmed what he already thought about the whole thing—this town, the spectacle—that it was a foolish waste of money. But he recognized that if he were not here, Parker or someone else would use that to their advantage. And so we came."

"Mother, I admit that I was surprised to see you. That you left Toronto, I mean."

This time, she reached for his hand. "He told me that you were going to be here." She squeezed it once and let go, clasping it again with her other hand.

"I know this is a difficult time, but I must ask you a few more questions about this morning." His mother's grip loosened as Winston spoke. He eased his hand from hers and picked up his pencil.

"I don't know what to tell you, Jack. But ask if you must."

"Where did Father go this morning? From the time he woke until I saw you at lunch."

"After breakfast, which we ate in our room, he went to view the trains a final time." She waved her hand in the air. "He was gone for no more than two hours. When he returned, I could see that he had lost some colour, but he said it was nothing more than his breakfast not agreeing with him."

Winston leaned forward. This is when his father had been struck his fatal wound. "Do you know whom he saw? What was the purpose of seeing the trains again?"

"I expect it was the same men we have seen at every event. Mr. Parker would have been there, of course. As would Howell." She tilted her head as if a memory was returning to her. "He said something about needing to retake a photograph. They had stood for one yesterday, but he'd received a note saying that it wasn't to Parker's liking. He'd asked him to return to have it retaken." She shook her head. "Can you imagine?"

"Did Father say anything about anyone approaching him, any uncomfortable moments when someone got too close?" His attacker would have needed to be close. "Were there many other people looking at the trains?"

"I don't know, Jack. I wasn't there. Surely there is now a photograph you can look at."

"Did he say anything else, Mother? Any comments at all?" He heard the desperation in his voice, how he was almost pleading for her to have the answers.

"I cannot answer these questions. You must speak with someone else."

Just then, the door opened and his Aunt Clarissa entered the room. Winston stood. "Jack. Good of you to sit with your mother. Shall I take over?" She kissed his cheek and took the seat Winston had just vacated. She leaned into Winston's mother. "Have a good cry," she said, rubbing her back. "There, let it go."

To his surprise, Winston's mother obeyed, and she dissolved in tears.

CHAPTER 27

Jack

WINSTON LEFT HIS mother in her room with his aunt and headed toward the hotel lobby, where he found Miller waiting with his hat under his arm. Miller raised an eyebrow and Winston nodded. There would be no further questions about the appropriateness of Winston's continuing the investigation.

"I've checked with the hotel reception," Miller said. "Mr. Howell is dining presently." As promised, they found Charlie Howell in the dining room, sitting with four other men. Full plates and empty glasses cluttered the table before them. The men had taken advantage of being the lone guests in the space, sprawling the remnants of what appeared to be a celebration among several tables. A waiter stood to the side of the room, awaiting their bidding. Although his face betrayed his weariness, he approached Winston and Miller at once as they entered. "The gentlemen are enjoying a private party, sir. The dining room will reopen for supper." He pointed toward the entrance to usher the men out.

"We are not here to dine. I need to speak with Mr. Howell. I believe he is one of the men attending the private event?" Winston met the waiter's eyes, unmoved by his request that they exit. "They must have paid a handsome price to remain the only diners?"

The waiter shook his head. "We had not planned to be open for luncheon today, with the picnic happening."

"The picnic?" Miller asked.

"Yes. Part of the festivities before tomorrow's crash. There is a tug-of-war this afternoon to predict how the crash will go tomorrow."

Parker's commitment to entertainment was impressive. His talents were many, it seemed. "And yet these men have chosen to remain behind. Do you know why?" Winston asked.

The waiter's cheeks coloured. "I do not." If he did, he was unlikely to share his knowledge.

"Very well. Which one is Howell?"

"The one on the left." The waiter gestured at a red-faced man in a well-tailored suit. He looked up as Winston and Miller approached. When he didn't recognize Winston, a frown crossed his face. "You have no business here, lad." His frown deepened when he saw Miller's uniform.

"Are you Mr. Charles Howell?" Winston asked.

The man offered a cautious nod. "And you are?"

"What is your line of business, sir?" Winston answered the question with his own.

The man's face reddened further. Howell was clearly unaccustomed to being ignored. "I'm not sure why my business is any business of yours."

Since beginning his work as a detective, Winston had become used to the deference he was usually afforded. Although Howell didn't know him or his rank, Winston was accompanied by a uniformed constable. Surely that was enough to suggest he had the authority to ask his questions. "I'd like to decide that for myself," Winston said.

As the man stood, his face softened. Had he realized who Winston was, or did he know people well enough to realize his bluster would not work with Winston? "It would help for me to understand why you're curious about my business so that I may know how better to answer your question."

The speed with which the man's voice had taken on a silkiness betrayed Howell's skills at reading people.

"It has to do with an investigation," Miller offered, no doubt to ease the tension. Beside Howell, his companions shifted. This was a man who commanded respect.

Miller's insertion into the conversation was enough to shake Winston from his anger. He adjusted his own voice to match that of Howell's. "As my colleague indicated, Mr. Howell, I'm seeking information in relation to an investigation we are conducting. It's somewhat sensitive, so I appreciate your discretion. I have no doubt you'll appreciate mine."

"In that case, I will let you know I have interest in several mines in the area, amongst other things."

"And what are those other things, Mr. Howell, so that my notes may be as complete as possible?" Winston asked as he pulled his notepad from his jacket pocket.

"I am involved in some importing from overseas. Does that help you with your investigation?"

Winston noticed the other men at the table shifting again in their seats. He pointed to a table removed a distance from the group. "Please join Constable Miller and me at the other table, Mr. Howell. We won't keep you long, and your companions can continue without our disturbing them."

Howell frowned and rose with an exaggerated sigh. He made his way to the other table as Winston held out an arm to usher him ahead. Once seated, Howell looked over to his companions, who had returned to their meals but clearly retained their focus on Howell's conversation.

Winston cleared his throat and waited for Howell to refocus on him. "Your mining interests today require transportation using rail lines?" he asked. Why else would the man have had heated words with his father?

"Yes. We need a way to transport what we find." He wiped his hands on a napkin.

"And which railway is it that you work with?" Miller asked, picking up the thread that Winston was following. He was coming along nicely as an investigator, Winston thought.

The man clasped his hands together. "As it happens, I've just negotiated a rather favourable deal with Parker."

"Had you previously been doing business with Pacific National Railway?"

At this, Howell coloured. "We had, but my interests no longer align with Montague's. He is not as honest as he'd like you to believe."

Shock spread through Winston from his toes. His father was one of the most honest men he knew … had known. Honesty was something his father had prided himself on. He had avoided having to lie or cheat to earn his accomplishments, yet he still managed to attain success. This man's suggestion that his father had been dishonest was akin to the man suggesting Winston's mother was unfaithful. It was unimaginable.

Beside him, Miller nudged his foot—a gentle prod that brought him back to the conversation they were having. "Was it a considerable sum, Mr. Howell?" Miller asked. "The amount that you thought Mr. Montague had cheated you?"

Confusion crossed the man's face. "Are you investigating his dishonesty? I haven't made a complaint to the police." He sipped from his wineglass and narrowed his eyes. "Which police force are you with?" he asked Miller.

"We're with the Vancouver Constabulary, Mr. Howell," Winston said. "I am a detective, and Thomas here is a constable, as I'm sure you've deduced. We were asked to provide police services here during the event."

"Shouldn't you be out amongst the people, then?" asked Howell. "I'm quite sure your services are not required here presently."

"As it turns out, they are. We are investigating Mr. Montague's murder," Winston said.

Shock registered on Howell's face. He mouthed the word.

Someone at the other table inhaled sharply at the news. Winston turned his attention to them and raised his voice. "Did any of you know Mr. Montague? Are you also importers, like Howell?"

One man turned in his chair to face Winston. "I own several factories. I'm considering opening one in the West, where land is plentiful. I've dealt with Montague in the past to get my goods east to Montreal. I'm sorry to hear he's dead."

"Your name?"

He gave it to Winston, but it wasn't one he recognized from the brief period he'd worked with his father and George. "Anyone else?" Winston directed his question to the whole table.

"I build locomotives. Montague purchased from me before," said a man on the far side of the table.

"Are they yours? The ones being crashed tomorrow?" Miller asked.

The man's chest expanded with pride. "They are. They are due to be replaced, but they've been restored to good working order for the event. I inspected them earlier and can attest that Parker has not in any way given one the advantage over the other." He appeared to suddenly remember why he'd been asked the question and became sombre. "Montague's death is a shame. I never had any complaints about the way he conducted business."

"I suppose we'll have to work on his son now that he's gone. He may be up for a better deal than his father," Howell said. He lifted his glass as if to honour Montague. "Perhaps Montague's death is not a tragedy for business."

Winston felt the heat rise up his neck. These men didn't know his connection to his father. What more might they say without that knowledge? Yet it pained him to hear his father being disrespected in such a manner. Before he decided how to proceed, Miller stepped in.

"Perhaps each of you could tell us when you last saw Mr. Montague. Did you see him here in Crasherton?" Howell took this as his cue to return to his original table.

"Aye, he was at that event the other night, wasn't he? With his lovely wife." The man winked, and a fire burned in Winston's stomach.

"And you, Mr. Howell?" Miller pressed on, and Winston silently thanked him for it.

"I spoke to him briefly. We exchanged pleasantries, as one does at that sort of thing. I found Montague a bore. Always talking of his sons. Say, you might know one. He's a..." When the realization of who Winston was hit Howell, the colour drained from his face. "Oh," he managed to say before sitting down. He stared at the table. "I'm sorry about your father, Detective."

Winston pushed away his anger. "I'm told I look like my mother. However, others have recognized glimpses of him in me." The words made him wince. His father had been proud of him, and ... he was proud of his father. Now he wouldn't have the chance to tell him. "Did you see him again after last night?" Winston heard the huskiness in his own voice.

"No." Howell cocked his head. "We may have passed in the hallway of the hotel, but we didn't exchange words again."

"What about Mrs. Harmony Fenton? Do you know her?" Miller asked. The three men shook their heads.

"I've been dealing with Isaac Fenton," said the locomotive man. "Is she his wife?"

"Why would we know her?" the other man asked. "I don't remember seeing Fenton at that dinner." Again, the other men shook their heads.

"Did my father cheat you? Or was it simply that he was an astute businessman?" Winston failed to keep the sting from his voice.

Perhaps Miller would be better to ask these questions and Winston merely observe. The rawness of his father's death was too powerful for him to prevent it from bubbling over. He was thankful they had had that final meal together, though words about Ellis's death had remained unspoken. He felt in his jacket pocket, and a surge of fresh loss passed through his body. He withdrew his hand at once, brushing at his jacket as if dislodging a piece of lint. Miller's hand at his elbow brought him back to the situation at hand. Four pairs of eyes were on him. What had he missed from the conversation? They were waiting for him to say something. Winston cleared his throat and repeated his question.

Howell answered. "Montague didn't do business with me, which caused me to spend more to transport my goods. That is, in effect, cheating."

"Why wouldn't he do business with you?" Winston asked.

"It was never 'the right time' was the only answer I could get. Instead, I was forced to deal with Parker, who is not the business mind he wishes he was. Montague, had he tried, could have moved everything in this country. Instead he was selective, sending the rest with Parker."

"So he didn't really cheat you?" Miller asked.

"Strictly speaking, no. It is not a situation in which he took my money and failed to deliver on a promise. He wouldn't take my money, so there was no opportunity to deliver on his promise."

"I'm not sure that's a crime, sir," Miller said.

"Certainly not one I would kill over, if that's what you're thinking, Officer." The man sipped from his glass with the confidence of a man with nothing to hide.

"What about you other gentlemen? Did you see Mr. Montague?" Winston asked.

"After yesterday," added Miller. Again, he had stepped in and covered for Winston's distraction. Winston offered a slight nod in thanks.

Another of Howell's companions answered. "But I saw him again, here, in the dining room. He was speaking with a well-dressed woman. I suspect she was also a woman of business, if you know what I mean." He snickered. "Though her goods had seen better days," he said through another laugh.

Winston flicked his gaze to the table. They must have enjoyed more than a few bottles of wine to be so loose with their opinions. Howell laughed, and Winston couldn't recall having such an instant dislike for someone. Still, he and Miller would need to try to find the woman. "What did she look like?" Winston asked.

The man coloured. "She had on a dark dress. Blue, I think it was. It caught the light in a rather fetching way, which I believe was the purpose of it. And her hair was dark. I didn't see her face."

Winston deflated. Searching for a woman in a blue dress would be nearly impossible. "Do you recall anything else?"

"I think I heard him call her Music. Or maybe it was Melody. Musical Melody." The man laughed at his own joke.

Melodia? She had dark hair, but so did many women. She wasn't a prostitute, but she could call attention to herself with her manner of dress. Winston made a notation of her name and turned to Miller. The constable frowned at the mention of Mrs. Spectre, but he shook his head to signal that he had no further questions. They had learned all they could from these men.

As they left the dining room, Winston considered the question that was now swirling through his mind. What had his father been doing speaking with Melodia? They were hardly likely to have acquaintances in common. *Unless...* Winston's stomach soured at the thought. Melodia could know women in Crasherton who had come here to ply their trade. But Winston's father wouldn't have been arranging to meet one. He was devoted to his mother. And on the very slim chance there was anything inappropriate about their encounter, he wouldn't have conducted it in such a public space. As for availing himself of Melodia's psychic services, that was equally impossible. So why had he been with her?

CHAPTER 28

Jack

WINSTON HAD DISPATCHED Miller to retrieve copies of the photographs taken at the rally. He sat on the bench outside the saloon, awaiting his return and trying to gather his thoughts.

"I heard about your father." Melodia stood a few feet away, waiting for his invitation to sit down.

"Did you know him?" Winston asked.

"Know him? How would I? Your parents live in Toronto, don't they?" Melodia sat next to him.

"You were seen speaking to him. Before he died." Winston slid away from Melodia.

She stood at once. Instantly, Winston regretted his movement, as he was now forced to look up at her when he spoke.

"After Harmony died, I needed to be surrounded by life. I attended an event last night. People were happy, celebrating. Nobody was thinking about murder. I heard someone call out your father's name, and in a quieter moment, I introduced myself. To him and to your mother." Melodia paced as she spoke, her shoes tapping a sharp rhythm with each step. "Perhaps it was not my place to do so. But he was a man who felt considerable pain. Your mother does too."

"What do you know of pain?" Winston whispered.

The tapping stopped as Melodia planted herself immediately beside Winston. "My sister is dead. Or have you forgotten in your own distress? Have you questioned her husband?"

Winston stood, heat rushing to his cheeks. "Melodia. I am sorry. For your sister. And for speaking so harshly. It is not fair of me." He turned her question over. "Yes, I have spoken to Fenton."

"And? How did he react when you mentioned her pregnancy?"

Winston had previously discussed cases with Melodia, but she wasn't involved in those the way she was with this one. He closed his eyes and continued. "I am not at liberty to discuss details of specific conversations with you." Winston did not want to admit to Melodia that he had not pressed Fenton further on the matter of the pregnancy. There remained questions he must put to him about what Kitty had mentioned. Did the man suspect his wife had been unfaithful?

"I think he knows something, Jack. Promise me you will consider him a suspect until you are certain he is not."

With his father's death, the likelihood that Fenton had killed his wife diminished in Winston's thoughts. Fenton didn't know Winston's father. What reason would he have to kill him? But Melodia was right. He must be thorough. "You have my word."

They moved closer together on the bench and instinctively reached for each other in their shared grief. After what could have been minutes, or hours, or days, Winston eased himself from her arms. "Thank you for sitting with me, Melodia," he said. "I will find who is responsible for these killings."

"And I hope that you do," she answered.

*

Winston remained on the bench in a hunched posture, weighted by a load of discouragement. Fenton was the only viable suspect for his wife's death, and he had no real suspects, as yet, for his father's. Maybe Melodia was right. Perhaps speaking to Fenton would provide other ideas for him to pursue. But he was in no fit state to speak to people on his own. He pulled himself from the bench and walked toward the constabulary tent to see if Miller had the photographs.

Inside the tent, Miller had arranged the images in neat stacks. "I've sorted them, sir. This pile contains people we know are involved with the case." He pointed to one that contained three or four. "Mrs. Fenton. Mr. Fenton. Melodia Spectre. Your father."

Winston picked up this last photograph. There was his father, standing beside his mother. They must have left the rally before Mrs. Fenton collapsed. The two had faint smiles—*picture smiles*, he thought. They were the kind one could hold for the time required to pose for a photographer. "They had no idea," he said. He placed the photograph on the desk and ran his finger along its border. "We must give this to my mother when we finish the investigation."

Winston picked up the next pile. "And these?"

"Oh, those are of little use. They show the crowd, but you can't make out anyone. The photographer was setting up when he took those." He pulled another batch of photos from an envelope. "While I was there, the photographer mentioned that he had been asked to take another set of photographs this morning. He gave me these." Miller handed the batch to Winston. "I haven't had a chance to sort them yet."

The men bent over the images. In these, the faces were clearer, and he could make out his father and Parker speaking to Charles Howell and the man whose locomotives were about to crash. Winston wondered why Parker wanted this particular image recaptured. He placed the image taken the day before beside the one taken just a few hours ago.

His attention was drawn back to the fuzzier photos where one of the men held what looked like a newspaper. In the retaken pictures, there was no such article. Was this significant? Winston wrote the question in his notepad and picked up the stack of crowd photos. He shuffled through each one, setting the stack down when nothing of import was revealed in them. "It's too far away to identify people, but let's hold on to them. Something in the crowd may lend a clue when we've had the time to study them."

Miller gathered the images. Winston stretched back in his chair, then snapped forward and said, "Let's go speak with Fenton." He knew his thoughts were scattered, but perhaps the answer to his father's murder was in Harmony's.

"Where will we find him?" Miller asked.

"I don't know, but let's start at the Crasherton offices. If Fenton isn't there, we will check the pub he was in before." Winston left the tent without looking behind to see if Miller followed.

The Crasherton offices were quieter than they had been earlier, with only two men sitting at the desk. They both looked more relaxed than the frenzied activity he'd seen previously. He envied the men their uncomplicated tasks that had nothing to do with death.

Craven, Parker's assistant, was speaking to the man Winston assumed to be the manager of operations. He waited until they finished their conversation. When he saw Winston, a pained expression crossed his face. Craven surprised Winston when he approached him. "Detective Winston. I didn't realize who your father was." He passed his clipboard from one hand to the other. "I didn't know him well, but he'd always been polite when we spoke." It was interesting to hear how others who knew Winston's father felt about him.

"Thank you, Mr. Craven. Perhaps you can help me. I'm looking for Mr. Isaac Fenton."

"You're working?" He failed to hide the surprise in his voice.

"I need to work," Winston said. He had no need to explain anything to this man, but there was nothing gained by being rude to him.

Craven nodded. "I haven't seen Fenton today. As you know, he is also mourning. Mr. Parker has told him to take a day to grieve. Have you tried his lodgings?"

Winston thanked the man, berating himself for not thinking of going to Fenton's lodgings first. In his state, the man was more likely to be found than at the railway offices. But they were nearer the pub, so he followed Miller across the street. The room was filled again—or perhaps still—with revellers. Fenton was seated at a table with four other men. From his slouched posture and overly loud speech, it was evident he had been drinking for some time. This was not ideal for questioning a witness, but perhaps his tongue would be loosened by the drink. Winston approached the table, and the five men stared up at him.

"Detective. Do you have news for me?" Fenton spoke clearly for a man who was in his cups.

"Not yet, Mr. Fenton. I have a few more questions for you. The answers may prove helpful."

Miller indicated with his head that they wanted to meet with Fenton alone.

Fenton stood. "Anything to help," he said. He waved to his friends and followed the policemen out of the pub.

Once they were outside, Winston led them back to the police tents. He pulled out a chair for Fenton. "Can I get you some water?"

Fenton waved away the question. "What are your questions, Detective?"

Winston took his seat, and Miller pulled up a chair beside him. Winston immediately got to the heart of the matter. "Tell me a little more, please, about your relationship with your wife. Specifically, did you have any suspicion that she was pregnant?"

"None. She had said nothing." Fenton pushed at a knot on the desk's top. "We had spoken of a family." He looked up at Winston, and his next words came out in a tumble. "Do you think it was mine? The baby, I mean."

The question—so simple—betrayed the additional level of grief Fenton felt. He'd lost his wife. He'd lost an unborn child, quite possibly his own. And if it wasn't his baby, his grief was still compounded by the sure knowledge that his wife had been unfaithful. If Fenton had been in possession of this knowledge, Winston reminded himself, it was a motive to kill her.

"I am not able to answer that," said Winston. He regarded the man across from him. Fenton bore none of the characteristics that he associated with liars. He met Winston's eyes, and his expression was open, devoid of deceit.

"Is that what you think, Mr. Fenton? That the child was not a product of your marriage?"

Fenton squared his shoulders. "I have no way of knowing for certain, but I believe that there is a possibility that it was not." He licked at his cracked lips. "I can see that this surprises you, Detective. But I am no fool. Harmony was always a happy woman, but in recent months she appeared more so, despite there being no change in our circumstances or our home life. I was pleased that she was happy, even if I suspected it wasn't because of me."

"And if she was unfaithful?" Winston let the question hang. "Would you have..."

"Would I have killed her? Never. I just don't have that within me." The man's voice was subdued and his eyes downcast. "If only she'd been honest with me. I could have made her that happy...I know it. And I would have found a way to love the child as mine." Fenton's voice hitched in a way that would be difficult to manufacture. Perhaps it was his own grief, but Winston was inclined to believe him. He'd learned to trust his instincts in these intimate interviews. But if Fenton wasn't the killer, who was?

CHAPTER 29

Riley

RILEY'S PHONE PINGED again. She'd received six "Where are you?" texts—most from Lucy, but others from Johnny and Jules. After skimming the messages to make sure there was nothing urgent, she set her phone on silent. She sat in the stuffy storage trailer with the journal in her lap, as she had done since reading Jack's message.

She reread it, touching each of the blots on the page as she did. Were they from Jack's tears? Her heart ached knowing that she could have warned him. She could have prevented his pain. Only she knew she couldn't. Telling Jack that his father was going to die would have changed the past in unintended ways.

A tear created a new blot as she stared at Jack's words. With a ragged breath, she considered whether she wanted to continue using it. What if she had to face a similar decision again and allow someone to die? She closed her eyes and focused on counting her breaths. As her breathing calmed, she realized that nothing had changed. From the moment she had realized what the journal was, how it connected her to Jack, she could have checked the police files and warned him about crimes before they happened. But she had no way of knowing what the impact of actively manipulating events would be, and they had agreed that she would not intentionally do so. She picked up her pen.

Dear Jack,

I am so very sorry. I know what it is to lose a father. But I cannot imagine what it is to have to investigate his death. It will be difficult, but you cannot spend time worrying about what you missed or the choices you made.

The newspaper write-up about two deaths at Crasherton, unrelated to the crash itself, flashed into Riley's mind. Why hadn't it mentioned murder? She pulled out her phone to search the archives again. Had she missed something? She was certain there was no reference to any cause of death beyond illness.

She added "murder" to the search terms. This time, different articles came back. MURDER TAINTS OTHERWISE SUCCESSFUL TRAIN CRASH and TRAIN CRASH MURDERER SET TO BE TRIED. Both were attributed to L. Smallwood. Riley checked the byline of the first article she'd found. It was also by L. Smallwood. How had she missed these? She checked the dates. A pit opened in her stomach as she realized her mistake. When she'd first performed the search, she'd limited the dates to the two weeks leading up to and following the crash. She had saved those results and continued to refer to them. The references to murder had been published a month after the crash. Why was the connection only made then? She read on. A railway employee was blamed for the two deaths. The name wasn't one that Jack had mentioned. Had the information about the deaths been suppressed to avoid panic among the people at the event? She had so many questions for Jack.

She reread Jack's description of the weapon the killer had used—a long, thin shaft. How would someone hide something like that in a crowd?

Jack, since your note about Harmony Fenton's death, I have been thinking of different ways the killer might have concealed a weapon like the one you've described. They would have to use something portable and so ordinary that it wouldn't attract attention. And it would need to be long or deep enough to hide the weapon.

I wondered if the weapon wasn't hidden inside an umbrella. But I believe there was no rain during the crash.

Riley lifted her pen and pictured a Victorian umbrella. One frilly image came to mind.

Women still carry parasols, though, so I suppose we shouldn't abandon the idea completely. Maybe the killer hid the weapon in a newspaper held under his arm or carried it in a satchel. I wonder if it might be difficult to retrieve from a bag, however.

She gave her chin a scratch with the top of her pen.

Perhaps the weapon was tucked into a boot?

She pictured the type of boot that would accommodate this long instrument. It would need to be tall, more of a riding boot, really. Any brief research she'd done into the fashion of Jack's era had revealed the footwear was dictated by specific activities.

Although I gather from your descriptions that people are treating the crash as a party and are dressed in finery rather than horse-riding attire, which might be better suited to hide a weapon.

Riley ran her finger over the last few sentences.

Of these suggestions, I think the newspaper or something else held in a hand is most likely, as the others would be cumbersome and hamper quick movement or draw attention to the killer. I hope that these ideas are of some value.

Her heart still ached at having been unable to prevent Jack's pain. She inhaled deeply and tried to organize her thoughts. *No.* She shouldn't feel guilty. As difficult as it was to accept, she couldn't tell Jack the killer's name and risk impacting other events.

I have never wanted to ignore my promise not to reveal anything about your future more than I do now. I will do everything I can from here to help you discover the truth and solve your father's death.

Riley set her pen down and stretched her arms over her head to shake off the heaviness of the moment. She reached into her backpack and pulled out the photos she'd found at Crasherton. Separating out the crowd pictures, she studied and compared them. Her pulse sped up when she noticed a contrasting detail between two photos. She pulled the journal closer. Maybe it wasn't too late to make a difference to Jack's investigation.

Today I found photographs taken at the crash. Perhaps they are the same ones that you referred to in your earlier message. There were only a few of the crowd. Most of the photos were of individuals. In the crowd pictures, I looked for attendees holding umbrellas, bags, and newspapers. It seemed as though everyone was holding something. So I compared the photos to see if I could find any-

where someone was holding an object in one photo but not in the next. In one of the photos, a man is holding a newspaper. In another photo, he carries nothing. I wonder, could this be the killer? I hope you have access to these same photos.

Riley

Never before had she wished she could physically be in the same time as Jack. She imagined herself chasing a lead with him, dressed as a woman of the time in a long summer dress, her hair tucked under a wide-brimmed hat. But if she were able to travel back in time, she'd want to wear running shoes. The footwear of the time did not look comfortable. She looked down at her own sandalled feet, dusty from her morning at Crasherton. She'd done all she could for Jack for the moment. She'd grab a quick shower and then figure out where to join the others. On cue, Johnny's text pinged.

Meet us at Main Stage, slowpoke.
Next band up in 15!!

CHAPTER 30

Jack

WINSTON SAT ACROSS from Miller and Philpott in the constabulary tent. "I'm at a bit of a loss," Winston said. "The method of killing is too similar for the deaths of Harmony Fenton and my father not to be related. Yet they shared no connection that I can identify. In fact, I'm not sure they ever met each other. Is it possible that their killer is simply a madman?"

Philpott leaned forward in his chair. "Have you considered if they knew anyone in common? Mrs. Fenton's husband. Does he work for your father?"

"He works for the Coastal Rail Company. He was recently promoted." Winston turned to Miller. "Do we know whether he ever worked for another company?"

Miller flipped through his notes. "He said he first worked on the locomotives when he began with Coastal Rail. He didn't mention another company."

"What about her friends? Would any of them have met your father?" Philpott asked.

"My father is never in Vancouver. What occasion would he have had to meet them?" As Winston spoke, he remembered what he'd learned about Melodia. "He spoke to Mrs. Fenton's sister. The night before he died."

"Could she have killed him?" Philpott asked.

"She had no reason to." Winston said.

Across from him, Miller stiffened. "You're speaking of Melodia Spectre?"

"Yes. But she had not met my father before that night. I've interviewed her, and I am confident that she is telling the truth. And why would she have killed her sister?"

Philpott nodded. "I agree. She doesn't sound a likely suspect." He tapped his chin. "What about Isaac Fenton? Did he know about the baby and suspect that it wasn't his?" Philpott asked.

"He seemed genuinely surprised about the pregnancy. And why would he have killed my father? When? He wouldn't have had an opportunity." Winston tugged at his beard. "This is the puzzle. The two victims share no common ground, at least none that we have discovered, and yet they were killed in an identical manner."

"Who else was at that event last night?" Miller asked.

"Mr. Parker, from Coastal Rail Company. He suggested I speak with Charles Howell, which I did." Winston flipped back to an earlier page in his notebook. "And when I spoke with Kitty Simmons, she remembered that she had seen someone at the Fentons' Vancouver residence visiting Harmony Fenton during the day. He left in a fancy carriage."

"Do you think this may be the father of the baby?" Philpott asked.

"Quite possibly. And he may be here," Winston said. He straightened in his chair as a passing thought surprised him. When he began speaking, he drew the words out slowly, allowing the idea to solidify as he spoke. "I wonder if it isn't Parker." The thoughts came thick and fast for Winston now that this floodgate had opened. "He arranged for Mrs. Fenton's husband to be granted a promotion, and he also arranged for them to receive tickets to the crash. Kitty Simmons said that Harmony Fenton invited her to the crash. She thought it might have been to silence her about the visit of the man in the fancy carriage. Parker could have arranged for these tickets as well."

The more he spoke, the more Winston felt sure about this train of thought. "Parker was at the event last night, and he saw my father again this morning before he died." Winston raked a hand through his hair. "If he knew of the pregnancy and dreaded the disruption it might bring to his life, his reputation..." Winston let the thought dangle incomplete, slumping in his chair. "But what reason would he have to kill my father?"

"Exactly," Miller agreed.

Suddenly, Winston thought of Riley's message. "Miller, where are those photographs you showed me earlier? Find the ones with the man holding the newspaper."

While Miller searched for the photos, Philpott tapped his finger on the table. "Let's focus on the woman first. Her pregnancy would be complicated for Parker. He wouldn't want to have to provide care for the mother and child," Philpott said.

"Would he have killed her to keep her quiet?" Miller asked.

Winston sat back in his chair. "These men are ruthless. It is how they are successful in business."

Philpott flashed surprise at Winston. "You include your father in this?"

"I would like to think that he was less ruthless than most. But I'm sure he made decisions that were in his interest that others would disagree with."

Philpott cleared his throat. "You're probably right, son. And perhaps that is sufficient reason for Parker to have wanted your father dead."

Miller pushed the photographs in front of Winston. "Are these the ones you meant?"

With a trembling hand, Winston snatched the photographs up. It was impossible to identify the men by looking at their faces. Assuming it was his father, Parker, and the others, he understood why Parker would have asked for a second version. He looked at their hands. In the older set, one man had held a newspaper. He picked up the newer set of photographs, again noticing that in these, nobody held anything. But, when he looked at each image, he realized that in one, the foot and hand of Parker's assistant, Daniel Craven, had been captured, identified thanks to the edge of a clipboard Winston could make out. He threw the photographs on the table. They were of no use.

The top photograph showed the unmistakable figure of Parker captivating the crowd's attention at the edge of the gathering. Winston liked the affable man behind the spectacle that had attracted thousands of people. He found it hard to attribute such acts to Parker, but Philpott was correct. He had a motive to kill both people. He rose. "We must find him."

"Do you know where he is?" Philpott asked.

Winston checked his pocket watch. "There is a picnic and tug-of-war this afternoon. I last saw Parker there, and it should be wrapping up within the next hour."

Philpott frowned. "It would be better if we were to find him in a less visible area. There's no need to embarrass him."

Winston failed to find sympathy for the man who had likely killed his father. "Wouldn't it be best to secure him now, before he has a chance to leave?" he asked.

"I doubt he would leave before the crash, given how much he has invested in it, but yes, we are best to make an arrest as soon as we can. I will come with you, Jack. Thomas, you come along too, but I'd like you to station yourself to be able to catch Parker should he try to run."

With a plan in place, the three officers set out.

*

PHILPOTT HAD SECURED a horse and cart to get them to the event grounds quickly. The three men squeezed on the bench while Miller drove. The roar of the crowd suggested the tug-of-war was underway. Winston had to remind himself not to leap from the cart and run toward it. Parker was sure to be there enjoying the moment.

They crested a hill and found the crowd divided into two sides, with people wearing colours of the train they supported. Two teams of ten men each held a thick rope suspended between them. Parker stood on a box with the rope in one hand and the other hand in the air. Winston saw that they would be unable to breach the crowd until the event finished. He and Philpott dismounted while Miller tied up the horse. Through the murmur surrounding him, he understood that two of the three attempts at tug-of-war had ended, with each side winning. This final attempt would determine the winner. The enthusiastic crowd would then be served a picnic in a shaded area to the left of the field of play. Once again, Winston was impressed by the planning that had gone into the event.

"Three ... two ... one ... go!" Parker shouted from his perch. The men, sweaty from their previous exertions, pulled in opposing directions. The sides were well matched, which, Winston had to admit, made for an entertaining time while they exchanged ground with each other, each team pulling fiercely. Eventually, the blue team faltered first and the red team, in a final burst of strength, toppled them. The good-natured crowd cheered and jeered and began moving toward the picnic area.

As the crowd thinned, Philpott signalled to Winston to approach Parker. Upon seeing them, he extended his hand. "Gentlemen. Did you see the show? I hope it took your mind off your loss for a few minutes."

"It was something," Philpott said.

Craven, Parker's assistant, appeared at Parker's elbow. "Sir, you will be presenting the awards in five minutes."

Parker thanked his assistant and turned to the police officers. "Everyone should have someone like Daniel working for them. It is as if he anticipates my every need. Is there something I can help you with before I get to the ceremony?" He stepped down from his platform. "You can walk there with me. And be sure to get some food. What's on offer promises to be delicious."

Philpott tried to steer Parker away from the picnic. "We need to ask you some serious questions, Parker. Perhaps someone else can give out the awards."

Parker searched Philpott's face. "Is this a joke? I don't want to miss anything. And neither should you."

"We think you killed Ernest Montague and Harmony Fenton," Philpott said quietly to avoid anyone else overhearing.

Parker's jaw dropped open. His face darkened. "Well, this is not funny at all, Lawrence. Not at all. Now, if you'll excuse me." Parker sidestepped Philpott.

"Mr. Parker, were you having an affair with Harmony Fenton?" Winston asked. "Did you kill her because she had become pregnant?"

Parker stopped walking. "She was pregnant?" He swallowed twice as colour drained from his face. "She didn't tell me."

"But you were having an affair with her?" Philpott asked.

"She was a remarkable woman. Beautiful. Funny." His eyes glistened. "I can't believe that she is dead."

"Did you kill her?" Winston asked.

"Of course not. I looked after her. That is how her husband has secured a position working in the office despite his lack of skills. Though I understand he has acquired many since his appointment." Parker wiped a band of sweat from his brow. He narrowed his eyes, as if he'd just made a connection in his understanding. "Why would I kill your father, Jack?"

"I would dearly like to know," Winston said.

"I didn't. I can assure you of that. We may have had differences of opinion when it came to business, but those are not something I could kill for."

It's as if he anticipates my every need. Parker's earlier words echoed suddenly in Winston's ears. "But someone else, perhaps," Winston said. He scanned the crowd and saw Parker's assistant a few yards away. Craven knew Winston's father. And he likely knew of Parker's reason for promoting Fenton. He was everywhere yet always in the background, while Parker was the showman.

Winston launched into a run, shouting at Miller. "It's Daniel Craven! Get him!" He dodged revellers carrying plates of food. Craven took less care, knocking people out of his way as he fled.

Miller ran faster than Winston and caught Craven on a downward slope, tumbling with him through the dust. When they rolled to a stop, they were under the shade of a tree. Miller flipped the man, turning him to sit with his hands behind his back. Winston arrived as a crowd started to gather, expecting, it seemed, that this was another spectacle arranged for their entertainment. Philpott and Parker caught up, bending at their waists to catch their breath. Philpott dismissed the crowd at once, pointing to Miller's uniform and using his commanding voice to gain their compliance. Parker joined him, turning on his charming host voice and encouraging those who had spilled their meals to seek replacements from the refreshment tables.

When he returned to where Miller sat constraining Craven, Parker stared at his assistant, then looked back toward the crowd. Uniformed officers had appeared and were ushering people away. "Eat, enjoy yourselves!" Parker shouted toward the crowd. "And return tomorrow for the main event!" He fumbled for his pocket watch. "Philpott. The awards ceremony. Can you find Theodore Bloomington? He is a suitable representative to step in for me." If Philpott was affronted at being ordered around by Parker, he didn't show it as he nodded and set off to follow Parker's instructions.

Bloomington. Publisher of the *Western Daily News*. That reporter, Lottie Smallwood. Winston shielded his eyes as he searched the crowd but did not see her face among the small number of people who had not dispersed. He doubted she would be far from the activity and stood to look deeper into the gathered onlookers. Unable to find her, he turned back to the spectacle unfolding in the shade. Parker moved to kneel beside his assistant—the man who had killed Winston's father. Winston balled his fists and forced himself to step back to distance himself from Craven. If he were within striking distance, he didn't trust himself not to lash out.

"Why?" Parker said as he ran his hands through his hair. "Daniel. Look at me. Is it true? Why?" He crumpled against the trunk of the tree, beside his employee. "Harmony," he said in a broken voice.

Craven shook his head and released a derisive snort.

"My…" Parker's voice rose in a keening moan. "My child!"

Craven stared straight ahead, focusing his gaze on the trains. "I was clearing the way for you, sir. You're building this company into greatness, and it cannot be held back." The words sent a shiver through Winston. Unlike other killers he had encountered, this man demonstrated no remorse for his actions.

Parker pulled his hand through his hair again. "But to kill. I never asked you to do that."

"You did not need to. I knew it needed to be done. Just as I knew what needed to be done to make this event a success. People will talk about it for years to come."

Parker lunged toward Craven. "I never wanted her dead. Or Montague. Why would you think I did?" Winston stepped forward to pull Parker away from Craven.

"I heard you, sir. One afternoon after you saw her, you said it would be easier if you had not met her."

"I simply meant that I would not be torn between my wife and her. Not that I wished her dead."

"And my father?" Winston asked.

Craven met Winston's gaze. Not an ember of regret shone in Craven's eyes. "Mr. Parker wanted a partnership with him. Your father was refusing to agree to his terms. This company. It could be great. If only your father wasn't in the way." Craven spoke as if he were explaining the mechanics of the train, not describing his reasons for killing two people. Winston's limbs felt inordinately heavy. He looked away from the man's eyes.

"How did you do it, Daniel?" Parker asked.

"In a crowd, it was easy to stand close enough to slide in my blade." He nodded toward his clipboard. Winston lunged to retrieve it, withdrawing the blade from its clever sheath with such speed that it bit into the flesh of his palm.

"Though I didn't manage yesterday to get to your father, which is why I arranged for the photos to be retaken this morning. It was lucky they didn't turn out the first time." Craven turned to look at Parker. "Now nothing is in your way." His eyes shone. "You can be truly great."

"Well," said Parker, "that, I'm afraid, is impossible now, Daniel."

Grief, anger, and frustration battled in Winston. He fought to keep his emotions in check. "And my father was a reasonable man." Winston heard the pleading tone in his own voice, even though no words could change anything. "He might have negotiated."

Winston turned his back on the two men. "Arrest him," he said to Miller and walked away, his heart a stone in his chest. Away from the central concourse, he found a tree and sat in its shade. He hung his head as he slumped against its trunk and held his wounded hand to his heart.

CHAPTER 31

Jack

"Mᴀʏ I sɪᴛ here?" Miss Smallwood's voice pierced through Winston's spiralling thoughts. Without waiting for him to answer, she lowered herself against the tree. "I saw a man being arrested. Did he kill both victims?" she asked.

Winston suspected that she knew the answer already, but as a journalist she needed to confirm her story. "This . . . this is not the time, Miss Smallwood."

"The murdered man. He was your father, wasn't he?" she asked.

Winston tried to think when Miller would have had an opportunity to reveal this to her. "Miss Smallwood, I really must insist. I cannot answer your questions." He rubbed his palm where it was now bandaged with his handkerchief.

"What if I promise not to print your answers? What if I simply want to satisfy my own curiosity?"

Winston turned his head to look at her. She stared at him with pleading eyes. "Please do not take this the wrong way, but we have only recently met. I have no way of knowing whether you can be trusted." She looked away, and he added, "Your trade is in stories."

"And you need to get yours straight?" Her tone had become more abrupt. "Is the male victim your father?"

Winston lowered his chin. "He was."

"And did he know the woman who was murdered?" Miss Smallwood squared her shoulders. "Were they acquainted? Or was their relationship more than that of casual acquaintance?"

Winston looked away. "They did not know each other." Despite his wish, she was getting information from him. "I cannot answer any further questions, Miss Smallwood. I will arrange for Constable Miller to speak to you when the investigation has concluded."

She stood and looked down at him. "I have a story to write, and I believe there is a story here, Detective. But I also see your pain. I can wait to write that story."

Winston rose. "Thank you, Miss Smallwood. That is all I ask."

∗

MELODIA FOUND WINSTON sitting on what he was beginning to consider their bench. He had walked there after the picnic crowd had left the crash site, collecting pieces of red and blue cloth along the way to give him something to focus on. He stared at the pile of scrap fabric piled at his feet. "I heard there was an arrest, Jack," she said quietly as she lowered herself next to him. "You must be satisfied."

He pushed a breath through pursed lips. "Satisfied? Perhaps with the idea that the killer has been caught. I would much rather be troubled by having to dine with my parents. I would trade satisfaction for the knowledge that I would see them again."

She slid her hand on top of his. "Will you not see your mother again, Jack? She still lives, doesn't she?"

Winston did not pull away from her touch. Instead, he leaned into her, sinking the side of his body into the softness of her. In response, she leaned back. "Yes, she does." He released a weary sigh. "There is much to be done, even though we have caught the man behind these senseless deaths."

"That can wait, Jack. I am in no rush. And, as you know, there is a crash tomorrow. You won't get attention from anyone, I expect."

"On this, I believe you are correct, Melodia. But there is something that must be seen to immediately." He shifted his position, bracing his foot against the boardwalk. "It is somewhat difficult to think about, but we must bury your sister. And my father."

As he expected, Melodia crumpled, and he supported her. "Here? In Crasherton?" The questions came in a raspy voice.

"Yes. Miller has spoken with Isaac. He agrees with the need to take care of this at once. The bodies cannot be preserved. It is too hot." He searched the horizon. "I had hoped to put them on a cooled railcar, but there isn't one available, and the scheduled runs cannot be disrupted to change the plans. On either railway," he said.

Melodia raised her face to look at Winston.

"This is a beautiful place," he said. "I think my father will be content to remain here for eternity. Though I may need to persuade my mother to accept the idea." He searched Melodia's face. "Do you not keep your sister in your heart?"

She brought her hand to her chest as if capturing her sister's spirit. "She is here." She moved her hand to her head. "And here. And your father?"

Winston nodded with a slow movement of his head. "The same is true."

Melodia leaned against the saloon wall and closed her eyes. Winston leaned back but kept his eyes focused on his hands. After a minute of silence, Melodia turned to him, her eyes wide with excitement. "In that case, may I suggest the location?"

Again Winston nodded, unable to find words.

She rose and beckoned him to follow her.

CHAPTER 32

Riley

RILEY STIRRED FROM sleep and wiped at her eyes, rubbing at the grit that had formed overnight. It was warm in the trailer, so much so that she'd slept on top of the covers. Or, more accurately, she realized, passed out on top of the covers, since she was still in the clothes she'd worn to the concert the night before.

As she woke, flashes of the evening played through her head. Dancing. Slipping her hand into Johnny's. Him squeezing her hand back. Inviting him for a drink in her trailer. Filled with warmth, she rolled onto her back and stifled a gasp. He was fast asleep beside her. His bright-coloured concert shirt—how had he gotten the memo about bright colours?—had ridden up so she could see the flesh of his stomach. Heat pulsed through her. The image of nuzzling against him while they'd sipped from their drinks and talked about the future came back to her. Their future. What had she said? "I'm connected to you, Johnny." Her cheeks flared. Had she said anything about the journal?

She carefully eased herself off the bed and crept into the main area of the trailer to retrieve the book from her bag. It looked undisturbed since she'd set it down the night before. Another flash of memory from the beginning of the evening—Lucy walking her back to the trailer, insisting that Riley leave her bag. "Just a few hours, Riley. It will be fine." Lucy had eased the strap over her sister's head, removing it from Riley's shoulder and setting it on the bench. Riley hadn't protested. She knew Lucy was right.

Now she opened the book to find that Jack had left another note. She read it slowly, her mind still not quite working as it should. His words stirred memories of those first days after her father died. She teared up as she read.

Dear Riley,

My father will be laid to rest in a few hours. He will be in a beautiful spot and, though he didn't know her in life, will spend eternity beside his killer's other victim. My mother accepted an offer from Parker to also have memorial stones placed in Vancouver and Toronto. Parker doesn't realize the significance of his gesture, especially to honour my father in Vancouver. I am going to invite her to stay in the city for a time, and she may be more willing to accept if she knows there is a place she can go to remember my father.

Riley thought of her own mother, now living with her. These connections, especially after a loss, felt important to forge. The arrangement was working better than Riley had expected. They'd come to an unspoken agreement about giving each other space and respecting boundaries. Nancy was more than a roommate, but she was also doing remarkably well at not treating Riley like a young child.

I look forward to returning home. My mother and I will need to find other accommodation. I fear she and Mrs. B will not be fast friends. And perhaps establishing my own household will settle me.

Jack

Riley picked up her pen to write Jack a reply when she noticed a paper tucked under the trailer's door. She eased herself from the bench and picked the note up. *Saw you and Johnny out cold so am crashing with a friend. Glad to see you've made a decision re Johnny. He's a keeper. Don't rush out of bed in the morning.*

How like Jules to end his note with a winky face. Had she made a decision about Johnny? Another fragment from the evening flashed in her mind. Whispering "I love you" to Johnny's soft snore before falling asleep herself.

Just then, he rolled over and murmured softly. Warmth spread across her chest. She picked up her pen to write a short reply to Jack before Johnny woke.

Dear Jack,

I speak from experience when I share that losing a parent is painful. It may not feel like it now, but with time it does get easier to accept. As does living with your mother again. At least, that is what I have found. What you describe sounds to me like a perfect solution for you and for her.

From the sleeping area, Johnny made another sound. Her heart fluttered. Her Johnny.

I have found that I am enjoying this time with my mother. It took a few weeks to figure out how to share a space with her again, but we are now in a place of comfortable companionship. I hope you find the same to be true and that you can turn to each other in your shared grief.

Riley signed off and returned her journal to her bag. She checked that the trailer door was locked and slid next to Johnny on the bed, melting into his arms as he pulled her close.

CHAPTER 33

Jack

WINSTON BUTTONED HIS waistcoat and slipped on his freshly pressed jacket. Doctor Evans had kindly suggested he avail himself of the services of the hotel's laundry. And again he'd extended to him the use of the bathing facilities available to hotel guests. He bent to polish the toe of his boot and spotted something in the shadow of one of the tub's claw feet—Ellis's stone!

The hotel staff must have swept it just out of sight. Winston picked it up, brushing it with the same cloth he'd used on his boot. He thumbed its familiar contours and slipped it into the pocket he'd been absently patting throughout the last day. Something settled in Winston. Something undefinable, but right. How remarkable that the restoration of this simple object could bring this sense of peace to heart and mind. Ellis.

It was crash day. Winston descended the stairs to the hotel's lobby and made his way to the front door through the growing crowd of visitors preparing to make their way to the site of the spectacle.

Winston's mother had elected not to attend the train crash. The noise, the crowd, the exuberance of the day were always going to be too much for her, even more so when she was so wrapped in grief. With this in mind, he explained to Miller that he would not be attending the crash. "Thomas, I would only sour the mood of the day," he'd told him, and he assured him that along with the assistance of the other constables, he'd be more than capable of handling the crowd. Philpott would also be there to lend authority, if required.

Over Miller's protests—"But you've come all this way, sir"—Winston had assured him that it was not the place for him.

Instead, Winston would lead a small procession of his mother, Melodia Spectre, and Isaac Fenton on a short walk from the Crasherton townsite. He made his way through the crowds to the Coastal Rail Hotel and spotted his mother waiting on the boardwalk that fronted the hotel. She wore a modest grey skirt and white blouse with a dark ribbon tied in a bow at the neck. It matched the ribbon she'd added to her simple summer hat. Winston's heart warmed toward her at once—the poor woman hadn't imagined she'd need to pack mourning clothes, but she'd managed to dress in a subdued manner befitting the occasion.

Winston had told her of the spot Melodia had found. It was Fenton who had suggested they go to see it while the crash was happening. "I wouldn't want to attend the crash without Harmony. And I don't think it's right for Parker to have any say in where she's buried," he'd said. To his credit, Parker had agreed. He'd also insisted that he pay for the burial as well as for a memorial stone to be installed in the cemetery in Vancouver for Harmony, and in cemeteries in Vancouver and Toronto for Montague.

"We cannot ask you to do that, sir," Winston had said when Parker had found him at the Crasherton Inn.

"I didn't hear you ask it, son," Parker had said. "I am as responsible for your father's death as Daniel is." When he spoke the killer's name, it came out as if he were spitting.

Parker had also arranged for Daniel Craven to be put on the next train returning to Vancouver. Winston had to agree that it was better that the man leave before the crash, when the constable accompanying him would not be bothered by other return passengers. When Winston returned to the city, he would make sure that the young officer was rewarded with an extra day's leave for missing the crash.

And so Winston and the other mourners walked through trees that grew denser with each step away from the town. Just as Winston was certain that he must have taken a wrong turn and was about to have them stop so they could retrace their steps, a small clearing appeared. He held up his hand. "Here."

"He would have loved this spot," his mother said, turning to view the area from all angles. "Your father was proud of you, Jack. Did you know that?" She grabbed her son's hand and squeezed it. "This is perfect."

"I'm glad you approve, Mother. The arrangements have been made, but I wanted you to see it first to make sure you felt as we did about this lovely place." He glanced toward Melodia. She smiled back at him.

Isaac Fenton was about to speak when the murmur of the crowd that had gathered to watch the train spectacle erupted into a cheer. "How long do you think it will take?" he asked.

"I don't know," Winston answered. "Parker told me there were to be some demonstrations of safety precautions before everything got underway. I believe we have just heard the spectators' reaction to the first demonstration."

The four huddled together a moment longer. A single tear ran down his mother's cheek. She held her head high, as he would have expected of her. Her grief was private, too raw to be shared with anyone yet. He stole another glance at Melodia, who had laced her arm through the crook of Fenton's elbow. She nodded at Winston and led Fenton deeper into the woods to give them some privacy.

Winston offered his own arm to his mother, and she accepted. He couldn't recall when she had touched him with such tenderness. Would she remain this softer version of herself? Or would she, in time, find a way to use her widowhood to her advantage? He shook the unkind thought away and placed his other hand over his mother's.

"After the crash is over, I will return to Vancouver, Mother." Winston waited for her to respond with a criticism of the city or his choice not to live with her in Toronto. When none came, he continued. "I was thinking. Perhaps you would like to come with me. It needn't be permanent. You could stay in the city, see what my life is like. Aunt Clarissa has room in her house, should you wish to stay with her."

Winston's mother planted her feet. "If I am to make that journey, it would be to stay with you."

He pictured the suite of rooms he rented and suppressed a smile when he thought of his mother and Mrs. Bradley sharing a space. Someone would be in tears within minutes of stepping into the house, and he wasn't entirely confident it wouldn't be him. He then thought of Riley and the recent change in her living situation. Her mother had moved back to Vancouver to live closer to her daughters. Should he offer his mother the same? "There are some beautiful homes, recently built," he said. "If you found the idea to be agreeable, I could look for one for us to live in. For however long you wish to stay."

His mother's reply was muffled by the sound of the engines blowing their whistles as they gained speed. Winston imagined the two machines racing toward each other, puffing steam as the distance between them shrank. He hoped the calculations were correct and the engineers were safely clear of their trains. The crowd cheered again, then the cheers were obliterated by the sound of violent twisting and tearing of metal. Winston put his hands over his ears. If the cacophony was so loud where they stood, it must be deafening for the spectators. The sound was both terrifying and awesome. He hoped Miller had the men prepared for what was surely to be an unruly crowd.

After what felt like a collective intake of breath, the crowd cheered once more, nearly matching the noise of the destruction just moments before. Winston turned to his mother, still waiting for her reply. Squeezing his arm, she closed her eyes and nodded yes.

257

Jack and Riley will return in *Skeletons in the Salish Sea.* When a sunken ship is found, Riley Finch is invited to be part of the recovery team on behalf of the museum. She turns to Jack Winston, a detective living 120 years earlier, to help solve the identities of the owners of the treasure aboard.

For a sneak peek into Jack's and Riley's lives before they met and to receive early notice of upcoming books, visit Sarah's website: https://sarahmstephen.ca/newsletter-book/ to sign up for regular dispatches.

Books in the Journal Through Time Mysteries:
The Dead of False Creek
The Hanging at the Hollow Tree
Murder in Mount Pleasant
Bodies in the Boundary
Skeletons in the Salish Sea (coming in 2026)

He chases crooks in the nineteenth century. She researches the past in the twenty-first. When a shipwreck is discovered, Riley Finch is invited to be part of the recovery team on behalf of the museum. She turns to Jack Winston, a detective living 120 years earlier, to help identify the owners of the treasure aboard while uncovering the truth of the bodies found with the ship.

Jack and Riley use their time-spanning journal to uncover the truth behind the events. *Skeletons in the Salish Sea* is the fifth book in the Journal Through Time historical mystery series.

Author's Note

A few years ago, my family took a road trip around the southern part of British Columbia. It is a beautiful part of the world, and I knew I had to write about it. When I found an article about the staged crash in 1896 at Crush, Texas, I had the perfect excuse to send Jack and Riley out of Vancouver.

Trains were essential to Canada after Confederation (and continue to be an important way to transport goods across the country). Train historians will recognize that I fudged the timing of when some routes were available to serve the story. I hope that hasn't impacted your enjoyment.

If you liked this book, please consider leaving a review, recommending it to a friend, or requesting that your library order a copy. These little gestures are so meaningful to authors.

Finally, hearing from readers is a joy. You can reach me at sarah@sarahmstephen.ca or follow me on social media to share your comments.

Warmly,
Sarah M Stephen
Vancouver, 2024

Acknowledgements

If you've ever read another author's acknowledgements, you've likely seen something along the lines of "putting a book together requires many people." It's true. I type the words alone, but so many others contribute in different ways. The words sound as good as they do because of my editor, Janet Fretter. Shelley Hudson is an excellent proofreader, and any remaining typos are my fault. My family puts up with my pecking away at all hours and pushes me to talk about my books more. Brook Peterson, who is more than my podcast partner, helps me sort through plot puzzles while writing her own wonderful mystery series. And you, dear reader. Your support encourages me to continue writing. Thank you.

About the Author

Sarah M Stephen started writing at an early age, first scribbling pages of notes while pretending to be a journalist before she could print. After mastering the alphabet, she moved into poetry and short stories. Following a few successes in grade school (a regional poetry prize) and university (a short story published), she traded her creative tales for corporate ones. A graduate of The Writer's Studio at Simon Fraser University, Sarah also co-hosts the *Clued in Mystery* podcast, where listeners can hear about her love of the mystery genre. She lives in Vancouver, Canada, with her family.

Contact Sarah:
Instagram: https://www.instagram.com/sarahmstephenauthor/
Facebook: https://www.facebook.com/sarahmstephenauthor/
Website: https://sarahmstephen.ca/
Podcast: https://www.cluedinmystery.com